Lost

Echoes

The Dark Asylum

Even the spirits of the dead have a story to tell

EJ CASTILLE

© Copyright 2024 EJ Castille

Cover Art by Muhammad Aryaputra

EJ Castille Books Inc.

This story is a work of fiction, a product of the author's imagination. Any resemblance to people, whether living or deceased, is purely coincidental and unintentional. The characters, events, and places depicted in this novel are entirely fictional and should not be construed as real.

No part of this publication may be reproduced, distributed, or transmitted in any form or by any means, including photocopying, recording, or other electronic or mechanical methods, without the prior written permission of the publisher, except for brief quotations embodied in critical reviews and certain other noncommercial uses permitted by copyright law.

All Rights Reserved

PREFACE

In crafting "Lost Echoes: The Dark Asylum," I ventured into the shadowy corridors of the human psyche, exploring the thin veil between life and death and the even thinner one between justice and revenge. The inspiration for this novel sprang from a fascination with forgotten corners of history—places and tales left to gather dust in society's collective memory. These forgotten corners, like Ravensbrook Hollow and its dark asylum, are rich with untold stories, whispers of the past that speak to our deepest fears and hopes.

This story is a tribute to those unquiet spirits of lore, the ones that linger at the edge of our dreams, seeking release or redemption. It is a testament to the power of unity, a beacon of hope in the face of unimaginable horrors, both human and supernatural. The journey of writing this novel took me through a labyrinth of emotions, from the depths of despair to the heights of hope. Along the way, I delved into the complexities of human nature, the darkness that lies within us all, and the light of compassion and bravery that can emerge even in the bleakest of circumstances.

As you join Alexandra Horren and her companions on their perilous quest, you will encounter mysteries that challenge the bounds of reality and witness the strength of spirit that binds them together. It is my hope that this story will not only thrill and chill you but also inspire reflection on the themes of redemption, the enduring power of friendship, and the indomitable human will to seek justice.

As you turn these pages, remember: the darkness you will encounter is as much a part of our world as the light. And sometimes, it is only by facing the darkness head-on that we can truly appreciate the brightness of day. May the journey through "Lost Echoes: The Dark Asylum" leave you with a newfound appreciation for the shadows and the stories they hold.

INTRODUCTION

Ravensbrook Hollow is a town steeped in shadows, where the line between reality and nightmare blurs. At the heart of these shadows lies Ravensbrook Asylum, a relic of a bygone era, shrouded in tragedy and mystery. The legends that cling to its crumbling walls speak of unimaginable cruelty and the indomitable spirit of those who sought to oppose it. But legends, as we know, are born from truths too troubling for the light of day.

"Lost Echoes: The Dark Asylum" opens a window into Ravensbrook's soul, inviting you to unravel its mysteries. Through the eyes of Alexandra Horren and her unique companions, each gifted with abilities beyond the ordinary, you will venture into the haunted halls of the asylum, seeking to liberate the spirits bound by sorrow and rage.

But be warned—the path is fraught with dangers, both seen and unseen. Matthias Blackthorne and Dr. Fredrick von Menschen's malevolence has not faded with their physical demise. Theirs is a hatred that transcends death, a darkness that seeks to consume all who dare challenge it.

This is not just a tale of ghostly vengeance. It is a story of courage, friendship, and the relentless pursuit of redemption. As you follow the journey of these extraordinary individuals, may you find within these pages a stirring testament to the enduring human spirit, capable of shining light even in the deepest darkness.

Welcome to Ravensbrook Hollow

Let the echoes of the dark guide you

TABLE OF CONTENTS

Chapter 1: A Shameful Secret ---------------------------------- 006

Chapter 2: A Haunting Vision ---------------------------------- 025

Chapter 3: Investigation -------------------------------------- 040

Chapter 4: A Past Unveiled ------------------------------------ 053

Chapter 5: The Sinister Physician ----------------------------- 064

Chapter 6: A Trial of Force ----------------------------------- 078

Chapter 7: A Temporary Reprieve ------------------------------- 095

Chapter 8: A Vision Unfolds ----------------------------------- 110

Chapter 9: A Dreadful Demise ---------------------------------- 125

Chapter 10: A Vision of Destiny ------------------------------- 142

Chapter 11: Shadows in the Attic ------------------------------ 157

Chapter 12: A Force of Wills ---------------------------------- 169

Chapter 13: Spiritus Filius ----------------------------------- 186

Chapter 14: Recollection -------------------------------------- 201

Chapter 15: Immersive Experience ------------------------------ 215

Chapter 16: Confrontation ------------------------------------- 229

Chapter 17: Havoc Unleashed ----------------------------------- 251

Chapter 18: Trapped Within ------------------------------------ 264

Chapter 19: Darkness Falling ---------------------------------- 280

Chapter 20: Evil Company, Good Manners ------------------------ 298

Chapter 21: Absolution -- 315

Epilogue: Reflections --- 338

Chapter 1:
A Shameful Secret

The skies above Ravensbrook Hollow were a dull, leaden gray, heavy with unshed tears of a storm that lingered on the horizon. Below this brooding canopy, nestled on the outskirts of the small town, stood Ravensbrook Asylum. The towering stone building, an imposing structure of Gothic design, cast a chilling shadow that seemed to stretch endlessly. Its sharp, angular silhouette cut through the skyline like a jagged scar, a stark reminder of its foreboding presence. The very air around it seemed to hold its breath as if in anticipation of the horrors that lay within.

The asylum, once a beacon of hope for the mentally troubled, now stood as a monument to despair. Like gnarled fingers, Vines clung to the cracked walls, crawling upwards as if trying to pull the structure back into the earth. The once-majestic edifice was now marred by time and neglect, its grandeur lost to years of abandonment. The surrounding trees, overgrown and wild, swayed in the gusty wind, their branches casting eerie, dancing shadows across the asylum's façade.

At the entrance, a wrought-iron gate, twisted and rusted, creaked mournfully on its hinges. Beyond it, a gravel path, overgrown with weeds, led to the main doors. The path, once well-trodden by doctors, nurses, and visitors, now lay forgotten, a testament to the asylum's isolation from the world outside. Flanking the pathway, statues of angels, their features eroded by time, stood guard, their sightless eyes gazing eternally at the decrepit building.

The asylum's sign, once proudly proclaiming its name, hung lopsidedly at the gate. Its letters, ravaged by the elements, were barely legible, the paint peeling and faded. 'Ravensbrook Asylum for the

Mentally Disturbed', it read, the words almost lost in the patina of rust and decay. The sign squeaked as it swayed in the wind, a discordant note in the symphony of desolation that surrounded the place.

A palpable air of melancholy hung over the asylum grounds. The manicured lawns and carefully tended gardens that once surrounded the building had long since given way to a wilderness of neglect. Thickets of brambles and wild undergrowth encroached upon the building, nature slowly reclaiming what was once hers. The once vibrant flowerbeds were now choked with weeds, their beauty smothered beneath a blanket of neglect.

As one ventured closer to the building, the oppressive atmosphere intensified. The windows, many of them broken or boarded up, stared out like empty eye sockets, void of the life that once flickered behind them. The grand entrance, with its once-polished wooden doors and ornate framework, now bore the scars of time and abandonment. The brass fittings were tarnished and dull, and the wood was warped and cracked, groaning under the weight of years.

Inside, the corridors of Ravensbrook Asylum whispered with echoes of a troubled past. The walls, once pristine and white, were now peeling and stained, the plaster crumbling in places to reveal the skeletal structure beneath. The floors, lined with checkered tiles, bore the scuffs and marks of countless footsteps, a silent testament to the souls who had wandered these halls.

In these corridors, the air was heavy, as if saturated with the lingering essence of despair and suffering. The faint, musty smell of decay hung in the air, mingling with a colder, more sinister scent — the smell of fear. It was as if the very walls of the asylum absorbed the emotions of its former occupants, holding onto them long after the last patient had departed.

The once-bustling wards were now silent, their beds empty and their equipment gathering dust. The rooms, which had once resonated with the sounds of life, now echoed only with the whispers of memories. Each room held its own story, the remnants of its past occupants still evident in the faded wallpaper, the abandoned personal items, and the names carved into the bedposts.

In this place, where hope was once offered and often lost, the shadows seemed to move of their own accord, playing tricks on the eyes of any who dared to venture within. The atmosphere was thick with the unspoken, the air ripe with tales of pain, sorrow, and madness.

Ravensbrook Asylum stood as a testament to human suffering, a place where the line between treatment and torment had been blurred. It was a monument to the misunderstood and the mistreated, a relic of a bygone era when the lines of morality in mental health care were often indistinct. The building, with its dark history and haunting presence, held within its walls secrets that were as chilling as the wind that howled through its broken windows.

Here, in this forgotten corner of Ravensbrook Hollow, the asylum waited, holding its shameful secret close, a secret that was about to be unearthed by those brave enough to delve into its dark past.

Within the foreboding walls of Ravensbrook Asylum, the chilling presence of Warden Matthias Blackthorne was ever pervasive. He was a tall, imposing figure whose stern features and cold, calculating eyes betrayed no hint of compassion. Blackthorne, clad in a dark suit that seemed to absorb the dim light of the corridors, moved through the asylum with an air of absolute authority. His footsteps, firm and deliberate, echoed ominously through the hollow halls, heralding his approach.

As he passed, the asylum staff, a mix of nurses and orderlies, tensed visibly. Their eyes would flicker towards him with a mixture of fear and respect, quickly averting their gaze as he neared. Blackthorne's presence seemed to cast a shadow that lingered even after he had passed, a suffocating blanket of dread that smothered the faintest whispers of defiance.

In the nurse's station, hushed conversations ceased abruptly as he approached. The nurses stiffened, their hands pausing over their paperwork or clutching at their aprons. Blackthorne surveyed the room with a critical eye, his gaze lingering on each face as if memorizing their features, etching them into his mind for reasons only known to him.

"Report," he demanded, his voice resonating with a depth that seemed to vibrate the very air.

An older nurse, her hands trembling slightly, stepped forward. "W-Warden Blackthorne," she stammered, "all is as per the usual schedule. Dr. von Menschen is with a patient, and the evening medications have been distributed."

Blackthorne's lips curled into a semblance of a smile, but it was devoid of warmth. "Good," he replied curtly. "Ensure that everything continues to run smoothly. I will not tolerate any... discrepancies."

His words hung in the air like a threat, a silent reminder of the consequences of failure. The staff nodded, their expressions a blend of relief and apprehension as he turned to leave. As he walked away, the tension in the room slowly dissipated, like air being let out of a balloon.

Blackthorne's path through the asylum took him past rows of closed doors, behind which lay the patients of Ravensbrook. Some doors bore scratch marks; others were adorned with drawings or incoherent scribbles – silent cries from the souls trapped within. Occasionally, muffled sounds would seep through the wood – a sob, a scream, a plea for help. But Blackthorne paid them no heed; they were merely background noise to him, the soundtrack of his domain.

His destination was the office at the end of the corridor, a room that stood apart from the rest. The door was heavier, the wood darker, as if absorbing the despair that permeated the building. Here, Blackthorne paused, his hand resting on the brass doorknob, a brief flicker of something – anticipation, perhaps, or excitement – crossing his otherwise impassive face.

As the door swung open, the contrast between the corridor and the office was stark. The office was meticulously organized, every item in its place. The walls were lined with shelves filled with books and documents, the desk was neat, and the chair behind it was high-backed and imposing, much like Blackthorne himself.

This was his sanctum, the place where he orchestrated the workings of Ravensbrook. Here, amongst the files and records, lay the true extent of his control. It was here that he planned his strategies, here that he reviewed the reports on each patient, and here that he decided their fates.

As Blackthorne sat at his desk, the chair creaking slightly under his weight, he opened a drawer and withdrew a file. The name on the tab was handwritten, and the ink was slightly smudged. He opened it and began to read, his eyes scanning the pages with a predatory focus.

Each file was a life, a story of someone who had fallen through the cracks of society and into his hands. Some were there for treatment, others for experimentation. Blackthorne saw them not as individuals but as opportunities, as means to an end he alone understood.

His mind was a labyrinth of plans and schemes, each more diabolical than the last. Ravensbrook was his chessboard, and he moved the pieces with a deft hand. His experiments, conducted under the guise of treatment, pushed the boundaries of both science and morality. But in his eyes, the ends always justified the means.

As the day turned to evening and the light faded from the windows, the Warden remained in his office, the dim light casting long shadows across his face. In the silence of his solitude, he reveled in the power he wielded within these walls. Ravensbrook Asylum was his kingdom, and he was its undisputed ruler. But beyond these walls, a storm was brewing, a tempest of outrage and retribution that would soon sweep through the corridors of Ravensbrook, threatening to topple the king from his throne.

In the shadowed recesses of Ravensbrook Asylum, Dr. Fredrick von Menschen, the Chief Physician, pursued his grotesque experiments with a fervor that bordered on obsession. His appearance was as unsettling as his reputation: gaunt, with sallow skin stretched taut over sharp cheekbones and a gaze that seemed to pierce through one's very soul. His unkempt hair and disheveled lab coat spoke of long hours spent in the bowels of the asylum, far from the prying eyes of the outside world.

The lower levels of Ravensbrook, where Dr. von Menschen conducted his work, were a stark contrast to the rest of the facility. The walls here were bare, the air thick with the antiseptic sting of chemicals, and the lighting harsh and unyielding. The rooms were lined with equipment that seemed more suited to a medieval dungeon than a medical facility: restraints, surgical tools, and strange, arcane devices whose purposes were best left unimagined.

In one such room, von Menschen stood over a patient strapped to a table. The patient's eyes were wide with terror, their body trembling uncontrollably. Von Menschen, however, regarded them with clinical detachment, his eyes scanning over the array of instruments laid out beside him. With a thin-lipped smile, he selected a scalpel, the steel glinting coldly in the fluorescent light.

"Fear not," he murmured, more to himself than to the patient. "Your suffering is not in vain. You are contributing to a greater understanding, a higher purpose."

As he made the first incision, the patient's muffled screams echoed through the halls, a haunting symphony that underscored the horror of Ravensbrook. The doctor worked with a precision that was almost artistic, lost in his own twisted world where the lines between healing and harming were irrevocably blurred.

Elsewhere in the asylum, whispers of von Menschen's activities circulated among the staff. Nurses exchanged worried glances as they overheard snippets of conversation or caught glimpses of patients being led to the lower levels, never to return the same. Orderlies spoke in hushed tones about the screams that sometimes reached even the upper floors, their words heavy with a mix of fear and guilt.

Despite the rumors, few dared to question von Menschen's methods. The combination of his intimidating presence and the Warden's explicit support silenced any dissent. Those who did voice concerns were quickly reassigned or dismissed, their fates serving as a stern warning to others.

In the staff lounge, a small group of nurses gathered, their conversation a muted murmur beneath the constant hum of the asylum.

"I heard Mrs. Thompson crying last night," one nurse whispered, her eyes darting around to ensure they were alone. "She said her son was taken to Dr. von Menschen's ward three days ago and hasn't been seen since."

Another nurse shook her head, her face pale. "It's not right. We're supposed to care for these people, not..." Her voice trailed off, unable to articulate the horrors they all suspected.

"But what can we do?" a third nurse interjected, her hands wringing her apron. "The Warden has given Dr. von Menschen free rein. To speak out is to risk our positions or worse."

Their conversation was a microcosm of the moral dilemma that pervaded Ravensbrook – the conflict between duty and conscience, between fear and the desire to do what was right.

Meanwhile, in his subterranean lair, von Menschen continued his work, oblivious to the undercurrents of unrest above. Each patient was a test subject, and each experiment was a step closer to some unfathomable goal. His notes, scrawled in a frenetic hand, filled volumes – records of pain and suffering that he viewed as necessary sacrifices on the altar of progress.

Night fell over Ravensbrook Asylum, casting long shadows across its halls. But beneath the cover of darkness, the most sinister activities were just beginning. In von Menschen's world, the night was an ally, a veil that shrouded his deeds from the eyes of the world.

But even the deepest shadows could not hide the truth forever. In the heart of the town, anger and suspicion were brewing, a storm of outrage that threatened to break upon the walls of Ravensbrook. The secrets of the asylum and the atrocities committed within were teetering on the edge of exposure, poised to ignite a conflagration that would consume everything in its path.

Outside the oppressive walls of Ravensbrook Asylum, under the pale moonlight, the town of Ravensbrook Hollow was stirring with unrest. The night air was thick with tension as a crowd of townspeople gathered at the town square, their faces etched with anger and fear. Whispers had turned into rumors, and rumors into outrage, as the true nature of the horrors within the asylum began to seep into the public consciousness.

The square, usually a place of community and celebration, had transformed into a scene of impending revolt. Men and women, young and old, stood shoulder to shoulder, their voices rising in a chorus of indignation. The flickering light from torches and lanterns cast ominous shadows, painting their expressions with a stark intensity.

At the center of the crowd, a makeshift platform had been erected. Upon it stood George Miller, a burly man with a booming voice known for his outspoken nature. A former employee of the asylum, Miller had witnessed firsthand the atrocities committed by Warden Blackthorne and Dr. von Menschen. His revelations had been the spark that ignited the town's fury.

"Fellow citizens of Ravensbrook Hollow!" Miller's voice rang out, cutting through the murmurs of the crowd. "We have been blind to the nightmare that festers on our doorstep. Ravensbrook Asylum, a place we trusted to care for the sick, has become a den of suffering and torment!"

Murmurs of agreement rippled through the crowd; their anger fueled by Miller's words. He spoke of patients disappearing without explanation, of screams echoing through the night, of families torn apart by grief and uncertainty.

A woman in the crowd, her face lined with worry, called out, "My brother was taken there for treatment, and now he's gone! They say he ran away, but I know that's a lie!"

Her voice was a catalyst, sparking a wave of similar testimonies. People shared their stories of loved ones admitted to the asylum, never to be seen again, or returned changed beyond recognition.

Miller raised his hand for silence. "We trusted them to heal, but they have done unspeakable harm. The Warden and his twisted doctor must be held accountable for their crimes!"

The crowd erupted in cheers and shouts; the collective voice of the community betrayed. Among them, a sense of solidarity was building, a shared resolve to seek justice for the wronged.

As the fervor grew, another figure stepped onto the platform. Sarah Jennings, a young nurse who had recently resigned from the asylum, her eyes haunted by the things she had seen. Her voice was soft but firm as she addressed the crowd.

"I saw the fear in their eyes, the patients who were taken to Dr. von Menschen's ward. I heard their cries. I can no longer stay silent about the horrors that occur behind those walls."

Her confession added weight to the growing suspicion and fear. The crowd's mood shifted from anger to a collective cry for action. The once hushed whispers of discontent were now loud proclamations of revolt.

"We must act!" Miller bellowed, his voice echoing off the surrounding buildings. "For too long, we have turned a blind eye to the suffering of those within Ravensbrook Asylum. It is time we put an end to this nightmare!"

The crowd surged forward, their shouts blending into a single, powerful demand for justice. As they moved as one, the decision was made. They would march to the asylum, confront the Warden and his doctor, and put an end to the atrocities.

The torches and lanterns bobbed like a fiery serpent through the streets of Ravensbrook Hollow, a symbol of the town's unified stand against the darkness that had taken root in their midst. Their destination was clear, their purpose singular – to tear down the veil of secrecy that shrouded Ravensbrook Asylum and expose the shameful secret that it harbored.

As they approached the asylum, the building loomed ominously in the distance, its silhouette a dark specter against the night sky. The crowd's resolve hardened with every step, their collective heart beating with a singular rhythm of righteous indignation. Tonight, the walls of Ravensbrook would echo with more than just the cries of the tormented – they would resound with the voices of a town awakened; a people no longer willing to be silent in the face of evil.

The clamor of the townspeople's march towards Ravensbrook Asylum grew louder, echoing through the empty streets of Ravensbrook Hollow like the drumbeat of an approaching storm. At the head of this determined procession, George Miller's towering figure was a beacon of revolt, his voice resonating with the fury of the wronged. Beside him walked Sarah Jennings, the young nurse whose revelations had lent a haunting credibility to the rumors that had long circulated about the asylum.

Their destination loomed ahead, its foreboding structure a stark silhouette against the night sky. The crowd, fueled by a potent mix of fear, anger, and sorrow, surged forward with a single-minded purpose. Each step was a testament to their resolve, a march towards a reckoning that had been long overdue.

As they approached the asylum, the crowd's fervor intensified. The stories of mistreatment and suffering once whispered in the shadows, were now cried out loud for all to hear. Among the townspeople, a figure emerged, drawing the eyes of the crowd. Mary Elizabeth Cartwright, a middle-aged woman of strong character and presence, stepped forward. Her son had been one of the asylum's patients, and his unexplained disappearance had been the catalyst for her transformation from a grieving mother to a vocal advocate for justice.

"Listen to me!" Mary Elizabeth's voice, clear and compelling, cut through the cacophony. "We have been silent for too long, blinded by our trust in those who promised to heal and protect. But no more! The truth of Ravensbrook Asylum must be brought to light!"

Her words, spoken with the raw emotion of personal loss, resonated with the crowd. Many among them had their own tales of heartache linked to the asylum. Her grief was their grief, her call for justice a mirror of their own demands.

The crowd gathered around her, their voices joining in a chorus of agreement. The stories of loved ones who had entered the asylum, only to vanish or return as mere shadows of themselves, were now shared openly, each account adding fuel to the fire of their collective outrage.

As they stood at the gates of Ravensbrook, the crowd's mood shifted from sorrowful reminiscence to a determined call for action. The gates, once a barrier to the outside world, were now the only thing standing between them and the answers they sought.

"Tonight, we tear down these walls!" Miller proclaimed; his voice thunderous. "Tonight, we expose the horrors that have been hidden from our eyes! For justice, for our loved ones, for Ravensbrook Hollow!"

The crowd roared in response, their voices a unified cry that shattered the oppressive silence of the night. They pushed against the gates, their collective strength forcing them open with a screech of protesting metal.

As they flooded onto the asylum grounds, the reality of their mission settled upon them. The building, an ominous and silent witness to their intrusion, seemed to stare back at them with a thousand unseen eyes. Yet, the townspeople were undeterred, their purpose clear and their resolve unwavering.

Among them, conflicting emotions swirled. While some were driven by a thirst for retribution, others harbored hopes of a peaceful resolution of bringing the perpetrators to justice through lawful means. The complexity of their motivations reflected the depth of the impact Ravensbrook had on their lives.

At the forefront, Mary Elizabeth, Miller, and Sarah led the way, their steps steady and determined. They knew the risks of their endeavor and the potential for violence and chaos, but the need for truth and justice overshadowed their fears.

As they reached the main doors of the asylum, a hushed silence fell over the crowd. The enormity of their task, the confrontation with the very heart of their fear and anger, loomed before them like a dark abyss.

With a collective breath, the doors were pushed open, revealing the dimly lit corridors of Ravensbrook Asylum. The air inside was stale, heavy with the weight of untold stories and unspoken horrors. The crowd stepped inside, their torches and lanterns casting flickering shadows on the walls as if awakening the ghosts of the past.

The march of the townspeople, once a distant rumble, had now become a deafening roar within the halls of Ravensbrook. Their presence was an invasion of light and life into a place long shrouded in darkness and death. They moved forward, room by room, corridor by corridor, in search of the truth that had eluded them for so long.

Their journey through the asylum was a journey through their own fears and doubts, a confrontation with the darkness that had lurked at the edge of their consciousness. But united in their purpose, they pressed on, determined to uncover the shameful secret of Ravensbrook and bring an end to the nightmare that had haunted their town.

The interior of Ravensbrook Asylum, now infiltrated by the determined townsfolk, echoed with the cacophony of their collective outrage. The once-silent halls were alive with the sound of footsteps and voices as the crowd spread out, their lanterns and torches casting eerie, dancing shadows against the peeling walls. The air was thick with the scent of mold and neglect, a tangible reminder of the asylum's dark and tortured history.

George Miller, leading the charge, moved with a resoluteness that belied his inner turmoil. Beside him, Mary Elizabeth Cartwright and Sarah Jennings shared a look of grim determination. They were the embodiment of the town's collective will, the focal point of its pent-up anger and grief.

As they advanced, the secrets of Ravensbrook began to unravel before them. The sight of empty cells, their doors ajar, spoke volumes of the despair that had once resided within. In some rooms, remnants of the past lingered: tattered remnants of clothing, faded photographs, and scribbled notes that hinted at the lives that had been unceremoniously uprooted.

Their journey was punctuated by the discovery of rooms that bore the unmistakable marks of Dr. von Menschen's experiments. The sight of rusted restraints and abandoned surgical tools sent shivers down the spines of the onlookers, their worst fears confirmed by the grim reality before them.

Amidst the chaos, a voice rose above the rest, a beacon of reason amid the storm. It was Reverend Thomas, a respected figure in the community, known for his calming presence and wise counsel. He had joined the crowd, not to incite violence, but to seek a peaceful resolution to the unfolding crisis.

"We must remember our humanity," Reverend Thomas implored, his voice echoing in the hollow space. "Let us seek justice but let us not stoop to the level of those we condemn. We are here to expose the truth, not to perpetrate further violence."

His words resonated with a portion of the crowd, a reminder of the moral line they teetered on. Yet, for others, the reverend's plea was but a whisper in the wind, drowned out by the roar of their collective anger.

The crowd's momentum led them to the heart of the asylum – the administrative offices where Warden Matthias Blackthorne and Dr. Fredrick von Menschen had orchestrated their reign of terror. The door to the warden's office stood ominously ajar, an unspoken invitation to uncover the depths of his malevolence.

Inside, the room was a stark contrast to the decay that pervaded the rest of the building. The desk was laden with documents, the walls lined with files – each a testament to the meticulousness with which Blackthorne had maintained his control. The air was heavy with the scent of old leather and paper, mixed with a more sinister undertone that set the townspeople's nerves on edge.

As Miller and the others rifled through the documents, the scale of the atrocities committed within Ravensbrook's walls became painfully clear. Patient records, experiment logs, and correspondences painted a picture of a man who had lost all semblance of morality in his pursuit of power and control.

The discovery of a hidden room behind a bookshelf only served to heighten the horror. Inside, the remnants of what appeared to be a private laboratory were revealed, its shelves lined with jars containing unspeakable specimens, the legacy of Dr. von Menschen's madness.

The crowd, once fueled by righteous indignation, now found themselves grappling with the overwhelming weight of the truth. The reverend's words echoed in their minds, a call to retain their humanity in the face of such inhumanity.

As they emerged from the office, a palpable change had come over them. The initial surge of anger had given way to a sobering realization of the depth of the darkness they had uncovered. They had come seeking justice but had found themselves confronted with a horror that transcended their worst nightmares.

The confrontation with the warden and the chief physician, however, was yet to come. The crowd, now a collective force of subdued rage and resolute purpose, moved through the asylum with a newfound sense of mission. They were no longer just townspeople; they were avengers, bearers of the truth that would cleanse Ravensbrook of its sins.

As they closed in on the quarters where Blackthorne and von Menschen were believed to be hiding, the air crackled with anticipation. The moment of reckoning was at hand – a confrontation that would mark the end of an era of suffering and the beginning of a journey towards healing for the town of Ravensbrook Hollow.

The doors to the quarters were flung open, revealing the warden and the physician, their expressions a mix of defiance and fear. The townspeople, their faces hardened by the revelations of the night, stood united in their demand for justice.

What transpired in those final moments would forever be etched in the annals of Ravensbrook Hollow. The warden and the physician, confronted with the consequences of their actions, faced the wrath of a community that had suffered under their reign for far too long.

In the end, justice, in its most primal form, was delivered. The screams of Blackthorne and von Menschen, echoes of the cries of their countless victims, reverberated through the halls of Ravensbrook Asylum, a chilling symphony of retribution.

As the dawn broke over Ravensbrook Hollow, the asylum stood silent once more. But within its walls, a new chapter had begun – one of liberation and closure for the spirits that had been trapped within, their echoes finally set free.

The townspeople, their mission fulfilled, returned to their homes, forever changed by the events of the night. They had confronted the darkest depths of human depravity and had emerged with a renewed sense of unity and strength.

In the aftermath, the tale of Ravensbrook Asylum would be told and retold, a cautionary reminder of the thin line between sanity and madness, between healing and harm. And at the heart of this tale, the echoes of the lost souls of Ravensbrook would linger, a haunting testament to the price of silence in the face of evil.

*****

As the first light of dawn began to seep through the horizon, painting the sky in hues of pink and orange, the town of Ravensbrook Hollow lay in a restless slumber. The events at Ravensbrook Asylum had unfolded like a feverish nightmare, one that had shaken the very foundations of the community. In the heart of the town, within a modest house nestled amongst rows of similar dwellings, Alexandra Horren tossed and turned in her bed, caught in the throes of a disturbing dream.

In her dream, Alexandra stood at the gates of Ravensbrook Asylum, the building towering over her like a malevolent sentinel. The screams and cries of its countless victims echoed in her ears, a cacophony of despair that sent shivers down her spine. She could feel the weight of their sorrow, their unfulfilled desires and unavenged wrongs pressing down on her, imploring her to act.

The dream shifted, and she found herself wandering the desolate halls of the asylum. The walls whispered secrets to her, each voice a fragment of a tragic tale. The ghostly figures of patients, their eyes hollow with suffering, reached out to her, their fingers brushing against her skin like tendrils of mist. Among them, she recognized faces from the town's history, their stories intertwined with the dark legacy of Ravensbrook.

As she moved through the asylum, the figure of Warden Blackthorne loomed in the shadows, his gaze piercing and accusatory. Beside him, Dr. von Menschen, his hands stained with the blood of his victims, leered at her with mad glee. The air around them was heavy with the stench of corruption and decay, a tangible reminder of their reign of terror.

In the dream, Alexandra felt a deep, visceral urge to confront these specters of the past, to bring closure to the souls that had been wronged. She felt their pain, their longing for peace, resonating within her own heart. It was as if the spirits of Ravensbrook had chosen her, seeing in her the potential to right the wrongs that had been perpetrated within those cursed walls.

But as she stepped forward, the ground beneath her feet began to crumble, and she found herself falling into an abyss of darkness. The voices of the spirits grew louder, their cries more urgent, as if urging her to wake up, to bring their suffering to light.

With a start, Alexandra awoke, her heart pounding in her chest. The remnants of the dream clung to her like cobwebs, the emotions it had stirred within her lingering in the morning air. She sat up in bed, her breathing heavy, as she tried to make sense of the vivid images that had invaded her sleep.

The room around her was bathed in the soft glow of dawn, a stark contrast to the darkness of her dream. But the sense of purpose that had been kindled in her heart was undeniable. She knew, with a clarity that was almost frightening, that her path was inexorably linked to Ravensbrook Asylum.

Alexandra's gift of precognition, often a source of confusion and fear, now seemed like a beacon, guiding her toward a destiny she could no longer ignore. The spirits of Ravensbrook had reached out to her, and she felt a responsibility to heed their call.

As she rose from her bed, the decision was already forming in her mind. She would gather a group of like-minded individuals, each with their own unique abilities, to uncover the truths that lay hidden within the asylum. Together, they would delve into the shadows of Ravensbrook, seeking to free the trapped souls and bring to light the atrocities that had been committed.

Her resolve strengthened with each passing moment; Alexandra began to plan her course of action. She knew the journey ahead would be fraught with danger and uncertainty, but the call of the lost echoes of Ravensbrook Asylum was too powerful to ignore.

Alexandra, standing by her window, gazes out at the town of Ravensbrook Hollow. The peaceful facade of the town belied the turmoil that lay beneath, the echoes of a dark past that whispered in the wind.

With a sense of determination burning in her heart, Alexandra Horren was ready to embark on a journey that would unravel the mysteries of Ravensbrook Asylum, a journey that would challenge her very understanding of reality.

Chapter 2:
A Haunting Vision

If anyone had been standing atop the Ravensbrook Hollow clock tower and looking down over the town, they would find themselves staring at the shadowy forms of the early-rising residents going about their day. The clock tower was perhaps the tallest structure in town by itself, surpassed only by the asylum, which loomed over it as it did the rest of the town because it was built on a hill. Alexandra had never been, but apparently, looking out from one of the top windows on an overcast day, one would only see a fog so thick it was easy to believe you were somewhere up among the clouds.

Down on the ground, the town was bustling to life as the morning grew old, promising in its absence the birth of a slightly less gloomy day.

Alexandra Horren crossed the busy street— as busy as streets ever got in Ravensbrook Hollow — as she made her way to the building on the corner.

The words Raven's Cove, written on a faded wooden sign that hung over the building, gave the building its identity. It was a cafe and bar that served as a common hangout for most of the teenagers in the town. Raven's Cove had taken on the town's name not because it was the only cafe and bar in town but because it had been one of the first businesses opened when the first of the settlers moved to Ravensbrook Hollow.

The bell tinkled as Alexandra walked through the door, and from across the room, Wesley Hargreaves looked up from the counter where he was in the final steps of making a coffee for a customer.

Wesley had been working at Raven's Cove for as long as Alexandra remembered, and although she claimed to hate the job, it was clear she had no intention of quitting it.

As the lunch rush passed and it was too early for alcohol, the place was mostly empty. The only other customers in sight were a middle-aged couple, an old woman and her cat, and a hooded man sipping on a bubble tea.

"Hello, Wesley," Alexandra said.

"Alex. You're here early," she noted. "This week's orders haven't come in yet?"

A few blocks to the left of the bar, there was a library, the only one in town. It was Alexandra's favorite place to be, beating the cafe by a narrow margin. In fact, it was because of the library that she had come to discover and take an interest in the cafe.

Alexandra loved to read, and for that reason, she loved the library. The only problem was that she hated it for every other reason.

The library was managed—if you could call it that—by the Cooper family, and in an attempt to teach his daughter responsibility, Mr. Cooper had employed his daughter; pug-nosed, bumptious Bethany Cooper, who Alexandra was certain had never opened past the preface page of any book in the library as librarian. Beth Cooper hated her job and did her best to make it clear. The books were hardly ever arranged in order. Worst of all was the fact that she did not care about keeping the library silent, and a bunch of kids, having discovered they could do whatever they liked as long as they slipped her a twenty, had taken to smoking cigarettes in the back office.

Finding the cafe had been a hallelujah moment, and ever since, she had been a regular, coming here to read in peace as she enjoyed her iced tea and grilled cheese sandwiches.

"No, I'm actually meeting some friends here," Alexandra said.

"Friends?" Wesley repeated, genuinely surprised. "Gee, Alex. I didn't know you had those."

Alexandra rolled her eyes.

"I could say the same about you, Wes."

She did not look, but she could tell a scowl was now fixed in her direction.

She found a corner booth which was a first as she usually took up the table by the window so she could relax in the town's peaceful ambience as she read. Today, however, she wasn't here to read, and the nature of her business required a bit of privacy.

"The usual?" Wesley said as she waved the customer off with a practiced smile. Alexandra looked up in time to see her turn her head towards her usual seat, then frowned in confusion before redirecting her gaze to where she sat. "That's...new."

"Yes, please," Alexandra said, pretending there was nothing strange to pay attention to.

A few minutes later, she sat staring at the entrance, nervously turning the now empty glass around and around in her grasp. The mundane action was meant to help her pass the time, but she quickly grew bored and moved on to folding and unfolding a napkin. They weren't late; she was just early, which was a force of habit.

Also on the table, next to the platter of half-eaten sandwiches, was a journal. It was hers.

She picked it up, turned it upside down, and flipped through the pages. The first three were blank, but on the fourth, she had written down something.

First was a name: James Parson. Then, his gender. After that, she wrote: Mind reader. Possibly empath?

By the side of the page, there were two tiny holes where she had previously stapled a cropped picture of him she had obtained from his social media before she had decided that that was probably too creepy and removed it.

The next page had similar information, except this time, it was about Lila Sakarov, the telekinetic.

She was about to flip to the next page when she heard the door open.

A girl with long black hair and the biggest brownest eyes Alexandra had ever seen walked in. Their eyes met, and the girl gave a toothy smile, almost as if they had known each other forever.

She wore a pink cashmere sweater and knee-high boots, and there was a pair of headphones around her neck.

Alexandra was aware of Wesley staring keenly as the girl approached the booth.

"Looks like I'm the first one to arrive," she said, looking around as though she expected the others to jump up from behind the furniture and yell, 'Surprise!'

Up close, Alexandra realized that the photographs she had seen did not do the girl before her justice. She had this warm inviting aura around her. It was soothing.

Catching herself staring, Alexandra cleared her throat.

"Yeah," she said, rising to her feet. "Samantha, right?"

The question was a formality more than anything else. Her name was closer to the bottom of the list of things Alexandra knew about her.

Before she answered, the girl pulled her in for a hug.
"Sam is fine," she said.

"Sam it is. I'm Alexandra. You can call me Alex."

"Not Alexandra the Not-So-Great?" The corner of her lips rose in a playful smile.

Alexandra cringed at the sound of her username being spoken aloud.

"No. Please, no."

The bell jingled, shifting their focus. They watched as a boy held the door open for a girl to enter ahead of him. The boy was James Parson, and the girl, looking every bit like the twenty-year-old she was, was Lila Sakarov.

They walked shoulder to shoulder as they came up to the table.

"I'm guessing you're our people?" Lila said.

"Sam," Sam said, pointing at her chest. She jutted a thumb in Alexandra's direction. "Alex."

"I'm Lila," she said, stretching out her hand.

Alexandra shook her hand, but Sam went in for a hug instead.

After that, Lila moved aside to shift their attention to James.

"I'm James," he said. "Hello."

His grey eyes were the most peculiar thing. They weren't a startling grey like a storm cloud, more like an overcast sky on a chilly day. It was oddly calming.

Sam opened her arms for a hug, but he shook his head.

"Don't take it the wrong way, but I don't do a lot of physical contact," he said.

He stretched out his hand, which was tucked away in a leather glove.

"That's one bold fashion statement," Sam said, but she obliged him in the same way.

"So, do you two already know each other?" Alexandra said.

"Oh no. We took the same bus down here, and we happened to make small talk. We came down, said our goodbyes, and ended up walking in the same direction all the way to this very place."

"Are we all here, then?" James said.

"Almost. We're one short."

From the corner of her eye, Alexandra saw the hooded man rise from his seat. To her surprise, he didn't make his way to the exit or perhaps the bathroom. Instead, he made a beeline for their table.

As he drew closer, the others noticed him and turned, but he remained unfazed as he took up a chair at their table.

He pulled his hoodie back to reveal short brown hair neatly combed and parted, contrasting his bushy beard.

"I'm sorry, but this is a private meeting," Alexandra said.

"I was hoping so," he said.

To her surprise, and that of everyone else, he peeled off his beard and shoved it in his pocket and then from another pocket he brought out a pair of wire-rimmed glasses which he slipped onto his face.

Without disguise, Alexandra recognized him at once.

"You're..."

"Masters," he said. "Daniel Masters."

"Well, you certainly know how to make an entrance," Samantha said as she sat next to him.

The other two were still staring at him strangely as they filled the remaining seats.

"You were here even before I got here," Alexandra noted. "I noticed you in the corner."

"And?"

"Why didn't you just come over?"

"I had to make sure I wasn't being set up or lured into a trap."

"Who would lay a trap for you?"

He shrugged and, with zero humor in his voice, said,

"Any one of my enemies."

Looks were shared all around the table.

"Aren't you a little too young to be having enemies?" James said.

"Cute." His tone was withering. "Can we get on with this meeting already? I'm sure some of us promised our mothers we'd be home before dinner."

James did not have the intended reaction as he merely shifted his chair forward and propped his chin on his hands attentively and it was clear that Daniel was disappointed. Everyone else turned to focus on her.

Alexandra was not a particularly shy girl, but as she looked around the table at the expectant faces, she felt a wave of nervousness wash over her. They were all here because of her.

The determination that had come following her dream of Ravensbrook Asylum had not waned with the passing of time; the determination to discover what had really happened fifty years ago and rectify the damage that had been wrought on that cursed land. That very determination had led her to seek out people who could help her in her quest.

Ever since she was a little girl, Alexandra could see the future. The first time it happened, she dreamt, and in her dream, she saw flashes of a horrible car crash and a very familiar face among the wreckage. In the evening of the next day, she found out that her favorite Aunt Priscilla and her husband had died in an accident.

The premonitions primarily came in the form of dreams, and as she grew older, the dreams took on more depth and details, but in her early teenage years, she found that if she focused hard enough and quieted her mind, she could will her powers to manifest to a lesser degree.

For the most part of growing up, Alexandra had searched for others like herself. People who were gifted with supernatural powers like she was. She had had little luck until she stumbled on a retired circus performer who could see the future just like she did, using reflective surfaces as a medium. She reached out to her anonymously and found her to be surprisingly friendly. Her name was Agatha, but back when she performed, she went by the stage name the One-Eyed One, although she had perfect vision in both eyes and merely covered one with an eye patch. They built an online friendship until Agatha passed away two years ago.

Before Agatha had passed, she had helped her understand that people like them would exist in secrecy and that the only way to find them was to search in the secret places. That led her to the anonymous chat app, where, guided by the subconscious nudging of her extrasensory abilities, she met all four of them.

Oddly enough, Daniel was the first she had discovered. He was pretty easy to find, almost like he wanted to be found. He had heard her out, and if he doubted her claims, he did not show, but he refused to join until she proved she could get more people together. When that happened, she added them all to a group chat, and they used made-up names and misleading profiles to protect their identities. They had trusted her with their pictures and real identities, but they were yet to trust each other. And now it was up to her to navigate until they did.

"Right," Alexandra said. She took her seat. "Hello, everyone. I'm Alexandra. My friends would probably call me Alex if I had any. I've shared this with you all individually, but I'll repeat it to recap: I have the gift of foresight, or precognition if you will. That means I can see the future and occasionally the past in the form of dreams and visions. At least, that's how it typically works. Recently, I've had a recurring dream about the Ravensbrook Asylum. At first, it would just be this aggressive blur of specters attacking me anytime I close my eyes, but the dreams have gotten clearer, and now I understand that they're coming to me, seeking my help. I'm sure you've all heard the rumors of what happened in that place. You know that people have died there. But they haven't crossed over, and I don't know why. They're trapped, and they want release from their suffering, and they want me to help them get that. But I, in turn, need your help."

There was a moment of silence and it was broken by the person Alexandra least expected.

"Okay," Daniel said.

"Okay?"

"I'm in. That's what you want, right? Or has that changed?"

"What? No. I'm just surprised, is all. That was easy."

"I see things too, remember?" he said.

It was clear he was not going to elaborate on that as he leaned back and folded his arms.

"Right..." Alexandra said.

"I'm in, too," Samantha said. "My mom says I should get out more often."

"To be clear, you're talking about a haunted asylum with actual ghosts and whatever else," Lila said.

"Yes, I am," Alexandra said.

She nodded as though ruminating on it.

"I'm not great with group projects, but this one sounds like it might be fun, so count me in."

James cleared his throat.

"Well then, I guess I'm in too."

A smile broke out on Alexandra's face. She had hoped most of them would agree, but somehow, she got all of them.

"So, what now?" James said.

"Well... I guess we could tell each other about our abilities. I already went first, so who's next?"

None of them seemed eager to go next, but eventually, Samantha sat up.

"I can see and communicate with ghosts," she said.

"Cool!" Lila said.

"No. Not cool. I mean when the ghost is all nice and friendly then sure, but malevolent ghosts exist and they can be... a handful."

She shrugged. "I still think that would be interesting."

"Well, tell us what you can do."

"I could tell you," she said. "But I bet it would be more fun just to show you."

She lifted a finger and Alexandra's book shuddered briefly before rising off the table, levitating till it was hovering over her head.

"Lila!" Alexandra snapped. She snatched up the book before it could go any higher and looked around to make sure no one else had witnessed the unexplainable sight. Fortunately, the other customers were not paying them any attention and Wesley had her back turned to them. "You need to be careful!"

Lila rolled her eyes. "Yeah, yeah. Telekinesis. I have telekinesis."

"That is wild!" Samantha said. "Wanna trade?"

"I don't suppose any of you has ever heard of Psychometry," Daniel said.

Samantha scratched her head. "I'm not great with math."

He huffed and facepalmed.

"It's not math. It's my power. I have the ability to discover facts about an event or person by touching inanimate objects associated with them."

Lila's brow went up.

"What?"

He reached across the table and grabbed hold of Alexandra's cup as he locked eyes with her.

"You arrived thirty minutes before the specified time. You had an iced tea and two grilled cheese sandwiches while you waited. When that was gone, you played with the napkins, folding them into swaddled pretend babies. Then you read from your journal where you've written all the information you have on us as well as all the visions you've had. Also, you're here practically every day, and you've used this particular cup a total of fifty-eight times throughout your life."

The silence that followed was absolute as everyone at the table stared at the boy.

"What... the hell?" Samantha said.

"That was incredible!" James said.

"I'm not buying it," Lila said.

"I beg your pardon?" Daniel said, his brows furrowing.

"You were here before any of us arrived, including Alexandra. And you were watching her the whole time like a creep, which means you knew what she ordered just by looking, and from her interactions with the server, I'm sure you could tell she was a regular. Everything else about the content of her journal and the number of times she's used the cup is pretty much an educated guess here and there."

Daniel looked well and truly offended now. Without warning, he lunged across the table faster than any of them could react, but all he did was grab onto her jacket sleeve.

"You took the bus here even though you have your own car," he said. "Before you left home, you got in a fight with your mother because she thought you were going to hang out with those no-good friends of yours that she doesn't approve of, and frankly, I agree with her. The jacket itself belongs to your older sister, but she doesn't wear it anymore because she... can't." He blinked profusely, and his eyes softened. "I'm terribly sorry. I... I didn't mean to—"

Across the table, Lila's countenance had darkened, and the look in her eyes promised death, or failing to grant that, a world of pain. She stretched forth her hand and Daniel clutched his throat as his eyes widened in alarm. His mouth opened and closed like a fish out of water, and it was just as his face started to take on a shade of red that Alexandra caught on to what was happening. She was choking him.

"You fucking bastard!" Lila seethed. "You had no right! None!"

Suddenly, everyone at the table was on high alert, but they had to be careful not to escalate the situation and bring attention to themselves.

Lila was livid, bordering on irate. Whatever Daniel had found out was sensitive to her.

"Lila, easy now," Alexandra said. "You're hurting him!"

"I'm well aware of what I'm doing," Lila snapped.

"Well, are you planning to kill him too?" Samantha asked.

All the while, Daniel gagged and sputtered as he tried and failed to take a single breath.

Alexandra looked to the far side. Wesley was looking in their direction, and the look on her face was of curiosity, but she didn't seem to have caught on to what was happening, much less the supernatural nature of said happening.

"Lila!" Alexandra said. "Let him go!"

"Just shut up! Shut—"

Her voice was steadily growing louder, and if she had completed that sentence, she would have been loud enough to attract the attention of everyone else in the cafe, but before she could, James moved.

In a split second, he took his glove off and put his bare hand on Lila's wrist. She turned to him, and as her eyes met his, they seemed to lose all their fire, and quickly, her anger fizzled out.

"Calm down," he whispered. The single word felt like a command the way he said it, and it might as well have been because her hand went limp, and as he loosened his grip, it fell to the table as she slumped in her seat.

For a moment, the only sound that could be heard was Daniel's wheezy breathing as he took in air like a thirsty man would water.

"Empathy," James said as he struggled to slip on his gloves. "That's... That's my thing."

The silence persisted until Daniel found his words again.

"Lila, I didn't know," he said. "I didn't mean to go that far, and I didn't mean to see what I saw. I'm sorry."

Lila nodded.

"You will never breathe a word of what you saw," she said. "That is if you wish to keep breathing at all."

"O...kay," Alexandra said. "I think that's enough getting to know each other for one day. We'll meet up in a few days and go over the plan together, but for now, let's not try to kill each other again." She rose from her seat. "For what it's worth, I'm glad I found you all."

Chapter 3:
INVESTIGATION

A week later, Alexandra and her new crew did meet up again, and everyone was present although Lila made a point of keeping her distance from Daniel. Then again, whether it was due to remorse or fear, Daniel was not too keen on being near her either.

Within the week, Alexandra had acquired a map of the town as well as a book on the history of Ravensbrook Hollow, which included the original blueprints of the Ravensbrook Asylum and a summary of the events that had led to the shutting down of the asylum, and so as they sat around in the garden behind Alexandra's house, they looked over the maps.

Alexandra lived with her sister, who left home early in the morning and came home late in the evening.

"I still don't get what we needed the maps for," James said. "The blueprints I understand, but why the map of the town?"

"We need to know the best route to take up to the asylum. Five young adults just walking right up the hill to the gates will raise suspicion if we're seen."

"What does it matter? The asylum has been abandoned for over half a century. No one cares. It's not illegal, is it?"

"Not quite, but it's not entirely legal either," she said. "Years back, squatters and especially travelers passing through the town with no money for rent used to take up residence there, intending to spend a night or two, but none of them ever made it through a single night. At some point between midnight and three in the morning, they could be heard running down the hill, screaming at the top of their lungs about strange occurrences, from hauntings to ghostly possessions to flat-out inexplicable attacks. The police tried to investigate on multiple occasions, but they never found anything out of the ordinary, and eventually, they decided to seal the place up away from the public. Long story short, if we're seen traipsing up to the place, someone's definitely going to call the cops on us, and we cannot have that."

"Agreed. So, what do we do?"

"There's a bush path that leads out of town, across a stream, and right up to the asylum," Samantha said, putting her finger on the map just behind the local school. "That's probably the least conspicuous way into the woods because school's out for the summer. From there, I can probably find the path. It cuts through the woods right up to the fence of the asylum not too far from the side entrance."

"And how... I really don't mean to pry, but... How do you know this?" Lila asked.

"I've been there before," she said.

"You have?" Alexandra said.

They were all staring in awe.

"Don't look at me like that. It was three years ago. A ghost friend told me about the place, and I decided to check it out one time. Never made it past the gate." She shuddered. "That place practically reeks of evil."

"Can you remember the way?" Daniel asked.

"I don't know, but Sally can."

"Who?"

"My ghost friend. Her name is Sally. She died in the early 1600s. You might like her if you meet her."

"No, thank you. The living are trouble enough."

"Moving on," Alexandra said. "We need supplies. Flashlights. Crowbars. Food supplies. Water. Proper clothes. That sort of thing."

"What about guns?" James said.

"Not to be a Bible nerd, but we're not going up against flesh and blood, genius," Daniel said.

"Whatever happened to 'better to have and not need'?"

"Do you have a gun?" Lila asked.

"I do not."

"Neither do I. Can you get one?"

"I cannot."

"Neither can I. So why don't we focus on what we can in fact control?"

He nodded resignedly. "Sounds fair."

"And we're not going there to attack whatever's on the other side of those walls, remember that." Alexandra said. "We're going there to help them. They reached out to me for help, and that is the only reason I'm doing this. Are you with me?"

The nods of agreement were unanimous.

"So how exactly do we help them?"

"To be straight with you, I'm not sure yet. But I have this feeling in my gut that we'll find the answers we need when we get there."

"Gut feeling," Daniel repeated blandly. "That's what we're going with. Neat."

"If you're having cold feet, you could always bow out before it's too late."

He scoffed. "As if. I'm just processing how crazy this is, doesn't mean I'm not all for it. "

They went over the list of supplies and planned for as much as they could for another hour, and by the end of the meeting, they had decided on the coming Saturday as the D-day. Before that, they had split into two groups, with one group in charge of gathering supplies and the other paying a visit to the library to gather more information on Ravensbrook Asylum.

Lila and James were on supply stocking duty together while Alexandra, Daniel, and Samantha visited the library. Alexandra had a feeling Daniel agreed to the library only to avoid having to be around Lila but she did not mind the company, especially as he somehow managed to get rid of the smokers in the back.

*****

The Ravensbrook library was no giant marble-finished building on the town square, adorned with lion statues and Romanesque pillars like Alexandra had seen in the bigger towns and the city. Almost as old as the town itself, the library stood at the center of the town, not too far from the mayor's office on an all-but-dead street whose primary source of activity was the cafe and bar. The library was a wood and brick building that had closed down due to lack of funding and neglect but was remodeled and eventually opened in the 1990s after the schoolteachers and local residents campaigned to complain about the lack of reading materials for the students.

Usually, Alexandra was the only one at the library doing any actual reading, but today, she had company, and it felt nice.

It was Daniel who eventually found a book on Ravensbrook Asylum, and ironically, he found it because he was slacking off in the back instead of searching the shelves with the girls. The book was not on the shelves like all the other books but was instead in a box in storage, almost as if someone had intentionally put it away to bury it along with the memories of that dreadful place.

They found Bethany scrolling through an old Archie comic book with a perpetually bored expression on her face.

"I'm checking this out," Alexandra said.

"Whatever," Bethany said.

She pushed the comic aside and flipped open the front page but stopped as she noticed the red stamp on it. Alexandra had not seen it before.

"Well, this says not to be borrowed," Bethany said. "Where did you even find this?"

"Storage in the back," Daniel said.

"Daniel!" Samantha elbowed him.

"Well, I can't let you check that out," she said.

"But we need this book!" Alexandra said.

"I don't know what to tell ya," she said. "Rules are rules."

"Oh, come on, Beth! What do you care?"

"I don't." She shrugged. "My father, on the other hand... yeah."

Alexandra felt around in her pocket for a bit.

"Okay. How's this? I give you this." She placed a ten-dollar bill on the counter. "And you let me walk out of here with that book?"

Bethany stared down her nose at the money.

"Cute."

"Alright then. How about a twenty?" She added another bill.

"I cannot believe this is happening." Bethany scoffed.

"What? Do you want more? Is that not enough?"

"Money! You're trying to bribe *me* with money? Do you not know who my father is?"

"Right. Of course," Alexandra said with a defeated scowl. With Bethany working as a librarian, it was easy to forget that her family was one of the wealthiest in Ravensbrook Hollow. "But..." She could have sworn she saw one of the smokers slip her some money one time before they went into the back. That was why she let them in the back, wasn't it?

Daniel cleared his throat, and Bethany turned to face him.

"Who are you?" she said, pretending to just notice him. "Starting a book club, are we, Alex? What comic convention did you get these ones from?"

If Daniel was fazed, he did not show it. He ran his finger over the counter and pretended to inspect it as though it was covered in dust, except the counter was spotless.

"So, you care what your father thinks, yes?" he said. "I mean, you don't want your allowance cut off."

"Of course. Why else would I even be here?"

"That's what I thought." He smiled. "So, what do you think would happen if he knew about what exactly goes on in here?"

She scowled at him.

"I have no idea what you're talking about," she said.

"Oh, but I bet you do. Those boys. With the cigarettes. In the back office. I'm sure they ring a bell. And you know what? I don't think daddy would approve."

For a second, Bethany looked well and truly worried, but then she bent over and laughed a long, hearty laugh.

When she was done, she wiped her eyes and sighed in amusement.

"I'm sorry, it's really hard to pretend to take you seriously," she said. "You think my dad's going to punish me for letting customers smoke in here? He cares, but believe me, he doesn't care that much. And if something did catch on fire and this whole place burned, believe me, he would love the insurance money. So maybe get out of here before you embarrass yourself any further."

Alexandra was stunned, and a sideways glance showed that Samantha was right with her. She could have sworn Daniel had her on the ropes.

But Daniel's smile had not waned in the slightest.

"Close, but that's not what I'm referring to," he said. "I know why you let those boys in here. You're doing a little favor, aren't you? A favor to your little boyfriend, Greg."

"Boyfriend?" Alexandra said, surprised. *How could he possibly know?*

She stared at Daniel. That was when she noticed his hand on the table. He was doing his thing. He could tell everything that had happened around the table.

Across from them, Bethany's face was a picture of pure shock.

"You don't know what you're talking about."

"You have no idea how much I know," he said. "His name is Gregory Becker. Brawny dude. He says he's in a biker gang, but that's all bullshit. He's way too old for you, and it wouldn't matter if he were your age, considering what he gets up to in his spare time. But you don't care about all of that when he's propping you up on this very desk and having his way with you, do you?"

Bethany's eyes were the size of quarters now, and her jaw had dropped.

"You can't... How do you know all of that?"

"Wouldn't you like to know? But you're not the one I'm interested in spilling secrets to. I bet your dad would appreciate that kind of information, don't you think? I mean the smoking he probably can overlook but his daughter going out with a hooligan and having sex," He dragged the word out into a chuckle, "oh that won't go well, will it?"

At this point, Bethany was red in the face, and Alexandra was starting to feel sorry for her.

Bethany threw the book down in front of him.

"Just get out."

Daniel smiled. "You're a darling. Also, he's got a girlfriend, and he's cheating on her with you."

Samantha grabbed him by the arm and dragged him out before he could speak any further.

*****

Alexandra was the first to arrive at the high school on Saturday, or at least she thought so until she saw Daniel coming out of the woods just by the school fence.

"Of course, you're here already," she said. "How long have you been here."

"Seven minutes and..." He glanced at his watch. "... fifty-eight seconds."

"Do you always do that?"

"Check my watch? Yeah. How else would I know the time?"

"No, I mean arrive at a meeting before everyone else."

"Why do you care?"

"I don't. Just curious."

"I've dealt with enough people to know that people cannot be trusted," he said. "So, I make sure to stay one step ahead."

"Well, that was awfully cryptic."

"Whatever." He folded his arms and rested against the gate post. "Any word from the others?"

"Yeah, James and Samantha are almost here. Lila got held up, but she should be on her way now."

Daniel did not speak again. He turned towards the woods and fixed his gaze on a point underneath the canopy of green. Alexandra, on the other hand, distracted herself with the sight of the school buildings on the other side of the gates.

Ravensbrook High was the only school in the town, and Alexandra, like everyone else in her generation and the one before, had attended it. Alexandra herself had graduated last year but looking back, it felt like ages.

The halls of Ravensbrook High held fond memories for her, and they reminded her of a simpler time when her biggest worries were homework and picking out what to wear. Now, here she was, embarking on a mission with people she barely knew to help literal ghosts with no idea what she would find waiting for them. Suddenly, homework didn't seem so bad.

James and Samantha arrived a few minutes later, wearing their signature gloves and headset, respectively, but it was another fifteen minutes before Lila finally showed up. And then it was time to head out.

"So, when's your ghost friend gonna show, Sam?" Daniel asked.

"Rude," Samantha said. "On their own, ghosts can't wander too far from the place they were killed. We'll find Sally in the woods right around where she was murdered."

"Well, that's a cheerful thought," James muttered.

"Lead the way then," Alexandra said.

With Samantha in the lead, they began the trek into the woods. The path they followed led them out of town just as Samantha said it would and after fifteen minutes of trekking, she stopped abruptly.

"What is it?" James said.

"I can sense her," Samantha said as she looked around, her eyes narrowed. "She's close by. But where?"

"Maybe you should call out to her?"

"Very funny."

"I didn't realize I was making a joke," James said, confused.

"She's a ghost, James. It doesn't quite work like—gah!"

She screamed and jumped away.

The rest of them froze in place.

"What just happened?" Alexandra said.

But Samantha wasn't paying attention. Instead, she was scowling at thin air.

"Jesus Christ, Sally! We talked about this!" she said. "This is why you don't have any friends!"

"Is Sally here?" Daniel inquired. He cautiously waved his hand around as though trying to feel her.

His actions caught Samantha's attention, and she looked at him with a raised brow.

"What exactly are you doing?" she said.

Daniel righted himself and cleared his throat.

"Nothing."

She rolled her eyes and held out her arm as though putting them over someone's shoulders.

"Everyone, this is Sally," she said. "Sally, these are my friends. That's Alex. He's James. She's Lila. The weird one is Daniel."

"You're talking to thin air, and I'm the weird one?"

"That is very offensive, Daniel." Samantha frowned. "You could hurt Sally's feelings. Then again, she does float around with an arrow in her lung, so you probably aren't doing much. Either way, be better."

"Can we get on with this?" Alexandra said.

"Right. Sally, we need your help getting to the asylum. We're trying to stay out of sight so we can't go through the town, but I don't remember the way through the woods. Do you still know the way?"

A pause.

"Of course you do."

Another pause.

"Fine, I'll fill you in on the way, but you won't like it." She turned to them.

"This way."

She stepped aside, presumably to let the ghost pass, then she went after, and they, in turn, followed her.

"I've done some weird things in my life," Daniel said, "but following a girl following a ghost through the woods is definitely high up there."

"Shut up, Daniel," Samantha said.

Chapter 4:
A Past Unveiled

It was almost midday by the time they got to the stream, and they could only tell by their watches as the foliage had now grown too thick to get a good look at the sky, although there was still enough room for the light of day to sufficiently illuminate the way.

In the lead, James and Samantha had fallen in step next to each other, keeping a space between them that was occupied by the ghost named Sally. Alexandra and Lila had paired up behind them, leaving Daniel trailing behind.

If anyone had told him a month ago that he would be out in the woods playing fifth— sixth?— wheel with his new friends, he would have laughed in their face.

For as long as he could remember, Daniel had always flown solo. Having grown up in a foster home several towns away from Ravensbrook Hollow, he found himself unable to connect to his foster family, especially as his powers began to manifest, making him feel more and more like an outsider, so when he was thirteen, he ran away from home.

The years that followed were spent living on the streets, stealing to get by with the help of his psychometry. All in all, it was a good stint, and he made enough to put a roof over his head and food on his plate. But with youth came stupidity, and Daniel's stupidity manifested when he stole from the wrong man: the head of the Blue Fangs gang, Dean Wright.

Although the same could not be said of his crew, Dean was a smart man. He quickly figured out that there was something different about him and interrogated him until Daniel revealed his powers. Then again, perhaps that was giving him too much credit, seeing as he had stolen his credit card and used his powers to figure out the pin.

Deciding that Daniel was more useful alive than dead, he recruited him into his gang, threatening to kill him and everyone he ever met if he refused.

From then on, life for Daniel took a turn for the worse as he was used like a tool by the Blue Fangs. He was made to break into bank vaults with passwords he shouldn't have known and threaten their enemies with information he had no right or reason to possess.

Daniel endured doing the Blue Fangs' dirty work for three years, but eventually, he had to find his way out, and after tipping the police on their hideout, he skipped town. After moving from town to town, he at last ended up in Ravensbrook Hollow, where he had been laying low ever since, refraining from using his powers. But that quickly got boring and that was why he got that message from Alexandra, he agreed to meet. And now here he was.

"Hey, slowpoke! Hurry up!" Samantha called out.

Daniel snapped out of his reverie to realize that the others had already crossed the stream and were waiting for him on the other side. The stream was deep, and the current was too strong to wade through. The row of stones peeking out on the water's surface showed him how they had made it across.

Checking that his backpack was secured to his person, he jumped onto the first rock. And then the next. But as he jumped to the third, he landed wrong, and his foot slipped out from under him.

"Shit!"

His eyes widened in horror, and his arms shot out, flailing about in a futile attempt to save him. Just as he accepted his fate and braced for the dive, he felt a strange force, like a cushion but firmer, slow down his fall and then hold him up while he found his footing.

He jumped the rest of the way, and only when he was back on solid ground again did he take note of Lila's outstretched arm, which she had just put away, and turned from the scene. She had saved him.

"Good save!" Alexandra commented, either aloof to what had really happened or playing along.

"Right, yes," he said. "That was... something."

Thankfully, the rest of the journey was uneventful, but Daniel could hardly take his eyes off Lila. There was no doubt in his mind that she still wanted to hurt him for what he had done back at the cafe, but she had just saved his life, reacting with no hesitation. She was a good person. What had happened... What he had seen... It hadn't been her fault.

But that was not how she saw it. He could tell from the guilt in her eyes.

The trees gave way as they stepped out of the woods and into a clearing that was characterized by tall grasses and rocks. And then there was the fence.

Standing at a good five meters, the fence made Daniel feel smaller. It looked like it wasn't just meant to keep the inmates inside but also to crush the hope of ever seeing the outside world.

"What the hell was this place?" Daniel said. "An asylum or a prison?"

"From what I read, it was much worse," Alexandra said.

They went around until they came to the entrance where the rusty metal gates, barely hanging on at the hinges, were chained together with faded yellow police tape. Both measures were in place only to discourage wanderers from entering but not quite keep them out as there was a gaping hole underneath where the gate had been forced apart. Perhaps they thought the state of the property itself was enough reason to turn any sane person back.

Before they proceeded, Samantha took a minute to say goodbye to Sally. While that happened, Daniel found himself standing next to James, who was smiling fondly in Samantha's direction.

"Don't tell me you're already in love with her," he said.

James' expression shifted to confusion, and then, as he processed Daniel's words, he was shocked.

"What? No. That's not it," he said. "I might not be able to see this, Sally, but I can sense her through Sam's emotions and the energy coming off of her... Well, it's nice. She's nice."

Samantha rejoined the group just then, and one by one, they ducked under the gate.

Gravel crunched underfoot as they made their way towards the front doors. The path had been completely overgrown with weeds, coming as high up as their knees.

They came to a stop just before the threshold and looked up at the terrifying building. Daniel had a feeling that in its full glory, the building looked like the kind of place an ancient Disney vampire would be found, but now, with the faded, moss-covered facade riddled with stubborn plants growing through the cracks in the stone walls, the asylum looked like something straight out of a Grimm's horror story.

"Am I the only one getting major creepy vibes?" he asked.

"No," the others chorused.

"Ah. Cool. Cool."

"Let's split up and take a look around," Alexandra said. "See what we can find before we go in. Make sure there are no surprises."

James squinted. "You're using video game logic right now, aren't you?"

Alexandra's face took on a reddish tint. "Maybe. Maybe not. Just go."

One by one, they spread out left and right, going around the building, but Daniel remained rooted to the spot at the entrance with a burning curiosity. Of the five of them, he had the least knowledge of what had happened in Ravensbrook Asylum. All he knew was what they had learned from the book, which was that it had been run by a madman by the name of Matthias Blackthorne until the people heard word of his cruelty and took action, bringing him to justice. But he knew from experience that there was more to every story than what was written down.

With that thought in mind, he climbed the threshold and came face to face with the front door of the asylum, unlocked and slightly ajar as it was. He put out his hand in front of him, and after a slight hesitation, he extended it until he touched the wooden surface.

At once, his head snapped back, and he lost his sight entirely for a second.

*****

As he came to, he found himself staring at the very same door, except it could not have been more different. It was brand new. The wood was vibrant, the metal fittings were polished to a pristine shine, and the framework was immaculate.

He suddenly became aware that he was not alone and turned to find not a person but a whole crowd of people gathered around the entrance, facing a small, elevated platform where a man stood addressing them. Several photographers took pictures, telling Daniel that he was someone important. Behind the man, there was a red tape that separated him from the asylum itself. It did not take a genius to figure out that this was the mayor and he was about to commission the building.

"It is not a thing of pride to say that among us, we have men and women, and even children, who have fallen prey to the illnesses of the mind. More than a few of us have lost brothers and sisters and parents and children to madness. I remember my dear sister who took ill in this manner after the death of her daughter, my niece. Councilman Johnson, my old friend. He had an accident and took a severe blow to the head, and while he has physically been with us since, his mind has been far from us. If we were to go around asking, I'm sure you all would have your stories to tell, and it is indeed a very sad thing. As you all know, my dear sister did not make it. Three months ago, she, um... she hanged herself in her home while her husband was away." There was somber murmuring in the crowd, and several women and a handful of men turned away to wipe their eyes. "I could not save my sister, but in her name and in the name of all those we have lost, I solemnly vowed to save your families. That is why we are here today to commission the Ravensbrook Asylum. Let it now and forever stand as a beacon of hope for the mentally troubled."

The crowd cheered rapturously until he silenced them with a raised hand.

From the side, someone approached with a pair of scissors. The mayor took it and moved to the tape.

"I dedicate this building to family members lost," he said. "Here's to hoping it never happens again."

At the snip of the scissors, the vision shifted. Before Daniel had fully acclimatized, he heard voices drifting into his ears from above, mixed in with scurrying footsteps.

The gates were open, and a black car was driving onto the premises. It came to a halt in front of the asylum, and before the engine had ceased, the doors exploded open, and a group of nurses rushed out.

They lined up on either side of the path, just in front of the statues. They were the welcome party, apparently. But for who?

Daniel was keenly watching the car, waiting to see the man who would emerge, and he completely missed the tall man who came out after the nurses until he was standing just beside him.

He all but jumped at the sight of the man's towering figure, and his fright only intensified as he beheld the man's face.

Daniel had met with a lot of scary men while working under Dean Wright, men who could invoke fear just by being, but none of them held a candle to the man before him. With eyes devoid of feeling and lips marred into a permanent scowl, the man was absolutely terrifying. Dressed in a suit so black that Daniel wondered if it perhaps absorbed light around it, he had a penetrating aura around him that was felt even by the nurses.

He recognized him from the book they had taken from the library. This was Warden Blackthorne.

The driver had stepped out to open the door for his passenger. The man's face was every bit as Daniel expected: a thin, pale layer of flesh stretched over his vividly defined skull. He certainly looked like the kind of man who would be acquainted with the likes of the warden. Daniel wondered who the man was and what his connection to the asylum was, but he did not get a chance to find out because just as the man's cane touched the ground, Daniel felt himself being pulled away to another time.

When his vision returned, Daniel righted himself and looked at the door once more. It was the very same one, except, somehow, it was shut now and seemed to have regressed in age by several decades, judging from the less damaged look of the finish and the missing smell of wood rot.

Night had fallen, and the brilliant gleam of the moon shone brightly on him, casting his shadow over the door before him.

He looked up at the building, and sure enough, it was in better condition than when he and his friend had met it. He had been transported to the past. But how far back?
The sound of angry shouting soon reached his ears, and Daniel turned. The sight he found made him freeze in horror until he remembered that he wasn't actually physically present. In the distance, he saw an angry mob marching towards the asylum. They carried with them flaming torches, sticks, and literal pitchforks, and they were yelling out threats, their voices rising as they neared, but with everyone shouting at once in disunity, it came out unintelligible. But words were not necessary to understand that they were here with violent intent, and someone on the other side of the door Daniel was standing at had gravely wronged them.

It did not take them long to reach the gate, and there they stopped. Their chants and threats were now reduced to angry murmuring. Then a woman spoke up, her voice loud and clear over the chatter.

"Listen to me! We have been silent for too long, blinded by our trust in those who promised to heal and protect. But no more! The truth of Ravensbrook Asylum must be brought to light!"

The woman's voice was rich with emotions of loss and pain, and Daniel could feel it all the way from where he stood. He could feel that the crowd shared her grief.

"Tonight, we tear down these walls!" a man spoke up, his voice booming even louder. "Tonight, we expose the horrors that have been hidden from our eyes! For justice, for our loved ones, for Ravensbrook Hollow!"

The response was so deafening that it reverberated within Daniel himself. They pushed against the gates with their combined strength until the gates gave way.

They stormed right up to the door which only managed to delay them for a moment as they sent it swinging in, almost flying off its hinges, with several powerful blows.

As one, they charged into the building, ignoring Daniel as they basically moved through him.

Soon, their voices, loud as they were, faded into the distance above before suddenly cutting off.

He could still hear them moving through the building, but for some reason, they were no longer making a lot of noise. He guessed that they had found the warden. Perhaps they were arresting him now and bringing him down.

The thought lasted, but a moment as the next thing he heard was a scream so raw and guttural it could only have come from a man in agony. He heard another, matching the first. Two men. And then, as quickly as the screaming had begun, they were cut off.

Daniel did not need to see to know what had happened. The warden and whoever had been with him had faced justice, but not in any courthouse or town square. They had faced justice in its truest form, blood for blood.

*****

An arm on his shoulder jolted Daniel back to reality. He blinked as he adjusted to his physical surroundings once again.

When his eyes had gotten accustomed to the light once more, he realized he was sitting on the ground, and Lila was standing over him with a hand on his shoulder. Behind her, James stood with a concerned frown.

"How... How long was I out?"

"I don't know," James said. "A minute? Two, maybe?"

He noticed that Alexandra and Samantha were absent. "And the others? What happened to them?"

"Still having a look around. James sensed that something had happened to you, and we came back."

"Ah. Thank you."

"Whatever."

"So, what *did* happen?" James said. "I was getting a lot of mixed signals from you, all of them bad."

"I... I touched the door, and I saw..."

"You saw? Saw what?"

"The past. I saw the asylum as it was from the day it was built. I watched as it fell away to neglect and became something sinister. I saw it that night. The night of the..." He smacked his forehead in a bid to clear his head. "The night that," He waved his hand in the direction of the building, "this happened."

Alexandra and Samantha rejoined them just then. Daniel noticed that Samantha had her headset on now.

"What happened to looking around?" Alexandra asked.

"Something came up," Lila said.

She and James stepped aside so they could see Daniel on the floor.

"What happened?"

"Nothing much," he said. "Just a little trip down the memory lane of this place."

He proceeded to tell them everything he had seen including the strange man who had visited the asylum, but none of them knew who he was and the descriptions did not match anyone that had been mentioned in the book.

Deciding that Daniel had probably provided them with every bit of information they could gather from outside, it was time to venture into Ravensbrook Asylum.

Chapter 5:
THE SINISTER PHYSICIAN

The eerie chill the team had felt outside the asylum was nothing compared to the one on the inside.

As soon as they crossed the threshold into the lobby, they all simultaneously stopped in their tracks to make sure the others had felt what they had felt.

Standing in the lobby of Ravensbrook Asylum felt like standing in the hollowed-out insides of some dead entity. The proof that there had once been life within these walls was very present, but it had been tainted with rot and decay. It had been tainted with death.

They felt it in the thickness of the air and in the stained, peeled walls and the dusty, faded tiles. The memories of all this place had been had seeped deep into the very fabric of its structure like a stain that would not wash out.

There was a soft crackle as Alexandra tugged on a piece of peeling paint, and it came right off the wall, falling to the ground where it crumbled.

She gestured to the flight of stairs, and they nodded in agreement. With her leading the way, they ascended to the floor above, footsteps echoing through the empty hallways.

Reaching the floor above, they came upon a corridor with rows of solid oak doors on either side.

She went up to the first and opened it. The sight that greeted then was a single unmade bed with a small storage chest at the foot of it and a small reading table and chair to the side. The only source of light came from a tiny window just above the table.

From the fabrics that covered the bed to the paint on the walls, everything was a depressing grey. Alexandra also found a pair of old, worn-out slippers under the bed. Those, too, were grey.

All the other rooms that they checked turned out to be the same, and in one of the rooms, on the table, Alexandra found what could only be scratch marks made by fingernails. It had to have hurt a lot, and yet the person had dug past the paint and even managed to leave indentations in the wood.

Alexandra could hardly blame them. The thought of spending day after day in this room had to have been enough to make a mad person even madder.

In another room, they found a suspicious brown stain splattered on the wall, and they shuddered to think of the possibilities.

The more rooms they checked, the more abysmal the sights they found. There was one with a crack on the wall and a similar brown stain. Another, they found torn clothes with the same stains. By now, they were completely certain that it was blood.

By the time they got reached the end of the hallway, they had started to form a mental picture of the kind of administration that had been in place.

They found the nurse's quarters next, but they found little of interest there, and so they quickly moved on to the next floor.

Upstairs, they found more wards, but before they could check them out, Samantha stopped them.

"Wait!" she said. It was the first time any of them had spoken since entering the asylum, and although her voice was a mere whisper, it felt harsh against the otherwise quiet. "Do you guys hear that?"

Glances were cast this way and that, and by the end, it was clear that they had not.

"Hear what?" Daniel asked. "And how can you even hear anything through that?"

Samantha slipped off the headset and let it rest around her neck as she looked around with a squinted gaze, but it did not seem to be as a result of Daniel's question.

"The crying," she said. "Someone is crying."

They listened, but again, none of them heard a peep, talk less of someone crying.

"Are you... feeling alright?" Daniel said.

Alexandra was quick to elbow him, and while he nursed his rib, Samantha approached a door. She took a deep breath, and then she opened it.

Almost immediately, she cupped her mouth and staggered back so fast she hit the door and slammed it into the wall.

"Oh, dear God," she muttered.

The others came rushing in at once.

"What is it?" they chorused.

James started to put a hand on her shoulder but decided against it.

"Ghost," Samantha said. "There's a ghost in the room. There's... There's cut marks on her arms and she has a strange helmet on her head like... Like the kind that's hooked up to the electric chair."

At once, they turned to look in the direction she was facing and backed away, but Daniel was the first to notice something peculiar, or at least the first to voice it.

"You're afraid of a ghost?" he said. "Isn't that your whole thing?"

James took it upon himself to respond, which was convenient because Samantha was still staring wordlessly.

"She's not afraid," he said. "She's... She's horrified. And not of the ghost... on behalf of it."

"What does that mean?"

This time, James did not get to speak as Samantha approached the ghost, but when Samantha knelt and put up her hands as though cupping a face, the meaning quickly became apparent.

"Oh my God," Lila said.

"It's... It's a child," Daniel muttered.

"Hello," Samantha said. Her voice was even softer now. "I'm Sam. What is your name?"

The others looked on expectantly.

"Sylvia Grace," Samantha said, apparently repeating after the ghost. "That's a beautiful name, Sylvia."

Alexandra was positioned to Samantha's side and so when the first tear streaked down her face, she saw it.

"Sam..." she said.

She proceeded to put her hand on Samantha's shoulder. Automatically, the girl jerked. She rose to her feet and exited the room in a hurry.

"Sam!" Alexandra and James called after her.

They did not attempt to follow at once, but they heard her footsteps come to a stop outside the ward.

James started to leave, but Alexandra caught him. She could tell he was feeling whatever she was feeling, and it was hitting him just as hard.

"Let me," she said. "Please."

James nodded and sank back against the wall.

"What is going on?" Daniel muttered.

Alexandra held up a finger to pacify him, and then she went out after Samantha.

As she expected, Samantha was just by the door. She was seated on the dusty floor with her knees pulled up to her chest and her head between them, and Alexandra could hear her breathing heavily.

She sat down next to her and tentatively put a hand on her knee.

At first, Samantha did not react, but after a minute, her breath became gentler.

It was another minute before she spoke.

"I read her name off of her uniform tag," Samantha said. "Sylvia... Sylvia can't speak."

Alexandra's lips moved to form an O shape, but she didn't quite voice the sound.

"She's a child and a handicapped one at that. It's not right! It's not... What did she ever do to deserve to be tortured like a criminal and then murdered?"

"I was hoping you could find out, but now it looks like we'll have to..."

"Oh, I will find out," Samantha said.

She lifted her head, and so suddenly, Alexandra leaned away in surprise.

"But she cannot speak. You said so yourself."

Samantha wiped her eyes on her sleeve and rose to her feet.

"I have other ways." She looked down at Alexandra, who was still surprised. "Coming?"

They returned to the room to find the others seated on the bed, their eyes on the corner of the room where Sylvia was.

Samantha went right up to her and dropped to her knees once more.

"Sylvia, I know you don't know me, and you probably don't have any reason to trust me, but I am a friend. These are my friends," She waved at them, "and they're your friends too. We want to know what happened here, and we want to make things right, but we need help, too. Will you help us?"

There was a pause.

"I know you cannot speak, but I have a way around that. Let me speak for you. I invite you to possess me."

"Wait, what?" Daniel said.

"Shut up, Daniel," Samantha said. "This is not the time."

"No, no, I'm with him on this one. Have you lost your mind?" Lila said.

"I know what I'm doing."

Lila turned to Alexandra, who was still stunned by how quickly the situation had progressed.

"Don't just stand there. Talk to her!"

"Sam," she said, softening her tone even further. "Sam, we didn't talk about this."

"There's nothing to talk about. We need to know what happened here, and she can tell us. I know what I'm doing. She's not a malevolent ghost. I'll invite her in, she'll talk to you, then she'll pop out. Easy as that."

"It's never easy as that, you crazy person," Daniel said. "Let's just go find another ghost that can talk." All heads turned in his direction. "What? What did I do this time?"

"A bit insensitive, don't you think?" James said.

Daniel rolled his eyes. "She was tortured and killed. I don't think stating the obvious is going to break her little heart."

"Enough talking," Samantha said. She put a hand on her chest and held out the other. If they had to guess she had placed it on the girl's chest. "Come."

Samantha's head snapped back, and she fell to the ground.

"Sam!" they chorused.

They rushed to her, but her head would have hit the ground if Lila had not used her powers to stop her mid-air.

Seeing that she was still conscious, Daniel and James grabbed her arms and helped her over to the bed, where they propped her in a sitting position.

"You alright, Sam?" Alexandra said.

Sam's eyelashes fluttered profusely as she looked around as though seeing the world anew.

"Sam?"

"What... What is happening?"

It was Sam who spoke, as in the words came forth as she opened her mouth and moved her lips, but the voice was not Sam's. It was the unmistakable voice of a child.

Daniel leaned away. "Well, you're not Sam."

Sam— who was not Sam— held up her hands in front of her face and then began to poke her cheeks and her arms.

"Sylvia?" James said.

Sam turned at the mention of the name.

"Yes. Yes, I'm Sylvia."

As soon as the words came out, she cupped her mouth in surprise.

"I can speak again!" she said.

They gave her a moment to get used to it as she mumbled incoherently.

She tried to rise but almost immediately lost her balance. Luckily, James was there to catch her.

"Easy there. That's a lot of body you're carrying around," he said.

He held her upright until he was confident she could stand on her own.

Her features were gentler as she relaxed, and she even cracked a smile. It was hard to believe she was younger than they were.

"So, you haven't always been mute?" Daniel inquired.

Again, the others turned to stare, stunned by his forwardness. But simultaneously, it was a question they wanted answered, so they were grateful for it.

"No," she said. "I stopped speaking when I came to this place. This... This used to be my room. My cell."

"How old were you, Sylvia?" Alexandra asked.

"I was ten."

"How long ago was this?"

"What year is it?"

Alexandra told her.

"Fifty and eight years ago."

"And how old were you when you... you know...?" It was Daniel speaking, and he filled in the unspoken word by gesturing with a thumb to his throat.

"I was about to turn sixteen."

That was a little more than half a decade younger than Alexandra was and closer to a decade younger than Daniel.

"Why... Why did your parents bring you to this place?"

"After my baby brother died in my arms, the warden came to my family. He convinced them that I was plagued with spirits, and if they did not send me away. that they would see another child die."

"And they agreed?" James said.

"They thought they were doing what was best. He made them believe that. And he never allowed any visits, so they had no way of knowing what he did to me. To all of us."

"Oh God."

"Things were always bad here, but they got so much worse when he came."

"He? He who?" Alexandra asked.

"The chief physician." She visibly shivered as she spoke the words.

"Please tell us about this chief physician. Who was he?"

"He had two arms and two legs and eyes and a nose and a mouth. He had pale skin like that of a normal man, perhaps paler than most, as he hardly ventured into the sun, but he was no man. You could tell if you looked into his eyes. The chief physician was nothing but a monster."

Her words were weighty, and as they dropped, they caused a moment of silence.

It was Alexandra who eventually broke it.

"Can you describe him?"

"Yes, I can. He had the kind of face you could hardly forget. The kind that showed up while you slept and turned your dreams into nightmares. His name was Doctor Fredrick von Menschen. He was a thin old man; built like he could be uprooted by the next strong wind. He was starting to grow bald, and what hair he had left, he left unkempt. His eyes were like nothing I'd ever seen. They were absolutely devoid of warmth, like looking into the eyes of a dead man. Except this dead man was also calculative in the most sinister ways. The warden was a terrifying man without question, but the chief physician... the chief physician could give the devil a run for his money."

Daniel backed away half a pace, but it was enough to get Alexandra's attention. Still, he made an effort to mask the reaction, and although it didn't quite work, she respected the effort and moved on.

"What did the chief physician do, Sylvia? To you... And to the others."

"The chief physician considered himself some form of revolutionary. He thought it was his destiny to bring about new discoveries in the sciences of the mind. He said there were secrets locked away in our brains, and it was his duty to unravel them. He conducted experiments on us, each more unholy than the last. To say his methods were cruel would be an understatement. Within these walls, Dr von Menschen sinned against man and against God. He pushed the boundaries of both science and morality in his quest for knowledge. He liked to talk while he worked, too, whether it was while hooking people up to strange devices or when he was carving them with sharp knives. He spoke of his legacy; of the way he would be remembered. He was a sadistic man. A madman."

"Can you tell us what exactly he was trying to do?" Alexandra said. "Whatever it was, it has to be the reason you and the rest of the spirits can't move on."

Sylvia paused for a moment; her head tilted at an odd angle. Just when Alexandra was about to repeat herself in case she had not been heard, Sylvia spoke.

"I must depart this body now," she said.

"Wait, what?" Alexandra said.

"I cannot stay any longer."

"But we need answers."

"And you will find them. I trust that you will."

"Before you go, just tell us where the chief physician's lab is," Daniel said.

"I cannot," she said. "I do not know."

"How can you not know? You've been there."

"Daniel, easy," James said.

"You're right," Sylvia said. "I've been there. But I do not know because every time I was taken there, the nurses came to sedate me, and I woke up there. If there is anyone who knew, it is the warden. You will find his office on the top floor."

"Thank you, Sylvia."

"Now, if you would like your friend to continue staying amongst the living, it is necessary that I vacate her body. The girl, Sam, is strong. She has exceeded the limits of her power to bind me to her body and has been holding on by sheer will alone. Any longer, and I will do damage to her mind, spirit, and possibly even her body."

"But what if we need you again?"

"The chief physician wronged a multitude of people. In your quest to undo the damage he has wrought, you will find help when you need it, you need only know how to ask."

Samantha's body began to convulse, and her eyes rolled back into her head. She let out a strained gasp, and then her knees gave out.

Daniel and James were more prepared and wasted no time in coming to her aid.

"Easy now," Daniel said.

"We've got you," James said.

Then, their eyes widened at the same time.

"Jesus!" James said

"My God, you're burning up!" Daniel said.

"I'm fine," Samantha said. "I just need to catch my breath."

They moved her to the bed, and she sat, slouching under her own weight.

Alexandra fetched a bottle of water from her backpack and gave it to her to drink.

Sam drank until the water was gone and the plastic was crushed between her fingers so she gave her another.

"Are you alright?" she asked when Sam was finally satiated.

She nodded. "But I've used up my battery on that one. And so did she. It'll probably be a while before I can commune with any ghosts and much longer before I see Sylvia again."

"Hopefully, we won't need you to do that again."

"Hopefully," Samantha agreed. "Does that mean you got something useful out of her?"

"Sure did," Alexandra said. "But can't be sure how useful just yet." And then she proceeded to fill her in on everything the girl had said.

Chapter 6:
A TRIAL OF FORCE

Leaving Sylvia's room, the group continued to explore the rest of the floor. No one spoke a word except for Alexandra, who asked Sam if she was feeling any better, and the response was a small nod.

Finding nothing else of interest, they returned to the staircase and ascended to the top floor. There they came to a door at the very end of the hallway with the words WARDEN M. BLACKTHORNE engraved on a silver plaque in bold lettering.

James, who was ahead of the others, turned to look at them, silently asking if they were ready. When they confirmed that they were, he turned the knob and pushed the door in.

The air was thick and musty, and the sight that awaited them left them mildly surprised, although it made perfect sense. The room had been thrashed. The desk was broken and overturned, as was the bookshelf by the wall, and there were papers everywhere.

The rest of the damage was harder to see as the windows were shut.

As James crossed the room towards the window, the others spread out to look around.

With a loud creak, he managed to force a window open, and the introduction of light brought everything into full clarity.

Tiny critters scurried into the corner, squeaking their complaints at the light.

"Rats," Sam muttered. "I hate rats."

He got the others open and they stood around assessing the damage. It was messy, uncoordinated, and without direction. Clearly, the people who had done this did not care about anything. Not to uncover evidence or even destroy it. This was all an act of rage.

"The mob must have done this," Alexandra surmised.

"I think so, too," James said. He bent down to pick up a piece of paper. Most of it had been eaten by the rats, and the ink had faded from its surface. "It's a wonder they didn't burn this place to the ground."

Daniel crouched and touched the floor. As he did, the scene around him shifted.

He watched as the door burst open and villagers flooded in. They stormed right past him to the window and rushed upon Warden Blackthorne and Doctor von Menschen, who Daniel had not noticed before, standing at the window.

The two men tried to fight them off, all the while screaming something along the lines of, "You do not know who you are dealing with!" But they quickly subdued him, and a handful of them dragged him out of the room.

Those that remained looked around the room with disgust. Then, without a word, they set about destroying the place with their crude weapons.

When they were done, the fire was gone from their eyes, and something more vulnerable was left: guilt.

One by one, with their shoulders sagged and their heads bowed, they left the room.

Daniel watched the time flow by within the room as the police arrived the next day and closed the windows and the door. He watched the adventurers come and go. He watched the rats make a feast of the papers. He watched the years take their toll. He watched and watched until, at last, he returned to the present to find everyone staring at him.

"I think they wanted to punish themselves," he said. "By building this asylum, trusting an evil man to run it, and sending away their mentally ill loved ones to be tortured by him, they let this happen. And so, they wanted to force themselves to remember what they had done. This was... is... penance."

"Damn," James muttered.

"If only they knew that evil still remains in this place," Sam said. "And that their loved ones continue to suffer."

"And that's why we're here," Alexandra said. "To save them. To give the dead peace. We should start by looking for clues."

James moved to the bookshelf and tested its weight.

"Okay, that's too heavy," he said. "Anyone wanna give me a hand? Lila?"

She shook her head.

"I can't lift something that heavy," she said.

"Come on," he said.

"Fine. I'll try. But when I fail, remember I told you I couldn't do it."

She came to stand by the bookshelf and took a deep breath; then she stretched out her hands, her fingers curled. As she did, the bookshelf shifted.

She widened her stance and turned her hands, and slowly, the bookshelf started to rise off the floor.

"You're doing it!" James applauded.

But his praise came too soon as the next moment she lost hold of it and the bookshelf hit the ground again.

She dropped to her knees, breathing heavily.

"Told you... I couldn't," she said.

James helped her up while Daniel looked on, perplexed.

Thanks to his visit into her past, Daniel knew more about her than anyone else. In that moment, the most important thing he knew was that Lila was lying.

But why?

"Don't sweat it," James said. Daniel, come give me a hand."

"What does it matter?" Lila said. "If there were any clues in this room, we're several decades too late to the crime scene anyway."

She kicked a few pieces of paper and sent them flying to prove her point.

"That's not a problem for me," Daniel said. "Gather the papers and bring them to me. I'll sort through them."

"Right," Alexandra said.

She and the others moved to pick up the pieces of paper, but Lila stopped them.

"Hold on," she said. "This I can take care of. Stand back. Up against the wall, preferably."

They did as she said.

Lila raised her hands and extended her fingers like a pianist. She took a deep breath like before, and then her fingers began to move. With the move of each finger, a piece of paper lifted off the ground and floated over to Daniel.

This went on for almost a minute before she finally stopped, there was a stack of papers in front of Daniel and the rest of the room was bare.

"That's all of it," she said.

"This will probably take a bit," he said.

He ran his fingers down the stack.

"How about the rest of us try to get the bookshelf up in the meantime?"

"Very well, but I need Lila," Daniel said.

Lila was confused, but Daniel maintained a poker face.

"Just the three of us," Alexandra said less confidently. "What do you say, James? Sam?"

Samantha shrugged.

"Fine, but for the record, I have less faith in us than I did in Lila," James said.

As they went to the bookshelf, Lila came to kneel next to Daniel.

"What do I need to do then?" she said, begrudgingly.

"Just answer a question," he said. "Why are you holding back?"

"I beg your pardon?"

He took out a few pieces of paper from the stack before he went on.

"You're more powerful than you let on, Lila. I know this, and you know that I know this. I'm curious as to why you're limiting your powers."

"Do you want me to finish what I started at the diner?" she said. "Is that how much you dislike living?"

"You want to choke me out again?" He smiled. " What? Is that the most you can do with your powers? Choking people and making papers float."

"You have no idea what I can do."

"Oh, but I do. That's why you hate me so much. I *know*. I'm sorry that I do, but I know."

"Clearly, you have no need for me here, so I'll go help the others."

She turned away, but he grabbed her hand.

"It wasn't your fault, Lila. Surely, you know that by n—"

In a flash, Lila whipped around and grabbed Daniel by the throat, except she wasn't touching him.

As she rose, he rose with her, and he kept rising until his feet were barely skimming the floor.

"I could snap your neck with a twitch of my fingers, Daniel."

"Whoa, whoa, whoa!" James said. "What's going on? I thought we were friends here!"

"Lila!" Alexandra said.

Daniel held up a finger.

"Everything is... totally peachy," he grunted. "I... deserve this. Nothing... to... worry about... here. Keep doing... what you're doing."

"I won't say this again," Lila said. "Drop it, and back the hell off."

She let him go, and he dropped to his knees before falling over.

"Jesus! Would it kill you to put me down gently?" Daniel groaned, nursing his neck.

Alexandra rushed to his side and helped him to a sitting position while James approached Lila and dragged her away to calm her down.

"Do you have a death wish?" Alexandra snapped.

"Not particularly, no." He coughed.

"Well, it's a wonder you've lived this long with that mouth of yours."

"I just say things as they need to be said." Daniel shrugged. "People are just so touchy these days."

"Why do you have to go poking the bear? All you had to do was look through the papers."

"I did."

"What? When?"

"Before I got lifted off the floor by Darth Vader over there," he muttered.

"And? What did you find?"

"Most of them are irrelevant documents. Inventory. A couple of patient files. Tax stuff. A letter applying for funds to carry out certain research addressed to the mayor's office."

"And the rest?"

He picked up the four small pieces of papers he had separated from the rest, handed two to Alexandra and pocketed the rest.

Alexandra looked at the papers, no bigger than a shirt pocket, and she raised a brow.

"Those are the blueprints of the asylum," he said. "Or at least they used to be."

"And have you found the chief physician's lab?"

"Oh, I haven't really looked at the plan. Just skimmed enough of it to know what it is."

He raised himself to his feet and dusted off his pants. Then he noticed that the bookshelf was upright now, and a pile of books— or what was left of them, to be more accurate— were scattered on the floor next to it.

"Well done," he said, addressing Sam as she was the only person still standing by the shelf.

As he crossed the room, a blast of cold air stopped him dead in his tracks.

"Sheesh!" He rubbed his arms and noticed goosebumps were already forming. "What's with this draft?"

He looked up to find Samantha running towards him.

"What did I say this time?"

"Move!" she yelled.

She jumped and tackled him to the ground.

"Ow!" Daniel moaned.

Samantha rolled off of him and scrambled to her feet, dragging him along with her.

"What the hell, Sam?" he said.

But Samantha wasn't looking at him. She had her eyes fixed on the floor.

He followed her gaze, and his eyes widened in horror. There was a hand thrust through the floor where he had been standing. To call it a hand was a bit of a stretch. It clearly used to be a hand, but now it was little more than chunks and bits of flesh glued to a skeletal hand.

"You all see that, right?" he said, looking over at Lila, James, and Alexandra. "You see the hand in the floor?"

"Yeah, we see it." Alexandra nodded.

"Good. Not much of a relief but good."

Another hand shot out next to the first and both pushed down on the floor. Between both hands, out came the head.

It was in no better condition than the hands: paper-thin skin stretched over a skull, a clump of hair to the side of the head, and eye holes that glowed an ominous green.

The legs followed, and at last, standing before them was a semi-transparent zombie with a dark grey smoky aura.

"What in God's name is that?" Daniel said.

"Malevolent spirit," Samantha muttered. "Everyone get behind me. Now."

"I thought you said you used up your necromantic voodoo channeling Sylvia."

"It's not voodoo. And it's just one spirit. I can handle one spirit. Probably. Just slowly back away, yeah?"

As if on cue, another decayed hand shot up out of the floor next to the malevolent spirit.

"Oh God..."

It crawled out of the floor just as the first had done.

"So, uh... how are we feeling about two?" Alexandra said.

"A little shaky, but thumbs halfway up," Samantha said.

Two more zombie hands appeared on different sides of the room.

"And how about four?" James said.

"Perfectly honest? We might be screwed."

As soon as the other two had fully arisen, four more started to rise.

"Scratch that. We are definitely screwed."

"Plan?" Daniel said.

"Run!"

The five of them turned and ran from the room. Bringing up the rear, Daniel pulled the door shut.

"Don't bother," Samantha said. "They're intangible. They can phase through solid objects."

They had barely made it forty meters when the door literally exploded off its hinges and slammed into the opposite wall.

"You were saying?" Daniel yelled.

"Shut up and run faster!"

No sooner had she spoken than the malevolent spirits burst out of the room with a cacophony of screeching in what could only be described as a mad frenzy. They were literally climbing over each other in a bid to catch them.

"Safe to say we're not popular with this crowd!" Daniel said.

The five of them were running as fast as their legs would carry them, but the spirits were steadily gaining.

"Quick question," Lila said. "Can they touch us?"

"They just blasted through a solid steel door, so it's safe to say yeah."

"Then I can touch right back!"

She looked over her shoulder and extended her hand. At once, a couple of spirits were sent flying backward.

She did it again and again, but with each telekinetic blast, the others simply kept running after them.

"That's not doing a lot of good," Daniel said.

"I don't see *you* doing anything!" Lila retorted; her voice strained.

"You want me to tell you their history? What I'm trying to say is you can do better with those powers of yours."

"Are you trying to annoy me while we're running for our lives?"

"Is it working?"

"Shut up, Daniel!"

"I've seen what you can do, Lila."

"Then you know why I can't ever do it again."

"Take it from someone who knows a thing or two about dwelling on the past, that is not—"

"Gah!"

Daniel's head whipped around in time to watch Lila trip and fall, but he was moving too fast to stop at once.

"Lila!"

He skidded to a halt and without thinking about his next course of actions and the stupidity of it all, he sprinted back for her.

Lila tried to push off the ground but failed. She stretched her hand out to Daniel, her eyes pleading.

He doubled his speed, but the spirits were both closer and faster than he was. Still, that did not dissuade him.

Three feet away, he watched in horror as the horde of malevolent spirits descended on Lila.

But in that moment, something in Lila seemed to change. The defeated look in her eyes dissipated, and she rolled over to face the spirits.

"Get back!" she screamed, throwing her hands out in front of her.

It was as if a shockwave exploded forth from her hands, because every single one of them was blasted back several meters.

But there was no time to stare in awe as they were quickly regrouping to resume their pursuit. Daniel grabbed Lila by the armpits and lifted her, but as he did, her knee buckled, and she screamed in pain.

"My ankle!" she said. "I sprained my ankle."

"Oh, come on!"

He turned around and bent his knees.

"Hop on."

"I think I would much rather die than endure the humiliation of being carried by you," Lila said.

"Don't be such a baby. Hop on already!"

When she hesitated further, Daniel took matters into his own hands. He scooped her up in his arms, much to her protest, and then he ran to join the others who were at the staircase landing.

"This is so much worse! Put me down!" Lila yelled.

"This isn't a picnic for me either," Daniel said. "It would be nice if you could watch my back instead of shouting in my ear!"

It was clear that she still wanted to hurt him, but she shelved the thought aside and focused on the ghouls.

Daniel was not sure how much was owed to Lila's abilities and athletic physique, but they made it to the stairs safely, reuniting with the others.

They proceeded down to the floor below, but before they could decide on the next direction to go, the evil spirits literally began to fall through the ceiling, cutting them off from the rest of the hallway.

As they tried to return to the staircase, another group cut them off.

Now, they were in the middle of the hallway, between two hordes of evil spirits with nowhere left to run. The spirits knew this, and they waited, savoring the moment before they struck.

"Sam, just how badly screwed are we?" Alexandra asked.

"Unfathomably," Samantha said. "I've never encountered them up close before, but from the accounts I've read about, apparently, they basically tear you to shreds from the inside out. It's both painful and slow."

"And when you say from the inside...?"

"The translations were unclear. It could have meant anything from our internal organs to our souls."

"Plan? Anyone? Now would be a great time!" James said, panicking. "I don't want to find out which one!"

"If I could just..." Samantha muttered.

She stretched out her hand and shut her eyes in concentration, but she soon collapsed, groaning in pain.

"I can't... Guys, I can't do anything."

Samantha's attempt failed to stop the ghouls. What it did manage to do, however, was rile them up.

They let out an otherworldly screech and launched at them from both sides.

"Lila..." Daniel said, urgency clear in his voice.

"Stop it, Daniel. I can't do it."

"You can. The only thing stopping you is you!"

She pushed away from him and planted her legs on the ground, favoring her injured ankle.

"Lila, you need to let go right about now."

"Daniel, I'm not playing. Stop."

"Lila, for fuck's sake, you're the only one who can save us now. Let go!"

"Shut up!"

"Lila!"

"Shut up. Shut up. Shut up!"

"Do you think dying here will earn you her forgiveness?" Daniel snapped. "You think the guilt will finally end? Do you think this is a way out? I saw a lot of things in your past, but I did not see a coward."

"I said, shut up!"

The air around Lila began to hum, and the sand and bits of rocks around her feet began to vibrate. She was a ticking bomb.

"Everybody down!" Daniel yelled in warning.

James was already kneeling next to Sam, but Alexandra was fully upright and slow to react, so Daniel tackled her. He twisted mid-air so his body took the impact of their fall when they landed, and for a moment, the wind was knocked out of him.

He opened his eyes to see the spirits bearing down on them, a second away from clawing off his face.

They never got the chance.

With a scream so raw that it grated against Daniel's nerves, Lila threw her hands out once more and let out a telekinetic blast that put the last one to shame.

The spirits were blown back and ripped to nothing simultaneously.

Daniel got back on his feet and tentatively approached Lila, who was hunched over, breathing heavily.

"Lila?"

She looked up at him, a burning fury in her eyes.

"You piece of shh..." She trailed off as her eyes rolled back in her head and her body swayed, but thanks to Daniel, she never hit the ground.

"I've got you," he muttered. "I've got you."

Chapter 7:
A TEMPORARY REPRIEVE

With the ghouls banished for the time being, the asylum returned to a quiet which was now more eerie than comforting. It was now midday, but the air was cold, and the direct rays of the sun did not seem to permeate the building.

Exhausted and still in recovery from the near-death experience, the group made their way down to the lobby to rest.

Lila was still unconscious and had to be carried, but Daniel did not seem to mind. There was a strange way he looked at her while she slept in his arms that Alexandra found almost touching. It was like he and Lila had connected on some level that the rest of them knew nothing about, and despite how much she seemed to hate him, they had an understanding.

Even after he had put her down to rest properly, he remained at her side, quietly poking at the campfire they had made, with a brooding expression on his face.

Sam, too, was exhausted from using her powers, but it wasn't until they forced her to rest that she agreed to stay put. And it wasn't long before she succumbed to sleep. Meanwhile, Alexandra and James went to fetch firewood from the edge of the woods just outside the asylum premises.

"So," James said after a long period of silence. "Is it everything you expected so far?"

Alexandra had been lost in thoughts and did not tune in in time to hear the entire sentence.

"I'm sorry, what?" she said. "Sorry, I wasn't all here."

"I know. I asked if this adventure so far has been everything you expected." When Alexandra did not reply at once, he added, "Sorry. I'm... trying to make small talk. I can sense the general direction of your feelings, and they're putting me on edge."

"Ah. Right. Sorry. It's just... the gravity of the situation is kinda settling in a way it couldn't have before we came here, and now I'm—"

"Anxious," he filled in with a smile. "I know."

"We almost died back there," Alexandra said.

"I know. But we didn't."

"We were this close."

"But Lila saved us."

"Yes. She did. But I'm the one who brought all of you out here, and all I could do was stand there and watch."

"Exactly," James said.

"Exactly what?"

"You brought us here."

Alexandra deadpanned. "There is really no need to rub it in, James. I'm well aware."

He smiled.

"Alex, you're not getting it. *You* picked this team. What we're doing should be impossible and yet Sam and Daniel have been

~ 96 ~

gathering clues from the past like it's nothing. Lila was a total badass back there. Me, I'd like to think I'll figure out my purpose here eventually, but that's beside the point. This team has come up against some impossible obstacles and we have made it through them *because* of each other, and we would not have that if not for you. It's not up to you to save us each time we get into trouble. By picking out the team you picked out, you made sure we could take on and survive the things we've encountered so far, and I choose to believe we can take on anything that comes next."

"When you put it that way I..." Alexandra trailed off. "Thank you, James."

"No need for that, really. Just know that I'm ready to follow you, whether it be to gather twigs in the woods at one in the afternoon, or to face the vengeful ghosts of our evil forefathers."

"I'd hug you if you allowed that sort of thing," she said.

"Sorry. The best I can do is an extended handshake." He stuck out his hand.

"I'll take it," Alexandra said.

She shook his hand.

"You say you haven't figured out your purpose, but I think you found yours before anyone else. You keep team spirit up, and you keep us away from each other's throats."

"Team spirit? I can do that. The other thing, though, that's just Daniel," he said. "I'm not particularly fond of him."

It was no secret that Daniel set most members of the group on edge, but Alexandra did not think of him as just that.

Of all the members of their merry little band of misfits, she probably found Daniel to be the most peculiar. He was the oldest of the lot, but he carried himself like one who had seen things and done things further above his age. Things that had aged him beyond his years.

She saw it in his eyes and in the way he reacted to situations, putting his feelings in the corner when it was time to make hasty decisions.

There was one other person whose personality was strangely akin to his, and it was Lila.

Speaking of Lila...

"But you are fond of Lila," Alexandra said.

"Lila's a good person," James said. "She doesn't like to show it, but she's kind and sweet, and when she's not all caught up in herself, she can be funny."

"That's not what I asked though, is it?"

To this, James said nothing.

*****

Back in the asylum, all was calm. The only sound that could be heard— and barely— came from the fire and Daniel's occasional heavy breathing.

Next to him, Lila was a picture of tranquility, nothing like her waking self, especially around him.

"If I didn't know better, I'd say you cared about her."

Daniel glanced over to the other sleeping bag and found Samantha staring up at the ceiling. Her voice was low, but as the rooms were empty and the walls bare, she could probably have been heard from the floor above.

He was mildly surprised that she was still awake, but he answered at once.

"Good thing you do know better then," he said. "What I care about is the success of our mission here."

"You work very hard to keep people at arm's length. It's actually sad."

"What are you? James' personal assistant?"

"Dealing with human feelings?" She chuckled. "No, thank you. I'd rather stick with ghosts. They're usually either overly chirpy or downright gloomy, and they're mostly easy to send off. That's easy to navigate."

"I can relate to that. The past is the past. No matter how deep I dig, the dead remain dead. Or at least that used to be the case until I met you."

"Well, aren't you a charmer."

He could not see, but he had a feeling the statement was accompanied by an eye roll.

"I pushed her," Daniel said after a brief period of silence. "Back in the warden's office and again while we were being chased. In the end, it worked, and she saved us, but I worry I may have pushed her too hard. That is the extent of my care."

"So, you do have a heart. James isn't entirely sure."

"Don't get sentimental on me, and I don't care what he thinks, or anyone for that matter."

"Why does it sound like you're trying to convince yourself more than you're trying to convince me?"

"Shouldn't you be asleep or something?" Daniel sighed. "I swear you were much better company until a minute ago."

Amused, she chuckled again.

"You act tough, but I see through the facade. You're a runner, aren't you?"

"Maybe I am. So what? You think it's easy? Being a runner?"

One moment, he was relaxed, and the next, he was getting defensive like an animal backed into a corner. Who was she to presume to know him?

But when Samantha turned to look his way, with a genuine, unassuming curiosity in her eyes, his aggression dissipated.

"You tell me," she said.

He sighed again and poked at the fire until the end of the stick caught alight, then he blew it out.

"I didn't grow up surrounded by friends and family, Samantha. I've never been around people who didn't want something from me or have something I wanted from them. When I wasn't a thief, I was a fraud and a crook, but most of it was against my will. It was not a great life, and more often than not, if you weren't fast enough, you were dead. As you can see, not dead."

"So why did you come here? If I recall correctly, you were the first to agree, too. An adventure to a mental asylum to help ghosts find peace, what part of that appealed to you? What is it you want?"

"What makes you think I'm not the one with something you all want?"

"For one, you're here by choice. For two, I sense that you have an inflated sense of self-importance, and I refuse to further inflate it."

"Ah, you hurt me, Sam," he joked.

"Don't change the subject."

Daniel was quiet for a while.

"This is the first time I've been around people like you and Alex and Lila and..." He made a gagging noise. "...James. And I don't mean people like you in the sense of the things you can do. I mean, who you are. And you're right; I'm here by choice. I don't want anything. Or perhaps I do, but not in the usual sense. What I want is to know what it's like to have healthy relationships that aren't based solely on how you can benefit me and vice versa."

"To be fair, we've mostly been using you for your psychometric thing."

"No one likes a smart ass, Sam."

Samantha laughed lightly. "Don't be mad at me. Be mad at your big mouth."

"I say what needs to be said, what people need to hear, and that's a fact."

"You know, Dan..."

"Daniel."

"Just because you think people need to hear it does not mean that they do. You don't get to decide for them, or most likely, they will resent you for it."

"Even if I'm trying to help?"

"There's a reason the road to hell is paved with good intentions. Humans have free will."

"It's an illusion."

"Maybe, maybe not, but that's not for you to decide on their behalf."

"So even though I know what's best for Lila, I probably shouldn't try to make her see it?"

"Correct. It's not your place. You can help her along the way, but you do have the gentleness of a jackhammer, so I don't see you doing any better."

"Hey!"

"What? I thought you're all for telling people what they need to hear."

"I mean, I am, but aren't you in the process of getting me to change my ways? Bit hypocritical, don't you think?"

"I'm going to go back to sleep now, Dan."

"Daniel."

"Yeah, yeah."

The lobby was quiet for a minute, save for the crackling of burning twigs.

"Just to be clear, I did the right thing helping her get over her mental block to save our asses back there, yes?"

"Oh, absolutely. Forced possession can be incredibly painful, or so I've heard, and that's just one of the things that could have happened."

"Cool. Cool."

Just then, Lila mumbled something incoherent as she stirred from her slumber.

Daniel moved closer to her, anticipating her full return to consciousness, but Samantha had another approach altogether. She laid back down and closed her eyes.

"Hey," Daniel said softly.

At last, Lila's eyes fluttered open, but almost immediately, they went wide as she sat up in alarm.

"Hey, hey, hey!" Daniel said. "Easy now. Easy. I've got you. You're alright."

He reached out to hold her hand.

Lila looked around wildly as though expecting malevolent spirits to start descending through the ceiling again.

"It's alright," he continued to reassure. "We're safe now. You did it."

After a few more seconds, Lila managed to calm down. She looked down, suddenly realizing that he was holding her hand, then she traced the hand back to its owner, and as her eyes fell on Daniel's face, the fear vanished from her eyes to be replaced by a sudden rush of anger.

"You... asshole!' she yelled, shoving him.

Daniel lost his balance and fell over. She must have added a bit of her telekinetic power to the blow because Daniel's feet went up over his head as he nearly tumbled over.

"Hey, chill out!" He awkwardly tried to regain a less embarrassing posture. He ended up on his hands and knees and looked up to find Lila standing over him.

"I have a good mind to do very bad things to you, jackass!" she threatened, pulling back her hand as though to hit him, although her fist wasn't fully clenched.

"Look! I'm sorry!"

That got her to stop for a second. Confusion was clear on her face.

"What?"

"I have been out of line on several matters, especially matters concerning you, and I realize that now. I shouldn't have done what I did to you. Even though it did pretty much save us back there."

"You egotistical son of a bitch!"

"Okay, what did I do this time? Sam got me to see the errors of my ways, and I'm trying to make peace with you, but even she admitted that if you hadn't acted when you did, we'd be in big trouble."

"Hey now, don't credit me for anything," Samantha said, her eyes remaining closed. "You're already screwing a simple apology up. I don't want anything to do with that trainwreck."

"Aren't you supposed to be pretending to sleep?" Daniel frowned.

"I was until you mentioned my name," Samantha said. She propped up on her elbow. "Hey, girl. Glad to see you're okay."

"Hey, Sam," Lila said. "Where are the others?"

"Alex and James went out to get more firewood," Daniel said.

Lila made no attempt to acknowledge his response.

"They'll be back soon," Samantha asked. "You feel alright?"

"Yeah. My body feels like I just spent an afternoon in the gym, but it'll pass."

"I get ya. My headache's gone now, thankfully."

"How long was I out for?"

"I can't say for sure. I haven't exactly been aware myself."

"An hour, seventeen minutes, and nine seconds," Daniel said.

Again, Lila pretended he wasn't there.

"I'm starving," she said. "You wouldn't happen to know where my backpack is, would you?"

"Nope," Sam said.

"I brought tuna sandwiches. You want some?" Daniel said.

Lila looked around and spotted her backpack against the wall.

"Oh, there it is!"

She reached out her hand, and the backpack flew over to her.

"Great. You're ignoring me now?" Daniel said.

"Be grateful; that's all I'm doing," Lila snapped.

He sighed and shook his head. Sure, he was wrong, and he got that now, but didn't the fact that his actions ultimately saved them earn him a little less aggression?

Resignedly, he retreated to the wall to eat his lunch in peace.

Just as he settled down, the front doors swung open, and Alexandra and James entered. James had a pile of sticks in his arms, and Alexandra had a flashlight.

"Oh look, everyone's awake!" Alexandra said.

They came to join them by the fire.

"Feeling alright, Lila?" Alexandra said.

Lila nodded.

"What you did back there was incredible. I don't know what we would have done without you."

"It was nothing," Lila said.

But Daniel noticed that as she said that, she cast a glance his way.

Before he could attempt to decipher what it meant, James interrupted, involving her in conversation.

The next ten minutes were spent on lunch, and when that was done, they gathered together beside the fire to share thoughts on what they would do next.

Alexandra mentioned that they had a lead and were met with surprised looks.

"A lead? I thought the warden's office was a bust," Lila said. "Those spirits came at us before we could go through the books."

"That's right, but we got our lead before that. Or should I say, Daniel got the lead."

She produced the pieces of paper he had given her before the attack and set them down in their midst.

Samantha picked up the papers, and as she turned them over, her face formed into a confused frown.

"They're blank," she said.

"Yes, but once upon a time, that wasn't the case," Alexandra said. "Both papers once had blueprints of the asylum drawn on them, and even though the ink has long faded, Daniel can still see them." She turned to Daniel. "Did I say that right?"

He shrugged. "Pretty much."

"Must've been in some pretty tiny writing," James said.

"This is merely a surviving portion of the original large paper," Daniel explained, not in the mood to be snarky. "Here, give it."

Samantha passed him the papers, and he set them down on the floor before him.

As he stared at the yellowed, faded pages, they began to renew themselves. As they did, they began to expand and unfold. The edges that had been eaten by rats began to reform, and the ink began to appear on the pages. When the papers had been fully restored, he had to place them far apart to see the full picture.

He looked over the pages and began to trace with his finger, muttering to himself.

On each page, there were two floors, but Daniel noticed something peculiar about the ground floor plan, and the only reason he noticed it was that, looking into the past, at one point, someone had held it over a flame to reveal some form of invisible ink. In dotted lines, there were outlines on it that did not match the interior walls of the plan itself, almost as if there was a...

"Basement," he said aloud. "There's a basement."

"I bet that's where the chief physician's lab is," Samantha said.

"Well, where's the entrance?" Alexandra asked.

Daniel studied the plan again, but after a couple of minutes, he realized there was no visible door.

"I can't tell. It doesn't seem to be indicated on the plan."

"What if it's not on the ground floor?" Lila said.

Daniel perked up, eyes wide, first of all, surprised that she was speaking directly to him and second because of the implications of her words.

He had already started studying the other paper when James asked the slow question.

"What do you mean by that?" he said.

"The basement is clearly meant to be a secret; even on the map, it's written in invisible ink and exposed only over naked light, so the entrance is definitely hidden," Daniel said. "At the same time, the basement is meant to be accessed by a select group of people who need to be able to move patients in and out without drawing any unwanted suspicions, so it's probably hidden somewhere above, likely within—"

He put his finger on the top floor plan, directly on an office they had not had the chance to enter.

"The chief physician's office," Lila filled in.

"You're a genius!" Daniel said excitedly.

He looked up to find the others looking at him, in equal parts surprise and amusement. Even Lila was surprised.

"What?" he said.

"Nothing at all," Samantha said with a grin.

Chapter 8:
A Vision Unfolds

Another ten minutes passed before the rest was over, and they prepared to continue the mission. Daniel spent those ten minutes poring over the mostly non-existent piece of paper in his hand while Alexandra watched him. He had earlier said that he still could not find the entrance to the chief physician's lab, and that was what he was still searching for. Alexandra wished she could be more helpful, but it was hard to assess a map she could not see.

She tried not to feel useless, and James's words from before helped, but it did not completely dispel the thoughts.

From the lobby, they went straight to the top floor. As they stepped out into the hallway, Alexandra had flashbacks of the haunting specters chasing after them. She remembered thinking that was the end for them. But somehow, they had made it past that, and here they were, back to the scene and pressing on, too.

The chief physician's office was adjacent to the warden's, and the only reason they had missed it was that they had been laser-focused on finding the warden's office.

Unlike the warden's, the chief physician's office did not have his name on the door, just the words 'CHIEF PHYSICIAN'S OFFICE'.

They opened the door to find a boring, typical office with a desk opposite the entrance and a bookshelf to the side. There were paintings on the wall and a couple of decorative vases in the corners.

Also, unlike the warden's office, the chief physician's office had been spared most of the destruction. There were papers on the floor, but it was impossible to tell— unless you were Daniel Masters, of course— if they had been thrown there or blown off the table as the windows were wide open.

Everything else about the room looked straight out of Google search without an ounce of personal touch. Even the books on the shelf, as Alexandra soon found, looked like standard university textbooks, and she had a feeling they had never been opened, much less read.

"So, the hidden entrance is somewhere here?" Alexandra asked.

"That's the guess," Daniel said. "The map's useless, but it's got to be close by, so just look around."

"And what exactly are we to look for?" James said.

"Pressure plates in the walls or in the floors. Check the shelves for any lever disguised as a book. Check behind the bookshelves for any buttons. Have a look in his drawers or under his table for something. Anything."

They split up to look around.

Alexandra opted to check the chief physician's desk. First, she looked into his drawers but found them completely bare save for rat droppings and cobwebs in the corners. She swept her hands under the desk, but all she found were more cobwebs. Thankfully no rat droppings.

She sat back in his chair to look around.

Come on, Alex, she thought. *If I were a sadistic madman, where would I hide my secret door?*

A minute passed, and nothing came to her. With a groan of mild frustration, she leaned back in her seat.

She was hit with a wave of vertigo and thought she was about to fall back in her seat, but as she jerked forward, trying to catch herself, the world around her spun out of control.

The next moment, she felt as though a cord had been attached to her stomach, and then she was yanked forward.

It lasted for a second, but when it stopped, her vision had a blurry tinge to it, and she was standing in some sort of closet. There were brooms and mops and buckets stashed against one wall, and then there was a shelf of cleaning supplies against the other.

Her body moved against her will, and she pulled the light switch out of the wall to find a red lever behind it. She pulled the lever down, and suddenly, she was enveloped in blinding light. when it ceased, she was standing in a cold, dark room.

It took her eyes some time to get adjusted to the darkness, but when that happened, she found herself staring at rows upon rows of hospital beds. On the nearest one, she saw shackles for arms and legs, and by the bed, there was a chair and a table with a tray of surgical tools sitting and waiting to be used.

A flicker caught her eye, and as she looked, it came into focus and began to take form. It was the form of a child. He was bound to the bed.

She started towards him but only made it two steps before she heard a rhythmic clacking coming from the far end of the hall, too far away to see in the dark.

The boy's eyes widened in horror, and he began to fight futilely against his restraints.

Alexandra tried to move again, but for some reason, her limbs were locked in place.

The boy looked over to her.

"Help me!" he cried. "Please, help me!"

"I can't," Alexandra wanted to say. "I want to, but I can't. I'm sorry. I'm so sorry."

But her mouth, too, had refused to move.

"Don't waste your breath, child." The voice came from the darkness, and it was punctuated by the ominous clacking. "From what I've come to understand, you will need it for screaming."

Out of the darkness, a man in a lab coat emerged, limping forward as a cane— the source of the clacking— kept him upright. It was the chief physician!

The boy's face was as white as a sheet now, and Alexandra had a feeling if she could see her own face, it would not be much different.

The man before her evoked pure terror. From his voice to his gait to the blank yet terrifying expression on his face, he looked ready to replace Satan in hell.

The chief physician came around and filled the seat by the boy's bedside. He picked up a scalpel and started to move to the boy but stopped. Then he turned around and looked right at Alexandra.

"Be a dear and wait your turn," he said. "I'll get around to everyone."

Alexandra's breath hitched in her throat. She was yanked again, and this time, with a gasp, she opened her eyes to her friends standing over her.

The four of them were on various points of the concern spectrum. It probably had something to do with the fact that she was covered in beads of cold sweat, her arms were riddled with goosebumps, and her knuckles were white and painfully stiff from gripping onto the arms of the chair for dear life.

But Alexandra was too focused on acclimatizing herself with reality to appreciate the concern just yet.

"Something on my face?" she muttered dryly.

"Hey there, sleepy head," Daniel said with an exaggerated grin as he waved at her. "Quick question." He held up a finger. "What the *fuck* was that?"

She got up and stumbled past him.

"I'll tell you along the way," she said. "We should keep moving."

"Moving?" Samantha said. "Moving where? We need answers."

But Alexandra did not offer any. The image of the boy about to be tortured by that man while she could do nothing to stop it set her on edge. She did not want to feel helpless any longer.

As she stepped out into the hallway, she looked around. Of two things, she was certain: one, the hidden entrance was in a false supply closet, and two, it wasn't far from the chief physician's office.

She tried the door right across from the office, but it was locked.

By then, the others had joined her outside.

"Alex, what is going on?" Lila said.

"Daniel, be a dear and kick this door in, will ya?" Alexandra said. She stepped out of the way.

"Now, wait one minute," James said. "We deserve an explana—"

His speech was interrupted as, with one powerful kick, Daniel sent the door swinging inward.

Alexandra almost smiled. She had picked Daniel because, despite his concern, he was the most likely to take action first and then question it later.

He looked around to find the others staring.

"What?" he said.

"What happened to getting answers?" James said.

He shrugged.

Alexandra peered in and was pleased to find a supply closet. She groped the wall to her side until she found the light switch. With little effort, she pulled it out of the wall, and there was the lever.

She pulled it down and heard the click. The shelf of supplies shifted slightly forward as the hidden door behind it unlocked.

She pulled it further ajar to reveal an open elevator with fluorescent lighting overhead, then turned to the others.

"Ta-da!" she said.

"The entrance to the basement is a lift! Of course!" Daniel chuckled.

The others were not quite as speedy on the uptake.

"What the...?" James said.

"How?" Lila said.

"While I was trying to figure out where the door could be hidden in the chief physician's office, I had a premonition," Alexandra said.

"That explains your eyes rolling back in your head." Daniel nodded thoughtfully. "Can't decide if that's creepier than Sam's thing."

"Hey!" Samantha said.

"Wait, I thought you see the future," James said.

"Mostly. But I told you all, I occasionally see the past too. It's less vivid and usually scattered, but it helps with guidance. Now, shall we?"

They entered the elevator, and Alexandra pressed the only button on the panel.

The doors jerked shut like the metal jaws of some hungry monster, and with a loud groan, the elevator began to descend.

"Just think how fucked up it would have been if the cables snapped right then, and we all just fell to our deaths," Daniel said.

In unison, the four of them turned to look at him.

"What? It hasn't happened. Jeez!"

The remainder of the ride took place in silence, but with nothing but squealing and squeaking and shuddering as the car made jerky motions and nothing to stare at than the grimy walls, Alexandra almost missed Daniel's voice.

At last, the elevator doors screeched open to reveal an endless darkness.

"Well, where's the light switch, Alex?" Lila said.

"I don't know. I told you; the visions aren't detailed.

"I've got this," Daniel said.

He put his hand to the wall, and as he did, he walked out of the elevator.

Alexandra and the others followed close behind, and just as the elevator closed behind them, rows of white bulbs flickered to life overhead. By the wall, Daniel had his hand on a switch.

Alexandra was prepared for the sight that awaited them, but the others were taken by surprise.

Their expressions were grim as they took in the hospital beds. Still, they advanced.

"What kind of horrors went on here?" Daniel said.

He was standing close to one of the beds. He put his hand out to touch the sheet as if to find an answer but changed his mind at the last second.

It seemed he was curious but not curious enough to find out by directly immersing himself in the horrors. Alexandra could not blame him.

"I sense a presence here," Samantha called out. "There's a spirit here."

Before she even knew she was doing it, Alexandra automatically sought out Lila and found her walking next to James. Daniel was one step ahead, having positioned himself behind Lila as casually as possible.

"What kind of spirit are we talking about?" Alexandra asked.

"I sense no hostility," Samantha said. Speaking to no one in particular, she commanded, "Show yourself!"

She turned around and quickly stepped back.

"Oh, dear God!" she said. "I mean... Hello."

"What is it? Do you see him?" Lila asked.

"Yeah, I see him," she said, her eyes fixed on the ghost. "He's a young man. Pretty tall and rugged-looking—no offense. He's got the uh... saddest eyes I've ever seen."

"He's dead." Daniel rolled his eyes. "What do you expect?"

"You say that because you haven't seen Sally," Samantha said. "What is your name, sir?" A pause. "Hello, Mark Waters. My name is Samantha Cunnington. You can tell already, but I have a strong connection to the spirit realm that grants me the ability to communicate with the dead. These are my friends." She introduced them to the ghost and they said their hellos. "We're here to help. I met another benevolent ghost before you. Her name was Sylvia. She was mute when she died, and so I had her take my body to speak to us. If it's alright with you, I could do the same with you. We would like to find out more about what happened here."

"There's no need for that. I believe I can offer a better solution." The voice came from thin air.

Stunned, Alexandra turned to make sure she was not the only one who heard him. Their expressions told her that she wasn't.

Samantha noticed their shocked faces.

"You heard him?"

"They did," the voice continued. "And in a moment, they will see me, too."

As soon as the words were out, Alexandra saw a smoky form standing in front of Samantha. It took on more detail within the next few seconds until they could see him almost as clearly as they could each other.

But he was not easy to behold. He was thin and malnourished-looking. The most jarring feature, however, was the blood flowing from one of his sunken eyes.

It was easy to assume that was why Sam had said his eyes were sad, but the blood aside, his eyes were truly sad. They were the eyes of a man who had died long before he breathed his last.

"Forgive my appearance," he said. "I am Mark Waters."

"How is this possible?" Samantha said.

"It is difficult to explain," he said. "But we ghosts are not exactly all equals. I suspect I have a few more tricks up my sleeves than your friend Sylvia." He moved to sit on the edge of the bed.

"That's unsettling," Daniel said.

"I can understand your discomfort, but I assure you I mean you no harm."

"And do you mean to help us?" Lila asked.

"Indeed. I know why you're here, so I know that helping you is the same as helping myself and all the other spirits.

"So, what can you tell us about the chief physician's laboratory?" Alexandra asked.

"For one, you're standing in it," Mark said. "Well, part of it, at least."

"Part of it?"

"Doctor Fredrick von Menschen's goal was to understand how our brains worked, but that didn't mean he had one singular approach. Sometimes, he poked with a stick and assessed the brain signals on the computer. Other times, he sawed heads open and dissected the brains to get a closer look. He did not use the same room."

"That's horrible!" James said.

"He didn't think so," Mark said. "If you spoke with Sylvia, then you probably know he considered himself an innovator of sorts. He was a very chatty man."

"She said he spoke of secrets locked away in your brains and how it was his duty to unravel them," Samantha said.

Mark nodded.

"This area was primarily used for short-duration physical studies," he said. "Reactions to experimental drugs especially. And most of the people who were here often were those he considered expendable. Those who did not show potential. They were the lab rats. Usually, they didn't last a week."

Alexandra's thoughts were cast back to the boy in her vision. She imagined him writhing in his restraints, begging for his life until a mercilessly slow death eventually claimed him.

"So, where are the other parts of the lab?" Alexandra asked, hoping to hurry things along.

"Follow me," Mark said.

He led them down the hall and through a door on the other side.

As they went through it into a dark room, he resumed speaking.

"Sometimes, the chief physician wanted to watch his lab rats bleed out slowly," he said. "Sometimes, instead of stabbing right through, he wanted to make multiple shallow cuts over months or even years. At times like that, he used this room. The light switch is on the wall to your right."

Alexandra found the switch and flicked it. Once again, light was introduced into their surroundings, and horrors were heavenly accentuated.

"Jesus Christ!" James said.

"Oh my God!" Samantha said.

"What the hell?" Lila said.

There were four prison cells in the room with two pairs of shackles attached to each of their walls.

The floors and walls inside each and every cell were stained brown, a sight they had now identified to be blood. The air was musty and hung heavy with old, bad smells that had long become part of the room, even though they could no longer be deciphered.

"I wasn't being entirely metaphorical when I said sometimes he wanted to make multiple shallow cuts, you know," Mark said.

"But to what end?" Alexandra said. "Why do this?"

"Doctor Fredrick von Menschen perfected the art of breaking people," Mark said. "He favored the tougher ones because they made his work feel difficult, and he liked a challenge. And with an unending supply of test subjects and all the privacy he could ever need, he was in his element."

"This... This is evil. It's so, so wrong."

"You're a little too late asking for reasons for the behaviors of a psychopath," Mark said. "Understand that within these walls, there was no god except Dr von Menschen. He decided the fates of living beings as easily as you picked out clothes or shoes, and he was ruthless to the very core. But I suppose no matter how much you discover in this place; it doesn't quite prepare you for the next discovery."

Alexandra noticed that Daniel continued to avoid physical contact with any part of the room. His hands were shoved deep in his pockets, and he stood between Samantha and James.

He seemed shaken, which was uncharacteristic of him. He had been better put together when they were running from the horde of malevolent spirits.

What was going on with him?

"Through that door, you will find the chief physician's third and final torture chamber."

"Are these three rooms the only rooms in this basement?" Alexandra asked.

"No, but you're not ready to go beyond these three just yet. You haven't understood what you need to understand."

"Why does it sound like you won't be accompanying us?" Samantha asked

"I'm a wandering spirit, Samantha," he said. "That means I, and the others like me, exist without true purpose or motives. That makes it difficult to interact with the physical world. It takes a lot of energy just to sustain a visible form. We remain here only because we cannot go on. Furthermore, while you may find that it does not look like much, the next room was the worst of them all, and I'm afraid I'd rather not experience even for a flicker of a second what it was like to be in there."

"We understand. Thank you for your help."

"I wish only that I could do more." He sounded genuinely morose. "But before I go, I leave you with one last piece of advice. During his time alive, the chief physician would have been very interested in you five."

"Because of our abilities?"

"Indeed." Mark nodded. "He would peel off your skins and smash your skulls to pieces just to find what makes you tick. Now, he may be dead, but you will find that this place has not forgotten his name. The ideals of a man like that don't just fade quietly into the night. His influence is very much etched into the very stone of these walls."

"We know," Lila said. "We've encountered his army of the dead."

"Then you do not yet know. What you have faced pales in comparison to what lies ahead. I encourage you to tread very carefully. There is unspeakable evil in this place, rotten and fetid, and it was born the day the physician came to Ravensbrook."

Mark's form began to dissipate.

"How do you know so much about this place and about the chief physician?" Samantha said.

He smiled. It was the tired smile of a man who wanted to lie down and sleep after a long, hard day.

"Because I was Doctor von Menschen's first patient."

Chapter 9:
A Dreadful Demise

The disappearance of Mark Waters was followed by a grave silence. At that time, no one made any attempts to go through door number three.

Daniel's behavior has not changed since Mark's departure, and Alexandra could not help but be concerned.

"Hey," she whispered. "You okay?"

"Fine," he said. It was an obvious lie because he averted his gaze and stared at the floor instead. "We should get moving."

Just then, James made a sudden jerky movement that got her attention. Samantha and Lila noticed it, not just her.

"James?" Lila said. "James, what's wrong?"

He did not respond. Eyes wide and pure, he looked around the room in horror.

"Oh God!" he muttered. "No! It's gonna happen again. Not again!"

He grabbed the sides of his head and dropped to his knees.

"James, what are you talking about?" Alexandra said. "What's going to happen again?"

"I wanna leave. I wanna leave!" he said.

"James!" Samantha rushed to his side, grabbing him by the

shoulders. "James, breathe for a second. I'm here. We're all here. Talk to us."

All of a sudden, James' body went slack in Samantha's arms. His eyes, now brimming with tears, glazed over. He let out a deep breath of relief and then another.

"You alright?" Samantha said.

"Yeah, you... Your touch snapped me out of it," he said.

"What was 'it'? What happened just now?"

"It's not..." he said. "It's not mine."

"What?" Alexandra said.

"The... The panic... The fear... Just now... It's not mine," he said.

"What does that even mean?"

"I... I don't... I don't do physical contact... because I'm highly... sensitive to the emotions of others. I'm an empath, as you've probably already figured out, and I don't mean that in the way you hear on social media. I'm the real deal, and unfortunately... that means I can become very overwhelmed by the intensity of emotions around me."

The words came out in a blur, and only when he was done did he pause to take a proper breath once more.

"But... But no one touched you." Lila frowned.

"If the emotions are intense enough, they don't need to."

"But then... If it's not your fear..." Lila started.

"Then whose?"

Eyes still wide and frantic, James looked around at each of them one after one until his gaze settled on Daniel, who had not moved an inch.

"Daniel?" Alexandra said.

Daniel's face remained towards the ground. From the moment James had collapsed in panic, he had understood what was happening. It was, after all, reminiscent of how he himself had reacted back then, and even though now he could at least keep from expressing his fears, he remembered what it had been like to live them.

"We're wasting time here," Daniel said, measuring his words and his tone evenly. "We should get moving."

"Are you kidding? Absolutely not. What's going on with you?" Alexandra said.

"Nothing's wrong with me," Daniel snapped, fiercely locking eyes with her. "Why don't you tell empathy boy over there to keep his powers under control?"

Alexandra was taken aback, and it showed on her face.

Samantha gestured to Lila to take care of James, and she came over to Daniel.

She tenderly cupped his cheeks, forcing him to meet her eyes.

"I'm your friend, remember?" she said. "Me. Lila. Alex. James. We're all your friends, and we're here for you. Talk to us."

Daniel breathed out his mouth and his shoulders sagged.

"I've been in a place like this before," he said. "Steel bars. Concrete walls. No sunlight. Barely any food or water. Praying for death. All this hits a little too close to home."

As Daniel expected, no one spoke. They were too busy being stunned by his confession. The only sound: barely audible, came from James, and it was just as Daniel mentioned the word 'death'.

"When I was younger, I was careless," Daniel went on. "I was a thief— a stupid thief— and one day I stole from the wrong person. His name was Dean Wright, and he was the head of a criminal gang called the Blue Fangs. I was caught by Mr. Wright's crew within the same day, and I almost died, but Mr. Wright figured out that I had powers. He made me prove it and when I did, there was the brightest smile on his face, and I could tell that he was thinking of all the things he could accomplish with a power like mine. He asked me to pledge loyalty to him in exchange for my life, and seeing as my choices were rather limited, I did. He also made it clear that the punishment for leaving would be death. Looking back, perhaps death wouldn't have been so bad.

"For years, I worked for the Blue Fangs, breaking safes, stealing private information, things like that. I was a priceless member of the gang. I earned them more money in three months than they had made since the gang was first formed. But eventually, that wasn't enough for Mr. Wright. At some point, he started to imagine what it would be like if it was he who had the powers instead. I guess I should have known something was up when he started making a point of keeping himself and everything he touched out of my reach. They came for me at night, took me from my bed, and then delivered me to a place not too different from this one. It was there Mr. Wright revealed his reasons. I was physically abused for a day: waterboarded, whipped, chained to the ceiling, and deprived of rest. It wasn't until the next day before he brought in the man who would be my true torturer; a brain surgeon named Emil. I had my head shaved, and portions of my skull sawed open so he could poke around my brain, looking for God knows what. He never found anything to show for it."

"Oh my God..." Samantha muttered. Behind her, Alexandra's face was frozen in horror.

Lila maintained a poker face, but she had tears in her eyes.

"Emil wasn't a bad guy honestly, but there's little a man won't do when you hold a gun to the heads of his wife and kids. The only reason I got away was because I promised Emil I could save his wife and kids. And I did. Emil, however, was not so fortunate. He paid the price for helping me. I tipped the police off and left them enough evidence to put Mr. Wright away for good, and then I skipped town and never looked back."

There was a long period of silence as they stood around processing the revelation.

"Freaking hell," Samantha said eventually.

"Daniel, I am so sorry," Alexandra said.

"Don't do that. You didn't know."

"But why did you agree to this?"

"I mean, you couldn't have known we'd find all this down here," Daniel said. "Alex, it has been a long time since I left all that behind. I didn't expect my trauma to resurface this way, and even now I have no regrets. Your invitation came at a time I had no clue what to do with my life."

"Just so you know, if you want to leave, we can leave. Maybe call it a day or a week. Whatever you need."

He shook his head. "This is just fear. It's hardly the end of the world."

"Maybe not," James said. He sounded much calmer now. "But I think I can help with that."

"How?"

"If it's alright with you, I could help you deal with the fear."

"You want to take it away?"

"No such thing. I mean to suppress the fear. For now. Just keep it down and out of reach."

"What are you talking about?" Lila said. "You were just exposed to his emotions and look what that did to you. Now you want to suppress them?"

"Not me," James said. "All of us. I could create a psychic link, and hopefully, our numbers will be enough to counter his fear. But I should warn you that you will all feel a little drained."

"Well, it's up to you, Daniel. What do you say?"

Daniel nodded hesitantly. "But this won't make me like you"

"Ditto."

James shifted into the lotus position and gestured for Daniel to join him on the floor.

"Uh, what are you doing?" Daniel said.

"Focusing. I took up meditation to help me learn to control my powers, and it stuck. This is hardly the time to be judging me. Just sit."

Daniel plopped down and tried to imitate James' posture.

"So, what do you need us to do? Hold hands and clench our butt cheeks?" Samantha said.

"Really, Sam?" Alexandra deadpanned.

She shrugged. "What can I say? He's rubbing off on me."

"No need to hold hands," James said. "Just stay close."

"Should we think happy thoughts?" Alexandra said.

"I mean, happy thoughts would be nice but not necessary," James said. "We're not trying to compel him to be happy. Just not afraid. Now, try to breathe easy, Daniel."

Daniel did not have a lot of faith in James or his powers, but as there was no harm in trying, he shut his eyes and took one breath, then the next, then the next.

It was only when he started to feel his breathing come easy that Daniel realized just how tight the knot in his chest had been. His brows relaxed, and the worry lines dissipated.

"There," James said.

Daniel opened his eyes and looked around. The chains and the bars still reminded him of that place, but suddenly, he did not feel the fear that came with the reminder.

He smiled. "Well, what do you know? Empathy really is a superpower."

James rolled his eyes and, with Lila's help, got back on his feet.

"You couldn't go ten seconds without antagonizing him?" Samantha said.

"I really couldn't," Daniel said.

She yanked him to his feet and patted him a little harder than necessary, but when she stopped, her hand lingered, and her expression softened.

"Just so you know, you're safe with us. We've got your back." She patted him a final time and walked away.

Dumbfounded and touched by the sentiment, Daniel could not help but smile fondly. He caught himself when he realized James was watching him and flipped him the bird.

*****

After their unscheduled and not-so-restful break, it was time to check out what was behind door number three.

The door opened to reveal a small room, completely bare save for two chairs and a flickering yellow bulb overhead.

One of the chairs was overturned as though its last occupant had gotten up in a hurry and never returned. The second chair, however... still had its occupant seated.

Strapped by arms and feet to the chair was a skeleton. On its head, there was a strange-looking helmet. Daniel suspected it was the same one Samantha had seen on Sylvia.

Thick blankets of cobwebs surrounded the seat and filled the spaces between the ribs and its mouth, which hung open as the lower jaw was subjected to the influence of gravity. It did not take a detective or a team of forensic scientists to decipher what had happened to the skeleton. The skeleton, once a patient of this depraved institution, had been tied in place and left to die.

Daniel cringed as he imagined the poor fellow, withering away, trapped underground where no one could hear their screams, craving a simple drop of water until, after several days in agony, they breathed their last. It was unsettling.

But Daniel had a feeling that whoever had abandoned them to die, most likely the chief physician, had not done so willingly, and that led him to be curious about the other chair.

He went to it and knelt in front of it, his hand hovering a mere inch away.

He looked up to see that the others had gathered around him.

"Are you sure?" Samantha asked.

"Whatever happened here was important," he said. "Or Mark would not have led us here. Besides, you've got me, right?"

"Of course." She smiled.

"You should know, if anything happens in there that leads to a panic attack, it will incapacitate us all. I can't tell for how long, but I'd rather not be unconscious in an evil physician's dungeon."

"So, no pressure," he breathed. "Gotcha."

Daniel clenched his jaw in anticipation and closed the remaining distance.

The world around him faded into a blur as time rewound. Days, months, and years all receded within the blink of an eye.

He watched as the decay process reversed and the skeleton became a bloated corpse; then he watched as that corpse became a barely alive human female, her chest barely moving with each shallow breath. More time passed, and the woman's skin regained volume, and her eyes were less sunken. He watched her scream for help. He watched her struggle futilely against her bonds.

Even though it was like watching a movie he already knew the end of, it was still very painful to watch. Thankfully, more time regressed, and then, at last, the chair was upright, and sitting in it was none other than Doctor von Menschen.

At the sight of him so close, Daniel felt a shiver race down his spine.

He was dressed in a lab coat and held a remote in his hand. On it, Daniel found two buttons, one red and the other green, and a dial.

Just then, he pressed the green button and turned the dial, and in the other chair, the girl began to scream at the top of her voice.

She fought against her restraints like a mad woman, even though it bit deep into her flesh as she did.

It was obvious that the remote controlled the device on her head, and whatever it did to her, it caused a tremendous amount of pain. And Doctor von Menschen was smiling.

Daniel ground his teeth together in frustration. He could not bear to watch her suffer, and he hated that there was nothing he could do about it.

But just then, the door burst open, and a guard ran into the room.

The chief physician pressed the red button and massaged his temple in annoyance.

"What have I said about interrupting me when I'm working?" he said. His voice was raspy and chilling.

"Sir, trouble is afoot. An angry mob is upon us!" the guard said.

Doctor Fredrick von Menschen sprang to his feet, and the chair was knocked over.

In a split second, the confidence diminished from his face, and it reflected in his tone when he spoke again.

"A mob?" he said. "What mob?"

"It appears to be the townsfolk. They approach with torches and pitchforks. We must leave, and fast!"

The girl now forgotten, he tossed the remote and hurried after the guard.

Soon, he was out of earshot, and Daniel knew he would never return. But what happened next? Did he escape?

He let go of the chair, and the girl became a skeleton once more. The empty room was filled with four familiar faces. Neither was of priority to Daniel at that moment.

"What did you see?" Alexandra said.

"Not enough," Daniel said.

He went out the door, following the doctor's footsteps.

When he got to the first room with the hospital beds, he put his hand on one. Once again, he was transported to the past, in time to see the chief physician and the guard walk past.

"Where the hell is Blackthorne then?" Doctor von Menschen said. "The warden. Where is he?"

"He's in his office."

"What for?"

"I'm not sure, but I don't think the warden will be coming with us."

The chief physician stopped in his tracks.

"What is that supposed to mean?"

"The warden asked me to inform you of the situation and escort you to safety if you so choose, then he retreated to his office and asked not to be disturbed."

"Has he gone mad?"

Not expecting an answer, the chief physician resumed walking at an increased pace.

He and the guard got into the elevator and disappeared as the doors closed.

Letting go of his last point of contact, Daniel made a beeline for the elevator.

"Yo, Dan! A little update here?" Samantha called after him.

"Right. Sorry." He stopped. "I'm following up on what happened the very last time Doctor Fredrick von Menschen came down here. Now, I'm trying to follow the events of one particular night from fifty years ago. I have to focus, so I will not be giving updates as I go along. Just follow me. I'll tell you the whole story when I know it."

He entered the elevator, held it open for them, and then pushed the button for the top floor.

Upstairs, Daniel picked a wall and resumed gleaning.

The chief physician sent the guard down to ready the car and went in the other direction towards the warden's office.

He barged in to find Warden Blackthorne standing at the window looking out into the yard.

"Matthias," he said. "I've heard the news."

"News?" Warden Blackthorne turned with an odd, amused expression. "They stand at our gates as we speak."

"Then explain to me why you stand and watch instead of making haste to leave."

"I understand what is to come," the warden said. "This is my end."

"You really have gone mad. Stop this foolishness. The guards have the car ready. We will flee through the back gates."

"You may go if you wish, although I don't have much faith that you'll make it very far. My fate is sealed. If I am not found within this asylum, I will be hunted down like a dog, and I would rather keep my dignity than preserve my head for a while longer."

"Dignity?" The doctor said. "What dignity? You are warden over a madhouse, and in the eyes of those people down there, you are a murderer. There's no such thing as dignity for men like us. We must flee!"

"Fredrick, my friend. Do you have no faith in the work we have done here?"

"My work is flawless!" Doctor von Menschen said, his pride taking over. "But it is also incomplete!"

"It was enough. We will persevere, and your work here will live on long after we are gone. We will not be erased."

The clamoring of the mob rose to their hearing, and Doctor von Menschen grew more and more uneasy until he threw up his hands resignedly.

"If this is your decision, very well," he said. "I, on the other hand, am leaving. I will not accept death by their grimy hands. Dignity be damned!"

He left the room in a flurry and raced for the staircase at impressive speed, considering his bad leg. Just as he got down to the landing of the first floor, the front door burst open.

Beating a hasty retreat, he hurried up to the floor above and then raced for the service staircase that Daniel had spotted on the map.

He emerged from the backyard and found that the coast was clear. On the other side of the gate, a car waited for him.

Just then, he heard voices drawing closer.

His eyes darted this way and that like a prey evading capture. From either side of the building, light from torches could be seen, and through light, shadows of dozens of men and women were cast forward.

They were not yet aware of his presence, but if he stepped out, they would see him. However, he was left with no choice.

He dashed forward as fast as his legs could carry him, but before he could cover a significant distance, someone in the crowd noticed the car and drew the attention of the others to it. And then everything went horribly wrong. With angry cries, they ran after the car. Flaming torches and big sticks were hurled at it, but the driver sped off into the night.

It looked as though he might escape, but then a deafening 'boom' went off, accompanied by the flash of gunfire, and the car careened to the side, crashing into a tree.

Quietly, Doctor von Menschen retreated.

Now a panicking mess, he went back inside and ran up the stairs to the top floor. He could hear the other half of the crowd moving around the floor right below him.

He returned to the warden's office and found him where he had left him.

"They're relentless!" the chief physician said. "They were waiting at the back gate. There's no escape!"

"As I already foresaw."

He still had a passive demeanor, but there were cracks in it now, and Daniel realized he was merely putting on a brave face. He was no less terrified than the doctor was.

"There has to be something we can do!"

"It is far too late for that."

The door burst open, and the mob came rushing in.

This part Daniel had seen already; they were quickly overpowered and dragged away, but this time he followed them.

They were dragged down to the lobby and thrown to the floor. There, a woman emerged from the crowd to say, "That's him! That's the devil himself!"

She was pointing at Doctor von Menschen as she spoke.

Satisfied that they had gotten the right targets, a beating of epic proportions commenced. And it wasn't just the men who wanted their pound of flesh; women too came forward to take a swing, and they swung hard.

The sight of two men getting absolutely pummeled should not have been as satisfactory as it was, except these were no ordinary men, and he deserved every bit of it and then some.

Someone called the crowd to order and had them back off, and then, from nowhere, gasoline was produced. Without hesitation, they doused the warden and the chief physician from head to toe while they writhed and sputtered and cursed their black hearts out.

"Matthias Blackthorne and Fredrick von Menschen," one of the men— a priest— said, "you have sinned against God himself and against the good people of this town. I am not one to condone violence, but as of this moment, I find myself in full support of it. The punishment for your evil deeds, as decided by the bereaved, is death by fire, a lighter sentence than you deserve, but we leave the rest to God. And while we cannot undo the damage that you have done, we can rest easy knowing that your evil dies here with you."

A match was lit and tossed, and a great big flame roared to life with two men dancing in it.

Black spots danced across Daniel's vision as the scene came to an end, and he took his hands off the lobby wall.

Unable to keep away the melancholic thoughts, he reflected on the priest's final words before the men went up in flames. If only they had held true.

As Daniel's vision snapped back to reality, the others were standing around waiting for him to respond.

"Well, don't keep us waiting. What happened?" Samantha piped up.

"They... left her here..." Daniel's voice trailed off.

"Oh god." Lila gasps, hand over her mouth.

"Menschen had brought her down here for experimentation, but before he could start, an angry mob had made their way to the Asylum. He went to Blackthorne's office, pleading with him to leave before they could get here, but he refused."

"I take it Menschen had no such desire to stay?" James said.

"He tried to leave. A car was waiting by the back gate for him, but so was the mob. He fled back inside to Blackthorne's office. The mob had finally caught up with them, and they... took care of the problem."

Everyone became wide-eyed simultaneously as they understood what he meant by that.

Just as everyone was processing what Daniel was saying, Alexandra became overwhelmed by extreme vertigo before her vision was enveloped in darkness...

Chapter 10:
A Vision of Destiny

Sarah Jennings was barely twenty-three when she first began to work at the Ravensbrook Asylum.

Having been born into a Catholic home and raised as a devout Christian, Sarah took her faith seriously. She tried her best to be good and to do good, not just because that was what her parents wanted of her but because that was what God wanted. Her parents were proud of her, but they were equally amazed at her dedication to all things that concerned God.

After graduating from nursing school, her intention was to join a convent, and that was the first time her parents ever opposed her choice. They figured the vows of poverty, chastity, and obedience were a big commitment to make so soon and feared that she would come to regret it.

Seeing that she merely wanted to serve God in whatever way she could, they came up with a different solution. The mayor had only recently opened the asylum, and nurses were wanted.

They encouraged her to apply, and even though she had no experience dealing with the mentally ill, she thought it was perfect. Service to humanity was a higher calling.

She applied for the job, and within the week, she was called in for an interview with the warden.

Upon arrival at the asylum, Sarah was truly awed.

The asylum was a towering stone structure that could be seen from far and wide, and the fact that it stood as a symbol of hope made it all the more refreshing. She found the Gothic architecture impressive, with the pointy arches and glass-stained windows and a roof so high and pointy it almost seemed to pierce the skies. The exterior walls had neatly trimmed creeping vines blanketing them, giving a feel like it was one with nature. She had seen such designs in magazines and newspapers but never up close.

Around the asylum, shady trees decorated the yard, and left and right of the gravel walkway, statues of angels carved from marble stood guard.

A security guard welcomed her at the gate, took her up to the warden's office, and knocked on the door.

"Enter," a gruff voice called from within.

She opened the door to find a man bent over some paperwork. The man was tall with broad shoulders, and when he looked up at her, there was a strange severity to his gaze for a split second before he offered her a smile.

"Sarah Jennings, I believe," he said.

"Yes, sir," she said.

He gestured to the seat across from him.

"Please."

As she sat down, he closed the file he had been perusing, and she realized it had her name on it.

"I've gone through your file," he said matter-of-factly. "Not very impressed, to be honest." He pushed the file to the edge of the table and let it fall into the trash bin.

Sarah was taken aback. Surely, her qualifications were not that bad.

"Well, yes, I uh... I don't have any work experience," she said. "But I did recently graduate from nursing school."

"And did this nursing school have anything to do with the mentally challenged?"

"No, sir. But I've been told I'm a fast learner, and I really am willing to learn."

"Why are you here, Miss Jennings?" he said.

"I want... I want to do good. I want to help people."

The man's brow rose slowly as he stared in disbelief.

"You want to help people?"

"Yes, sir."

"And you mean the psychos and the loonies and the rest?"

"I'd prefer not to call them that, sir. But yes."

"Oh, is that so?"

Never had Sarah been made to feel stupid for saying she wanted to do good.

"I wonder what it's like inside that tiny head of yours," he said.

He let out a hearty laugh that lasted a good half minute, and then he propped his elbows on the table and leaned in.

"Have you ever been this close to a lunatic before, Miss Jennings?"

"N-no sir, I can't say that I have."

"And if I were, perhaps, to do something like this." He lunged forward and grabbed her by the neck. His eyes widened, and his lips curled in a smile. "What would you do to *help* them?"

Sarah's eyes bulged, and her mouth hung open in a pointless attempt to breathe. His grip had cut off her air supply.

"Can't... Breathe..." she managed to say.

He held on a bit longer, and just as Sarah thought he just might kill her, he let her go.

Coughing and wheezing, she backed away as soon as she could and didn't stop until she was against the wall.

The warden gave her an emotionless glance, then got out of his seat and moved to the window.

"Perhaps I was a bit too harsh just then," he said. "I apologize. But there is a message I hope I was able to get across to you with that simple demonstration: This is not a hospital, Miss Jennings. These people are not your regular patients. They're not weak and helpless. They are very dangerous, uninhibited by morals or good conscience or even the fear of God, and if you are not smart, if you let your guard down and treat them like you would normal people, you will get hurt. You might even die."

As she nursed her neck, fearing that he might have bruised her, Sarah took in the warden's words. She was horrified to hear him talk like that about his patients; almost as much as she was that he had basically nearly killed her.

"Don't misunderstand me; we are truly here to help in whatever way we can," he said. "But to do that, we are required to use a sterner hand than you're used to. Think of it as breaking a few already-cracked eggs to make an omelet. This interview is over. Bernard will see you out. Take the rest of the week to think about what we have discussed here. If you decide you still want to work here, then I will see you Monday, but if you're not sure you have the stomach and the spine to tolerate the methods we apply here, then save both of us the trouble and stay home."

Sarah was determined not to let the warden see her tears, and so she held them in, staring defiantly at the back of his head, but when she eventually left his office and the door was shut behind her, she broke down and cried.

Bernard turned out to be the guard who had brought her in, and just then, he returned. He told her a car was waiting to take her home and then handed her a handkerchief.

For the rest of the week, Sarah thought of little else than the interview. At first, she was certain she never wanted to see the warden ever again after what he had done to her, but a couple of days passed, and her mindset changed.

This was God's way of testing her. Surely, it had to be. He had put the warden in her path as a challenge. She would not give up. She would not fail. She had gone to that interview because she knew she wanted to help people, and even if the methods were different and she would have to grow a thicker skin, she was willing.

She would not fail.

And so, the next morning, bright and early, she was back at the asylum. She thought back to her last time and happened to look up at the window of the warden's office, and there he was, watching her make her way to the front door.

When she reached his office, he was already standing there with the door open.

"Miss Jennings," he greeted. "I must admit I had a little wager in my head over whether or not I would see those bright eyes again."

"Oh?"

"I bet against."

"Well, I'm sorry to disappoint you, Mr. Blackthorne."

"Oh, please. I am nothing if not impressed," he said. "So, I take it you've decided you have the skin for this?"

"No," she said and watched as his eyes widened in a mix of surprise and disappointment. "But I am willing to grow a thicker skin."

"Oh, you impress me more and more, Miss Jennings." He smiled. "Come, let me give you a tour of the asylum. We'll start with the nurse's quarters and then move on to the cafeteria. I hear they're serving fudge cake."

It was such a natural thing to say that Sarah could not help but laugh.

"Of course, Mr. Blackthorne."

"'Warden' will do just fine."

"Yes, Warden."

And this was how Nurse Jennings came to work at Ravensbrook Asylum.

Sarah soon found out she was the first nurse to apply for the job and the first to be hired, but in two days, the number had risen to ten. The first few days of employment were mostly assignment of duties and detailed orientations on the nature of said duties, and then, under supervision by the warden himself, they began to do their jobs for real.

From conducting patient intake screening, evaluation and triage assessments to providing case management as well as educating them about self-care, there was a lot to learn, but just as Sarah promised, she was a quick study. Eager to prove she was worth her salt, she picked up the routine faster than anyone else.

A month passed, and then a few more, and Sarah started to realize that the job was not quite as challenging as the warden made it out to be. She had certainly not been choked out by any inmates. A great deal of them were barely aware enough to even move their hands.

She could not help but wonder if it had just been a ploy to see if she was really serious about working here.

As for the warden, after the probationary week had passed, they saw less and less of him. He was mostly locked away in his office during the day, but every once in a while, he would conduct an unscheduled inspection of the entire premises.

The warden was every bit as scary as Sarah remembered, but it wasn't because of anything he did. He was just a frightening man by default. All the other nurses confirmed that his presence alone made them feel uneasy, and they never wanted to be in the direct path of his fiery gaze.

Warden Blackthorne did not only keep an eye out for the nurses, however. Occasionally, he would summon a patient to his office for several hours. What was said during the meeting was supposed to be strictly between him and the patient, so Sarah never thought to pry, but one of the other nurses did and revealed that the patient refused to spill. According to her, it was almost as if the patient was afraid of Warden Blackthorne and not like they were; it was more like deathly afraid. Another nurse claimed she peeped in one time and found a patient tied to a chair.

Sarah did not like to entertain gossip, and so she did not think much of it. For one, while there were not many, there were certain patients who had violent spells and could hardly be contained, so perhaps it was a mere precaution. For two, neither nurse was entirely trustworthy to begin with.

Life in Ravensbrook Asylum went on as normal, and as though suspicions persisted around the warden, they remained nothing but suspicions, and Sarah paid them no mind. But that all changed when the chief physician arrived.

The day before, Warden Blackthorne had called them in for a meeting to inform them that a very important man was coming. The warden wasn't lenient with the details, but apparently, he was a German doctor by the name of Fredrick von Menschen who had extensive experience dealing with severe mental cases. They were to welcome him, and as he would be staying for an indefinite period, they were to make him feel at home.

That was the first time Sarah had a sense of foreboding about the warden's administration.

Early the next day, they were summoned again by the warden to inform them that the doctor was in town and was expected to arrive within the hour.

It was a mere ten minutes before the honking of a car signified his arrival. As instructed, the nurses went out to welcome him.

Sarah's first impression of Doctor Fredrick von Menschen was that he reminded her of those little children who caught insects just to pull all their legs off one by one.

It was strange because the doctor was a frail man who did not seem capable of sudden movement. How, then, did such a small body seem so threatening?

The answer to that came exactly two days later.

Doctor Fredrick von Menschen had quickly moved into his office, and after taking one day to rest from his journey and another to familiarize himself with the ins and outs of the asylum, he got to work.

He called his first patient into his office, and ten minutes later, a scream of pure terror could be heard nearly throughout the building.

Nurses rushed to the scene, Sarah among them, in time to see the patient dash out of the doctor's office. Doctor von Menschen emerged a few seconds later with a look of annoyance on his face. He stared at the nurses like they were nothing but nuisances, then reentered his office and slammed the door shut.

The warden himself appeared on the scene soon after. He went into the doctor's office for a minute, and when he returned, he looked at them as if they were somehow responsible for what had happened.

"What are you standing around here doing?" he said. "Don't you have somewhere to be?"

The nurses started to disperse, but Sarah stood her ground.

"Sir, that patient was very much in distress," she said. "If it's our job to take care of them, don't we deserve to know what just happened?"

The warden was visibly surprised by the sheer cheek of her, and if Sarah was to be honest, so was she.

He approached her, and just as she prepared for a reprimand, he put a hand on her shoulder.

"That was nothing to concern yourself with, Nurse Jennings," he said. "The patient will be fine. I assure you the situation was greatly exaggerated. Doctor von Menschen's methods can be a bit intense, and it may seem harmful to the patients, but he knows what he's doing. Breaking a few cracked eggs, remember?"

He turned and started off the way he had come.

"So, this is going to be a regular thing?" Sarah blurted. "Patients running and screaming?"

"I'll talk to Doctor von Menschen. If all the ruckus can be avoided, I'd very much like that too, but if you're asking if the doctor will continue with his treatment, then yes. It is going to be a regular thing." He looked over his shoulder. "Is that going to be a problem for you?"

"No, sir."

If only she knew what was to come, she would probably have said yes.

But how was she to know?

The situation grew worse very quickly, and eventually, the screams of patients became a normal part of the day. If they were lucky, it only happened once or twice in a day. And on bad days, it got up to eight.

And then, after months upon months of this nearing a whole year, the screaming suddenly stopped. There were no more patients begging for the torture to stop. No more of them running in the halls to escape the madman in a lab coat. It was as if it never happened in the first place.

Sarah should have felt relieved by this, except she noticed that the doctor became scarce as well. She knew for a fact that he was still within the asylum because someone always took his food up to him every morning, but she hardly saw him aside from the evenings when he took a walk around the backyard and smoked a cigarette.

Sarah also noticed that there were cases of patients vanishing for long hours only to be found later in their rooms, too exhausted to speak and covered in cuts and bruises. She had to watch as her wards suffered in silence as they could not bring themselves to speak of what was going on. With time, the bruises grew worse, and the cuts ran deeper.

Sarah's mind ran wild with speculations, but there was no way to confirm, and even if she did, what could she possibly do? The other nurses fancied a good gossip, but when it came to doing something, they were cowards. Who would take her word over that of the warden?

The warden must have noticed her suspicions, and for some reason, he considered her more of a threat than all the others because her duties began to consist of more and more activities that kept her away from the top two floors.

Soon after, patients began to disappear altogether. No bodies were found, and the only clues left behind pointed to the chief physician. At first, the warden kept silent on the matter, but when too many nurses began to notice, he claimed they had been moved to special cells for experimental treatment.

Whether or not they were dead or alive, only the warden and the chief physician knew, but they were never seen again.

This went on for years, and then, one day, a patient passed out in the cafeteria. Sarah went in search of the chief physician while the other nurses on site tried to stabilize his condition. On reaching his office, she found his door unlocked and, after knocking, went in.

The office was empty, but her attention was drawn to the folder on the table.

Before she could stop herself, she went to it and flipped through it. It was full of patient files, and at the end, she found a list of all the patients. Most had been crossed out, but the rest were ticked once, except for a few that have been marked X after being ticked.

Sarah noticed that the names marked X were patients that had gone completely missing, and the ticked names were patients that had been disappearing for hours to days on end. It was almost as if the doctor was picking out certain people, except she couldn't find a pattern. There were old men and women as well as children yet to even reach puberty.

She went back to the files and sought out certain names that had been marked X, and to her horror, the first three she found were labeled 'DECEASED.'

Sarah had to clamp her hand over her mouth to keep from screaming as she continued to read. The doctor had killed them!

There were a few other labels like 'COMPATIBLE' and 'PROMISING,' but before she could find the link, Sarah heard a knock on the door.

Her heart leaped to her throat but then she realized Doctor von Menschen would not knock on his own door.

It was probably the warden, in which case she would simply tell him she had just entered looking for the chief physician.

Although she wished she could find more, Sarah acknowledged that she had accidentally discovered a lot.

She hurriedly put the files back together and went to the door, but when she opened it, it wasn't the warden but another nurse.

"Sarah?" she said. "I came looking for the—"

"I know. Me too. He's not here."

She exited the office, and they started down the hallway. It was just then that Doctor von Menschen rounded the corner and came into view.

"Doctor von Menschen!" the other nurse said.

"What are you doing here?" He eyed them suspiciously.
Not wanting to draw any attention to herself, Sarah let her continue to answer.

"We came looking for you. We have an emergency! A patient is having a seizure."

Seizure? *The situation had escalated.*

"A seizure?" he said.

"Yes, sir. In the cafeteria. Come quick!"

The doctor followed them to the cafeteria and, after assessing the situation, had some guards pick up the boy and follow him.

A few days later, the warden informed them that he had flown out for an emergency operation, but by now, Sarah knew the truth. She knew that the boy was dead.

*****

Opening her eyes to find Daniel staring down at her was not among the top ten ways Alexandra preferred to wake up, but alas, that was how it was.

"Personal space, ya creep," she muttered, pushing his face away.

He rolled his eyes and backed away.

"If you're going to black out like that, the least you could do is give us a heads-up," Daniel said. "Maybe just say 'going dark' or something like in those spec ops movies."

"Ha ha," Alexandra laughed dryly. "What happened?"

She realized she was on the floor and the others were standing around her.

"Daniel was in the middle of telling us about that night, and you passed out," Samantha said.

That was right. They had followed him downstairs while he was using his abilities.

Then what happened?

"Right. Of course," she said. And then she remembered... "The woman... You talked about a woman, didn't you?"

"Uh... What?" Daniel said.

"The woman who identified the chief physician."

"Oh, right. Yeah. What about her?"

"She was a nurse here. Her name was Sarah Jennings."

"How do you know that?"

"I basically just had a speed run of her life. Especially the important bits from her time here."

"And?"

"I know where we need to go next."

Chapter 11:
SHADOWS IN THE ATTIC

Sarah eventually worked up the courage to report her discoveries to the townsfolk with the help of her parents, who were quick to vouch for her honesty and good conduct. However, before then, there was one last discovery that hastened the process. It was the accidental discovery of an attic within the asylum.

To be fair, the discovery wasn't quite the straw that broke the camel's back because, at that point, its back was very much broken. How it happened was that Sarah, despite her findings, knew that she needed some sort of proof that the doctor and the warden were torturing and killing off patients, and she needed some kind of proof as to why.

She decided that if she were to find that proof, then she would have to know just where the warden and the doctor took the patients to. Clearly, it was still on asylum grounds and most likely within the building, so she did not expect it to be too hard to find as she was looking for it.

Aware that she was already under suspicion from the warden and the chief physician— and they probably had guards watching her— she bribed her fellow nurse, Greta, offering to do her morning chores for a month, to stake out the top floor and spy on the doctor. She did not mention why, and if she did, Nurse Greta would likely have refused, considering that, like everyone else, she feared the man, but she had her positioned along the hall around the time Sarah had noticed the guards usually came for the patients.

It took a while before the stakeout yielded results because Greta chickened out the first few times, and she was busy with a patient at other times. Once, the warden came out of his office, and she fled the scene before he could spot her.

After about a month, Greta came to her table during lunch and sat down with an excited look on her face. She had seen something.

Apparently, a guard had taken the patient up to the doctor's office, and after a brief moment, that guard and another emerged, carrying the now unconscious patient with the doctor right behind them. They took him into the supply closet and didn't come out for at least fifteen minutes, which was how long she waited.

Before she had left the scene, Greta had checked out the supply closet, much to Sarah's surprise, but she had found nothing but a supply closet within.

Now armed with a lead, albeit a strange one, Sarah plotted to check it out for herself. The only problem was there was no chance of her being on the floor without raising suspicion.

Luckily, a solution presented itself. The warden was invited to a party at the mayor's office, and the doctor had a personal errand to attend outside the asylum.

While they were both away, she snuck into the supply closet. It was dark inside, so she tried the switch, but it didn't work. As she continued flicking it, she accidentally dislodged it. To her surprise, there was a lever underneath. The lever was not up or down but balanced in the middle.

Taking a guess and hoping she did not unknowingly cut the power to the entire building, she pushed the lever up.

*****

"Up?"

"Yes, Daniel," Alexandra said. "Up."

She had just explained to them how she knew about the attic, and now they were standing inside the supply closet.

"So, what? Down is the basement, up is the attic?"

"You sound offended that it's so simple."

"'Offended' isn't the word I'd use. Suspicious perhaps. Disappointed even."

"So, there's another elevator?" James cut in.

"I don't know yet," Alexandra said. "All I know is we push the lever up this time."

"But you didn't say what would happen after, only that the vision shifted, and she was in an attic," James said.

"Are you worried about booby traps?" Daniel said.

"Aren't you?" James retorted. "A number of things could be waiting for us."

"Calm down, Indiana Jones," he said. "We've been traipsing around this place for hours. Pretty late to start thinking about booby traps now."

"That's no reason to let our guards down." He shrugged.

Alexandra rolled her eyes and pushed the lever, then backed away.

"There. Now we can see what comes forth: booby trap or hidden entrance."

They turned towards the shelf of supplies, but it did not move. Instead, they heard a scraping sound as though the stone was sliding across the stone.

"This way!" Lila called out.

They looked at the opposite wall, and there they found that a portion of the wall was sliding into itself to reveal a secret flight of steps.

"So, not an elevator," Daniel said. "A staircase."

"Shall we?" Alexandra said.

"Lead the way. It's your vision."

"So much for chivalry," she muttered.

"I'm all for female empowerment."

They got out their flashlights and ascended the stairs.

The space was small, with a ceiling so low they had to hunch over it, which was doubly uncomfortable because cobwebs and dust littered it, just enough to give mild cases of claustrophobia and arachnophobia. Thankfully, it was a short climb before they got to the top.

The doorway opened into a small room with a vaulted ceiling, and they stretched to full heights, grateful to be in a wider space again. The ceiling was far out of reach, so they were safe from the cobwebs, but they still had to duck under the beams as they moved.

The rest of the space was just as old and dusty. Light streamed in from the small window. Alexandra speculated that based on its position, it could not be noticed from outside.

The space stank of dust and dry rot, and the air left a stale taste in her mouth.

As Alexandra had seen in the vision, the attic was a storage of some kind. But not the usual kind because clearly, someone had gone through a lot of trouble to make this place.

There were two things in the room. The first was a wooden chair that crumbled to pieces when Daniel kicked it. The second thing was a chest. It was locked but, for fifty years, had done severe damage to its structural integrity, and so with a couple of blows with the end of his flashlight, Daniel broke it off.

Inside the chest, they found a large binder.

Daniel took it out and dumped it on top of the chest, raising a cloud of dust.

"Hey, watch it!" Lila coughed.

"Sorry. Sorry."

When the dust had settled, they gathered around the binder. Inside it, they found patient files. They had been well preserved in the chest, and the prints and writings remained.

Each file contained personal records of each patient: age, sex, body measurements, family members, as well as medical records, but there were also brain scans and mental health diagnoses.

"Why would patient files be hidden away here?" Alexandra wondered aloud.

"Maybe they take doctor-patient confidentiality very seriously?" Daniel said.

"What do you think the colors mean?" Lila said.

"Colors?" Alexandra said.

She pointed at the bottom corner of the file they were on. It was colored red.

"They're color-coded," she said.

Alexandra flipped through the others and found two other colors: green and yellow.

As she flipped back, a paper flew out and landed on the floor.

"How did I miss that?" she said. "Every single one."

James picked it up and read through it.

"It's a legend," he said. "It explains the colors. Red is for unsuitable candidates. Green is for suitable candidates. Yellow is for... deceased candidates."

He put the paper down for them to look at.

"Candidates for what?" Lila said.

"I don't know."

"Are there preferred categories of insanity? Like an Ivy League asylum?" Alexandra said.

"Why don't we leave the dry humor to Daniel, eh?" Samantha teased.

"So, someone does appreciate the work I do around here!" Daniel said.

"Shut up."

He rolled his eyes and picked up the binder.

"What if they were trying out some new, experimental drug to cure them, and those were the cases that fit?" James said.

"I guess that would make sense," Alexandra said. "But I'm not sure the warden or the chief physician was ever that keen on helping the patients."

"Maybe it was about money." Lila shrugged. "Maybe they used the patients as guinea pigs while trying to come up with new drugs. Antidepressants and all that, maybe."

Until now, Daniel had been flipping through the binder. All of a sudden, he stopped and perked up.

"Everybody shut up. You're all wrong," he said. "Very wrong." He picked out the first five green files and handed them out, taking one himself.

"What's going on?" Lila said.

"Turn to the end of your file, the bit with the doctor's note. Read what's written there. Sam, you can go first."

Samantha did as he asked, and from the final page, she read,

"Subject has tested positive for the gene and has shown immense promise. A series of tests have shown potential in extrasensory perception, low-level psychokinesis, and a newly discovered ability I've named phobiapathy. The latter ability causes the victim to experience terrors conjured up by their own minds. An experiment on a lab rat caused it severe distress coupled with elevated heart rate and behaviors consistent with panic. When used on a human subject, the human screamed himself hoarse and balled himself in the corner of the cage. Afterward, he claimed to have seen the devil himself, among other things."

For a few seconds, no one spoke.

"I'm no comic book nerd, but... those are powers, right?" Alexandra said.

"Like actual superpowers like the kind we have?"

"Yep," Daniel said, smiling almost proudly.

"What's got you all glib?"

"I'm just excited." He shrugged. "I mean, think about it: we each went most of our lives thinking there was no other person out in the world like us, and then we found each other, and the world felt a little less lonely, or at least it did for me, and now we learn that not only are we not alone but also fifty years ago there was so many of them. It really does make you wonder, doesn't it?"

Alexandra paused, taking in his words. She hadn't thought about it that way, and now that she did, he was right. It was a bit refreshing to feel less like a freak.

"Who wants to go next?" Daniel said.

"Um..." Lila began. "The subject tested positive and at first only showed low-level psychometric abilities, only able to glean a few minutes into the past in vague details, but after spending time in my care, her range has improved to a few hours with clearer details. I look forward to seeing what she will do with a year of continued training."

"Are you all starting to see a pattern here?" Daniel said. "I'll go next. The subject tested positive. Yadda yadda yadda. The tests revealed potent psychokinetic abilities and even apporation. The maximum load so far for psychokinesis is 215 pounds, which is over the weight of the average human being. Maximum apportation distance was seventy-three meters, with a load of about 7 pounds."

"What's apporation?" Lila said.

Daniel took out his phone and fiddled with it for a moment. He must have gone to the dictionary app because there was no cell service anywhere near the asylum; Alexandra had checked.

"Apporate is to produce a material object without any apparent physical means," he said. "So, like a summons, I think."

The gears had already started to spin in Alexandra's head since the first file, and she could see she wasn't the only one.

She looked at the file in her hands.

"Subject positive for the gene," she read. "A new psychic ability has been discovered. The subject possesses pyrokinesis, the ability to create flames out of thin air. The subject does not have substantial mastery of her ability and has set herself on fire twice now, but her potential is stunning. During initial testing, she set fire to the entire room and left the door red-hot by the time she finally ran out of fuel. An ability like this is rare but also dangerous. For the safety of the subject and myself, a new testing field will need to be arranged before more experimentation can be undertaken."

"Pretty sure it's clear now," Daniel said.

"Oh my God..." Samantha muttered.

"That's the correct response."

"These patients—the green ones and the yellow ones—they all have psychic abilities," Alexandra said.

"Well *had,* but that is also correct."

"So not all of them were actually mentally unstable," Samantha said. "They just had untapped psychic abilities that manifested strangely enough for their family to seek out help from the asylum."

"Do you think it's a coincidence?" James said. "Like maybe there's a link between mental illnesses and psychic abilities?"

"With the number of patients even showing signs of the ability at all, I'd say it's possible," Samantha said. "Either that or the warden went house to house testing people and making up mental illnesses, and that's unlikely."

"So, if we had been born fifty years ago, we could have ended up like these people?" James said.

"Well, you're awfully cheery," Samantha said.

"I don't mean to be a downer, but we're just discovering that these people were just like us. It feels..."

"Personal?" Daniel said.

"Yeah."

"Good," he said. "So, let's take it personally. Find whatever's haunting this place and show it to the door."

"Surprisingly great speech there, Shaggy," Samantha said.

Daniel deadpanned. "He better be Scooby, or we'll have problems."

"Can we get back on track here?" Lila said. "We've covered that about..." She did a quick count. "...twenty to thirty percent of the patients at least showed signs of psychic abilities, but what did the warden and the chief physician want them for?"

"I mean, the answer's right there, isn't it?" Alexandra said grimly. "Every way I try to think about it, it's not pleasant, but at the very least, we know they wanted to control their abilities somehow."

"Do you think maybe they were trying to sort of take the powers out of them?" Samantha said. "Make it their own somehow, just like..." she trailed off, but the rest of her sentence was clear as she looked right at Daniel.

Daniel looked away.

"I think so," Alexandra said. "It doesn't seem like the patients died from the testing alone."

"But what could they want with all this power?" Lila said. I mean, one or two, I'd kind of get it, but we're talking over fifty patients. And that's just the surviving ones among the 'candidates.'"

"I don't know, but the more I think about it, the more I worry that their plan did not stop with the death of Doctor von Menschen or Warden Blackthorne," Alexandra said. "Maybe it continues to this day."

"You think the doctor's ghost is still roaming these halls?" Samantha said.

"I mean, the other ghosts are still here, so it's plausible," Alexandra said. "And besides, before he left, Mark said something along the lines of the doctor's influence is etched into these walls. What if he wasn't speaking as figuratively as we thought?"

"Well, there's an unsettling thought," James muttered.

"Speaking of Mark," Lila said, "he said there were more rooms in the dungeon, but we were not yet ready to explore them."

"Yeah," Samantha said. "He said we were yet to understand what we needed to understand. Do you think this is what he was referring to?"

"Everything else we've learned since the basement hasn't been useful by itself," Alexandra said. "It's just been a trail leading us here. Not to mention, we now understand the reason for all of this."

"If that's the case, then I guess we're ready for the next step," Daniel said.

Alexandra nodded.

"I guess it's time to return to the basement."

Chapter 12:
A Force Of Wills

The elevator opened, and for a second time, they stepped out into the basement. The atmosphere felt less desolate, though slightly so, as they had left the lights on when they had left earlier.

"Well, we're here," Lila said. Do you know where the other rooms are?"

"Over there." Daniel pointed towards the far wall adjacent to them. "There's another door."

Lila had, at this point, noticed that anytime he spoke, she felt a sudden urge to punch him in the throat. She despised him for the things he knew about her and for what he had done during the ghost attack. The fact that his means were justified by the end did not make it better. Perhaps if she had not been forced to step up, someone else would have. Or maybe things would not have turned out as bad as Samantha predicted. Maybe they'd had been tickled to death as opposed to being torn from the inside out. That was a better way to die, right?

Either way, her emotional baggage was hers alone to unpack when she was good and ready. Even a threat to their lives did not constitute justification for forcing her to just get over what had happened.

To get over what she had done...

The others were talking now about something or the other, but it was engaging enough for them not to pay attention to her as she quietly trailed behind them. She did not mind feeling left out. In fact, it was quite the opposite. Ever since she tended off the spirits, they were either checking up on her or reminding her of how badass it was. Except it didn't feel badass. It felt like she had broken her promise to never let her powers go like that ever again, and she felt bad. Not just bad. She felt cruel and dirty, like some sort of monster.

Even as she walked, flashes of memories danced across her subconscious, stubbornly refusing to be swept away no matter how hard she tried to focus on being present.

She remembered the terrified scream of her sister Bobby. All four seconds of it before impact came, and her voice was suddenly cut off. She remembered the words "What have you done?" playing over and over in her ears. To this day, she has yet to figure out if she had imagined it or if it was her mother's voice. She remembered her sister lying on the floor like a rag doll. She remembered the smell of the hospital and the look on the doctor's face. She remembered counting the worry lines on her forehead as she prepared to drop the bomb.

"It wasn't your fault," Daniel had said.

Bobby had also said the same thing: "How long are you going to keep punishing yourself for this, Lila? It wasn't your fault."

But they were both lying. She knew they were. Of course, it was her fault. And the only person who was honest enough to tell her was her mother.

It was her fault and these stupid powers...

Lila did not notice that they had stopped and bumped right into James.

"Sorry," she muttered, snapping out of her reverie.

She looked around and realized that they had gone through the door and were now standing in a semi-dark room. In front of them, there were rows of strange-looking white statues.

She counted seven of them with a vacant spot, four spaces from the right where an eighth was supposed to be. Ahead of the first row, there was at least one more row.

The statues were each twice the size of human beings, and most of them were slightly humanoid-shaped. Something about them seemed oddly familiar, but she could not put a finger on it.

The two statues at the ends were long and cylindrical with slight overhangs. The two next to each looked like medieval knights, complete with armor and swords. After them were Catholic priests holding large crosses. And then there was a woman in a gown next to the vacant spot.

There was no way to go between, around, or over them, so it was safe to say the statues blocked off the path ahead.

Next to her, the others seemed equally stumped.

Daniel, ever the curious one, went close to one of the statues and knocked on it. It sounded like stone, and judging from the way he winced in pain, it also felt like stone.

Alexandra tried the walls to see if there was any pressure plate concealed in the stone while James tried to see if he could somehow crawl between them. He could not.

"So, this is a dead-end," Samantha muttered.

"It doesn't feel like it," Daniel said. He rubbed his hand over the statue. "Strange. I can't glean anything off of it."

"Like your powers aren't working?"

"Like no one has ever been here," he said. "No living person, at least."

"So, how did these statues get down here?" James said.

Lila was still fixated on the empty space, and her curiosity was getting the best of her; she tentatively approached it.

"Guys, is it me, or does this look sort of like a—" Alexandra started to say.

But then, Lila came to stand in the vacant spot, and without warning the very earth beneath her rose, lifting her with it.

Panicking, she let out a scream.

"Lila!" the others called out.

After a terrifying few seconds, the earth became still once more. Lila looked around to find herself atop what looked like a stone throne, slightly above the height of the rest of the statues.

She heard whirring behind her head, and before she could move, a band of thorny metal wrapped tightly around her head and locked her in place. The thorns pricked the skin of her head so hard she expected to find a river of red running down her face any second now.

"Oh my God!" Lila screamed. "Help! Help me!"

"Lila!" James yelled.

"Lila, we can't see from down here," Daniel said. "What's happening?"

"I'm... It's... It's some kind of chair, and there's a metal band around my head, like a crown with spikes, and I can't get it off! It hurts! Oh my God, it hurts!"

"Oh, dear God..." Alexandra said.

"What?" Samantha said. "Have you figured out something?"

"She's on a throne with a crown on her head," Alexandra said. She pointed to the statue at the far end. "Rook." The one next to it. "Knight." The next one. "Bishop." The next one. "Queen. And..."

"King," Daniel filled in. "Oh my God."

"What?" Lila said.

"Lila, this is... This is a chessboard. And you're the king."

"I'm the *what*?"

She looked ahead and realized it was true. There was another row of statues right in front of her, except these ones were identical—men carved in casual medieval clothing armed with short swords—and across the board, which she could barely even see, two rows of statues mirrored the ones on her side, except they were black and in place of the king there was a statue of a man with a crown on his head, holding a scepter. All their eyes glowed a threatening green, just like the malevolent spirits.

"Oh shit! Shit! Shit! Shit!"

"Calm down, Lila," Alexandra said. "I know you don't want to hear this, but calm down. It's just a game of chess."

"I don't want to be a king! I want out of this freaking chair! Why did it have to be me? Why not one of you guys?"

The sound of stone moving against stone drew Lila's attention to the ceiling. She watched as a hole opened, and an hourglass hovered over her head before being lowered into the hall. It turned over, and the sand began to pour.

"Guys!" Lila called out frantically.

"What's going on?" James said.

"What's that sound?" Daniel said.

"There's an hourglass hovering over me right now, and it's emptying."

"Oh crap."

"What now?" Lila said.

"Calm down..." Alexandra said. "Lila, you have to play the game, and you have to win to clear the path forward. That's the only way to get out of the chair. Also, I'm pretty sure you have to finish the game before the timer runs out."

"How can you tell me to calm down and *then* say that?" Lila screamed. "I've never played chess in my life!"

"Lucky for you, I have," Daniel said.

"So have I!" Alexandra countered. "I was vice president of the chess club back in high school."

"Cool story. Do you want a ribbon?" Daniel said. "I've had actual experience playing against actual professionals."

"Yeah, right. Lila, listen to me and ignore him."

"No, listen to *me*!" Daniel said. "You have to end this as soon as possible. Pawn to E4!"

"What the hell does that even mean?" Lila yelled back.

"You're white, so you get the first move?"

"I'm *what*?"

"The pieces. White goes first!"

"Oh. And how the hell am I supposed to actually play?"

"Maybe try giving the commands out loud?" Alexandra said.

"Pawn to E4!" Lila said. "Pawn to E4!"

Nothing happened.

"Didn't do anything?"

"Lila, Sam here," she heard Samantha say. "Call me crazy, but I think there's a reason you're the one in that really highchair."

"I'm not too good with heights, so I highly doubt that," Lila said.

"That's not what I mean. I mean, I think you need to move the pieces yourself. As in with your powers."

"Are you kidding me? Do you not see the size of these things?"

"You can do it, Lila," Daniel said.

"You... You shut up," Lila said. "No more stupid motivation from you."

"I hate to agree with him, but he's right," Samantha said. "You can do it. That's the only thing that makes sense. And we believe in you. I hate to say it, but the only person who can truly help you now is you."

Lila shut her eyes to block them out. She hated everything and everyone at that moment. Why did it have to be her? Why?

The sound of sand pouring into the hourglass brought her back to focus.

"Fine," she said. "Pawn to E4 it is." She took a pause and looked around. "Uh which pawn?"

"The one right in front of you," Alexandra said.

"Right. And what's E4?"

"Push it forward two spaces."

Lila took in a big breath and then thrust out her hand in a pushing motion.

The stone statue began to move. At first, it was slow, but then she redoubled her effort, and it increased in speed.

One space. Two spaces.

Done!

"I did it!" she called out. "What happens now?"

Before anyone could answer, the black pawn walked forward and came to a stop in front of hers.

"What's happened?" Alexandra asked.

"Their pawn is in front of mine!"

"E5. Okay. Okay. You see the pawn one space to your left? Move it forward two spaces. That's D4."

"Hey!" Daniel yelled.

"What?" Alexandra said.

"Actually, that's what I was going to say."

Lila locked onto the statue and began to push. It felt as though the weight had increased slightly, and she had to use both hands to get it all the way.

"So, who is responsible for the strategy exactly?" Samantha asked. "I'm no grandmaster, but isn't it a bad thing if both of you are butting heads?"

"We won't lose if that's what you mean," Daniel said.

"Besides, if we lose, maybe we can ask for a rematch," Lila said.

Just then, the black side made their move, and it was swift and deadly.

With a powerful swing of his sword, the black pawn stepped diagonally and split the white pawn down the middle, and as both sides of it hit the ground, it crumbled to dust, then it stepped up to take its place.

That was all it took for Lila to lose what little mind she had left.

"Oh God!" Lila screamed. "That pawn just got destroyed! I'm gonna die!"

"Lila!" Alexandra called out. "Lia, calm down! It's under control."

"Stop telling me that! I'm gonna die! I'm gonna die!" she continued to scream. "I'm going to freaking die!"

"Lila!" Daniel yelled out.

Somehow, the sound of his voice silenced her at once.

"You dislike me, don't you?" Daniel went on.

"What?"

"How do you feel about me?"

"Why are you—"

"Don't think. Just answer the question."

"I... I..."

"Come on, it shouldn't be that hard. It's me, remember?"

"Sometimes I want to punch you in that smug face of yours or even kick you in your nuts."

"Good. Good. Focus on that. What else?"

"I hate..." She balled her first and shut her eyes. Tears burned behind her eyelids, and she could not tell for the life of her if it was because of her fear of the situation or anger or just frustration at everything. "I hate you for knowing what you know about me and about my sister. I hate you for trying to tell me what to feel. I hate you so much for lying to me and telling me it's not my fault when I know damn well it is!"

Daniel was quiet for a brief moment. When he spoke again, his voice was softer, like he was trying to recover his footing.

"Yes. Right. So, bottom line, you hate me, right?"

"Why are you saying these things?"

"Because this isn't the time to be scared, Lila," he said. "I'm trying to give you something to focus on so you don't spend all your time and energy on yelling."

"And you picked hate?" Samantha said, the deadpan clear in her voice. "Really? You couldn't pick love or something? Maybe even the power of friendship?"

"Love? Grow up, please," Daniel said. "Now, Lila, yes, I did all those things, and you know what? I think I was right to do it."

The words burned in Lila's ears. "What?"

"You were acting like a big baby, and I refused to let you. Now, here's the thing: I'm down here, and you're up there, so if you want to show me just how much you hate me, you need to win this. Do you understand me?"

Lila didn't speak. She was already seeing red, and it helped to pretend every single piece on the board had Daniel's face attached to them.

She could decide what she was feeling now. It was anger. And boy, did she have a lot to be angry about!

She looked around the map and studied the moves she had made so far.

E4...

E5...

D4...

Letters... Horizontal... Numbers... Vertical

She was no chess wizard, but she was a quick study, and the directions they had been calling out started to make sense.

"Tell me what to do," she said.

"Right Knight to F3," Daniel said. "That's—"

Before he could finish speaking, she reached out telekinetically and grabbed the knight. Then, summoning inner strength she hadn't been acquainted with in quite some time, she lifted it over the row of pawns and set it down on F3.

If not for the crown holding her in place, she would have collapsed from exhaustion.

"How did you...?" Daniel said.

"I'm a fast learner," Lila breathed.

On the crosswise end of the board, the black knight mirrored her play, except rather than levitate, he pushed past the pawn with fully automated movements to move to his new position.

"Black knight to C6," she called out.

"Knight to G5," Daniel said.

She pushed it into place, and as soon as she let go, the black side made their play.

"Black pawn to H6," Lila relayed.

"Knight to F7," Daniel said.

Mustering her strength, she lifted the knight over the pawn at F7 and let it fall, watching with satisfaction as the pawn was crushed beneath it.

Her satisfaction was short-lived. Swiftly, the king stepped up and, with a swing of his scepter, knocked the knight's head clean off his shoulders. As soon as his head hit the ground, the rest of him crumbled.

"King took knight?" Daniel asked.

"Yeah."

"Bishop to C4. Check."

She did as he asked. At this point, her arms were burning, almost like she was going through a physical workout.

The king stepped back to his original position.

"The king retreated," she said.

"Queen to H5. Check."

Her muscles screamed in protest, but she continued to push.

Black made their move.

"Pawn to G6," she called out.

"Queen to G6," Daniel said. "Take it down."

She tried to do as she had done before with the knight, but her strength failed her. She could barely hold the piece in the air, so she opted to knock the pawn down with it instead.

"Done."

"Check," Daniel said.

The black king stepped forward to one place, and she relayed it to Daniel.

"Black queen to F7," he said. "Check."

She moved the piece.

The black king moved again to D6 this time.

"Move pawn at E4 to E5," Daniel said. "Check."

She moved the piece.

The black knight at C6 moved this time, and with a vengeance, it hacked the pawn to pieces.

"Knight took pawn?" Daniel said.

"Yeah."

"Good. Queen to D5."

"The black king moved back to E7."

"White queen takes black knight," Daniel said. "Checkmate."

Lila raised her hands to push, but she could barely hold them up, much less move the statue. Her vision blurred, and she felt a sharp pain behind her left eye.

"Lila?"

"Working on it!" she said.

It was one space. One measly space. She could push a stupid statue into one space.

She glanced up at the hourglass and saw that there was barely any sand left.

"Come on, Lila!"

Inch by inch, the stone statue moved.

"You can do it, Lila!"

At this point, she could barely feel anything. Not the pain or the fatigue or even the blood trickling from her nose. All that mattered was one more inch.

One more inch.

One more...

"Gaaaaaaah!" With the last of her strength, she gave a mighty push and moved the queen into the space.

Black spots danced across her vision as she teetered on the brink of unconsciousness.

"Lila?"

"Lila, can you hear us?"

"Lila, what's happening?"

The words swam in one ear and out the other as she tried to hold on and stay awake.

Her vision came into focus, and she found the king on his knees.

"I... did it," she mumbled. "The king is... on his knees. Is that... Is that a chess thing?"

"Not really," Alexandra said.

"The timer has... stopped running, but nothing... else is happening."

"I think you're meant to finish the job," Daniel said.

"Daniel!" Alexandra said. "Ignore him, Lila. Maybe it's just taking a minute."

"No, I think he's right," Lila said. "The other pieces. They're looking at me. It's like they're waiting for something."

"Can you finish it?"

"Yeah, I think I've got enough juice left in me."

She made a grabbing motion and took firm hold of the king's head; then, casting her hand to the side, she ripped it off and tossed it aside.

The king's body crumbled, and with it, all the remaining black pieces. Then, the whites began to follow suit, and the throne on which Lila sat sank into the ground. She must have faded out at some point because when she came to, she was in Daniel's arms with the others standing around.

"Is it... over?" she said.

"It is," he said. "You did well. You did very well."

"Yay," she muttered weakly.

And then she let the darkness swallow her whole.

Chapter 13:
S𝗽𝗶𝗿𝗶𝘁𝘂𝘀 F𝗶𝗹𝗶𝘂𝘀

It was a while before Lila regained consciousness, so the rest of the team made camp just past the giant chessboard.

While they rested, they snacked on granola bars, peanut butter cups, and cookies as it was too soon for a heavier meal, and the musty smell of the basement did not help with their appetites.

There was not much to talk about, but whispers of conversation came up and died down almost as quickly until, in the end, they had split up into pairs. Alexandra and James sat shoulder to shoulder talking about something, and that left Daniel as Samantha's temporary buddy, except he wasn't in the mood to talk. He did sit next to Samantha, who was next to the unconscious Lila, but his eyes were fixed on the black and white flooring a few meters away.

After he had confirmed that Lila was fine and only needed rest following the chess match, Daniel had kept his distance and barely finished a candy bar. Something seemed to be eating at him.

"You alright?" Samantha asked eventually.

Daniel showed no sign that he had heard her, but just as she was about to turn away, he let out a despondent sigh.

"I have enough self-awareness to know I'm not very likeable, Sam," Daniel said "You probably can't relate because you're this warm human being that everyone just takes to. You're easy to talk to." He chuckled. "I don't have enough experience with good people, and that's not me making up excuses."

"This is about Lila, isn't it? The things she said up there?"

"You know, when the stupid throne descended, and I held her in my arms, I touched her clothes, and I accidentally gleaned the previous ten minutes. I saw her up there, terrified and alone. We saw a chess game, and sure, we understood the stakes, but she lived it."

"Daniel..."

"And all those things... All those things I said to her... Those mean things."

"You didn't mean it, Daniel."

"Except that's the thing, Sam. I don't know what I meant and what I didn't. I just know that I said whatever was necessary to get her to do what she needed to do. For the second time today, I manipulated her. I used what I knew about her against her."

"You did what you had to do."

"Did I? Or am I exactly like the people that used me?"

"Daniel, that's not fair. The situations were not the same. If we didn't have Lila with us, we'd be dead by now. We have all had to play a significant role at one point or the other on this mission."

"So, what? If I didn't know what I know about her and used that against her, we'd be dead because she froze. Both times, she froze, and if I hadn't forced her past that, she wouldn't have done anything. I pushed her. But who's to say there wouldn't have been something else to do?"

"There wasn't, Daniel. When we talked about this earlier, I merely wanted you to understand where she was coming from. It's not your fault that what happened. But you got her through it."

"You don't know what I know, Sam," Daniel said. "There's so much weighing on her, and she's just a teenager. I know what it was like. I should be the last person to do this to her."

"You're not a bad person, Daniel," Samantha said. "You're not like the people who used you in the past."

She pulled his head down to her chest, and after a moment, she felt him exhale.

Something bumped into Samantha's leg just then, and she looked down to see that Lila was stirring.

"Lila?" Samantha said.

She let out a groan as she opened her eyes.

Automatically, Daniel pulled away and stealthily shifted away as Lila sat up. From across the hallway, Alexandra and James noticed and came over.

"Lila!" Alexandra said. "You're finally awake. Again."

"Had us worried for a second there," James said. "You alright?"

Lila nodded.

"How long?"

"About seventeen minutes," Alexandra said.

She looked around, and when her eyes set on the black and white floor, she retreated.

"Why are we still here?"

"We had to let you rest, and we couldn't move forward without knowing what was ahead."

Without a word, Daniel casually moved a few steps to the side. He averted his gaze the whole time, but Samantha knew he was trying to block Lila's view of the traumatic chess board.

"I'm awake now," Lila said. "So can we keep moving?"

"You should probably eat something first."

"I can do both simultaneously."

"Of course," Alexandra said.

She went to gather up her stuff, and after a quick pat on the back, James went with her.

Lila looked up at the same time Daniel happened to look right at her, and their eyes met. The expression in her eyes was difficult to read, but Daniel's remorse was rather vivid. He looked away first but did not move until Lila got up and turned towards the path forward.

As they resumed their journey through the basement, Lila munched on a comically large bag of cookies. She must have been either famished or nervous still, reeling from the effects of her experience, but she made quick work of the cookies.

Despite her fears— or perhaps because she feared what she had experienced much more than she feared the unknown— Lila walked in front with Alexandra and James walking next to her. Daniel brought up the rear, walking half a pace behind Samantha. It was clear he wasn't in the mood for conversation, but she wasn't about to leave him alone.

The path forward turned this way and that like a maze, but it did not branch off, so they knew they were still on the right path.

Samantha glanced over to find Daniel staring intently at Lila. He wasn't done beating himself up, and it was obvious. She turned away before he could catch her staring, but she felt the need to say something to help.

Just as she was trying to decide on what exactly, she felt him grab her by the wrist. There was an urgency to the gesture, and she whipped her head around at once, but to her surprise, Daniel was still looking straight ahead... and both his hands were at his side, in no way near her body.

Jolted, Samantha stopped and looked down. There was indeed a hand holding onto her. It was small, and so was the person to which it was attached. It was a little boy, much younger than Sylvia.

He had disheveled hair and sad eyes, and he was dressed in worn-out asylum clothes.

"Can you help me find my Mommy?" he said.

"Oh, dear God!" Samantha said.

The rest of the group stopped and turned.

"What is it?" Alexandra said.

"Ghost child," Samantha muttered.

"My mommy," the boy said. "Have you seen her?"

Before she could speak, James said, "Where is he? What is he saying?"

Samantha looked up and frowned curiously. They were looking around in the boy's general direction but not quite at him.

"You can't see him, can you?" she said.

"No," James said.

Lila and Alexandra shook their heads.

Samantha pondered it as she turned her attention to the boy again.

"Uh no... I haven't seen your mommy," she said.

"His mommy?" James repeated.

"What is your name?" Samantha said.

"Billy. Billy Winters," he said.

"Hello, Billy," she said. "I'm Sam. These are my—"

"Where's my mommy?" Billy pressed.

"I don't know."

"I want my mommy!" he screamed, yanking on her arm.

"I don't know where your mommy is, Billy!" Samantha repeated. "I need to go, and for that, I need you to let go of my hand!"

"No!" Billy yelled. "I want my mommy!"

She tried to pull away, but his grip on her was strong and painful too.

"Hey! Let go! You're giving me a headache!"

"What is it?" Daniel said.

"He won't let go of my hand!" She tugged harder. "Let go!"

But that did nothing, and she was beginning to realize that he was literally giving her a headache, and the longer he held on, the worse it got.

"Hey! Take it easy," Daniel said. "He's just a child, isn't he?"

"A child ghost," Samantha corrected.

"Yeah, that's what I meant," Daniel said.

"No, you don't understand. He's a child ghost, and while he might not be a malevolent ghost, when children become ghosts, it's very unpleasant. They're unpleasant. The tantrums of a child can be cute, bordering on irritation at worst, but the tantrums of a child with supernatural powers..."

"Oh."

"Oh, is right. And when I say he won't let go," She winced, "I mean he's crushing my hand, and his whining is layered with psychic energy, which is giving me a headache."

She doubled her effort, but even that did not help, and there was now a sharp pain behind her eye.

"Okay, maybe hang on a minute," James said.

"What?" Samantha snapped.

James smiled patiently as he came to put his hand on her shoulder.

"He's still a child one way or another, so talk to him like a child. You know, comfort him."

Samantha wanted to snap at him some more, but his advice was solid, and it was one more idea than she had. Additionally, she felt a strange calm wash over her, and she was certain it had to do with his touch.

Taking a deep breath to help her push past the pain, she got on one knee so she was at eye level with the ghost boy.

"Billy," she said. "I need you to listen to me. Your mommy is somewhere around here, and my friends and I are trying to help not just your mommy but everyone else. I'm a friend. Do you want to be my friend?"

Billy hesitated, then he slowly nodded.

"Well, you're hurting your friend, Billy, and that's not nice, is it?"

He shook his head.

"Your mommy needs you, and if you want to see her again, you need to be a big boy. I was hoping you could stop crying and keep it together. Can you do that, Billy?"

Billy tentatively let go of her hand and bowed his head shyly.

"Now, I'm going to hold your hand, and maybe you can take us to the last place where you saw your mommy. Can you do that?"

He nodded.

She held out her hand, and this time, he put his hand in hers.

"Very good," she said. She looked up at the others and nodded to let them know everything was alright. "Alright. Let's go."

Taking the boy's ghost along, they resumed their journey through the basement until they came to a dead end. Unlike the last dead end, this one was, in fact, a giant door, but it was a dead end because when they tried to open it, they found that it was locked. There was a keyhole implying the need for a key, and further still, there was a key in the keyhole, but when Alexandra tried to unlock it, it didn't budge.

"It's stuck somehow," she said.

"Well, that's not ideal," Samantha muttered, growing more aware of the boy once again. If they had no way of finding out what happened to his mother, it was only a matter of time before he became a nuisance once more, and she could not imagine having to use her powers against him.

Surprisingly, not only did Billy remain calm, but he also gently tugged on her arm to get her attention.

He pointed down the hallway in the direction they had come from.

"What is it, buddy?" she said.

James and the others were staring expectantly.

He tugged her wrist again.

"I think he's trying to show me something," she said.

"This is hardly the time to go exploring," Alexandra said. "We should figure out how to get this door open."

But Billy was insistent, and at last, Samantha disregarded the others and went with him.

They did not go very far before he stopped and pointed at the floor just by the wall.

"What's that?'

She moved closer to take a look, but as she did, she felt the floor beneath her sink slightly. When she looked down, she realized that she was standing on a hidden pressure plate switch.

"Billy," Samantha called out warily, "what exactly did I just do?"

Billy did not respond. Instead, he pointed to the floor by the other wall.

This time, Samantha saw it, and only because she was looking for it.

"Daniel, come over for a second," she said.

The others, who are making no progress with the key, have turned to follow their actions now.

"Stand over there," she said.

Daniel raised a brow, but he moved to where she had pointed. When the floor sank in, he looked to her, eyes slightly widened. He did not get to ask any questions because, just then, they heard the unmistakable sounds of gears moving in the walls.

Instinctively, Alexandra tried the key again, and this time, there was a loud click, and the door swung wide open.

Alexandra, James, and Lila went on ahead, but as Daniel and Samantha followed, stepping off their respective switches, the door began to close.

"Hurry!" Alexandra yelled.

They sprinted forward, but it was clear they were not going to make it in time.

Just as Samantha was about to give up hope, she felt something grab hold of her and yank her through the air. She did not stop until she was through the barely open doorway, and then she fell against James, who managed to hold her up as the door behind them closed completely.

The room they had entered was completely dark, but not for long, as flashlights came on, showing the way. They were in yet another long corridor that bent to the side as it progressed, making it impossible to see where it ended.

Her thoughts shifted to Daniel, and in a panic, she straightened neatly and looked around. There he was, on his hands and knees next to her.

As Alexandra went to help him up, Samantha looked forward and saw Lila lower her hands, her expression still tense. It was she who had gotten them through.

"Thank you," Samantha muttered.

Lila nodded and quickly turned away.

"Where are we?" James said.

"I remember this place," Billy said, appearing just by Samantha and startling her as she had, for the moment, forgotten about him. "The doctor took her here."

"Your mother?" Samantha asked.

He nodded and pointed.

"His office. It's there."

The doctor's office? Samantha thought about it, and it made sense. Of course, a man like that would have his real office hidden away. That explained why the office above ground was bare.

The others were waiting expectantly, so Samantha filled them in.

"Doctor's office straight ahead," she said.

They walked down the corridor until, just as Billy had said, they came to a door. But it wasn't the only one. There was a door on either side of the corridor leading to other rooms.

"First, the doctor, then we check out whatever else is hidden down here. Agreed?" Alexandra said.

They all showed signs of agreement, and Alexandra turned the knob. To their surprise, it was unlocked.

With the aid of flashlights beaming all over the room, they confirmed that it was an office space. Daniel found the switch, and soon, the room was bathed in fluorescent white.

A table and chair in the center and bookshelves to the back, it looked pretty similar to the upstairs office, except it was vastly different. The bookshelves were stocked with old books. The table was covered in open books and what looked like a well-preserved brain in a jar, right next to a human skull.

"Well, Billy's mom isn't in here," Samantha noted.

"Let's not talk about that," Alexandra said. "Just look around. This is the chief physician's office. This has to be the most important room we've discovered so far."

While Alexandra and the others scattered about the room, looking for clues to guide them forward, Samantha sat on the floor and beckoned Billy over for a word. She could sense that he was starting to get frustrated, and she wasn't about to have another tantrum on her hands.

"Tell me about your mom," she said. "What is she like?"

"My mom is super tall," Billy said, holding a hand over his head to show how tall he was. "Taller than you even. She's skinny, too, and her eyes are always sad. The doctor is mean to her, and that makes her cry, but only when she thinks I'm not watching."

Samantha sighed. She had been hoping for a fonder memory.

"But what was she like before she came to this place?"

"I... I don't know what you mean," he said.

"This... hospital," Samantha tried again. "Before you and your mother came to this hospital. What was she like? What was life like outside this place for you? Was she happy? Were you happy?"

"I don't..." He seemed genuinely confused, as if he could not answer her questions. "I don't know."

"Sam," Daniel called out urgently. He was sitting in the chief physician's chair, and the others were next to him, hunched over the table, looking at something. "Could you..." He cleared his throat. "...come over here a moment?"

"I'm kind of in the middle of something."

"Trust me, you want to see this," Alexandra said.

She raised her brow questioningly, but they gave her no clue.

"I'm sorry, Billy. Give me a minute. I'll be right back."

She went over to the table.

"What is it?"

Daniel's expression was grim as he turned the book they had been reading over to her.

Her eyes skimmed the open page at first, and then a second time, she read more thoroughly. And as she read, her brows furrowed in confused anger. The words on the page were simple, but the implications were difficult to process.

She glanced over her shoulder at Billy, who was still waiting for her, and then she looked back at Daniel.

The words were written by hand, like some kind of diary or memoir, and according to what she read, in the early years of the asylum, a woman by the name of Martha Winters had been admitted into the hospital suffering from severe mental issues which included manic rage and violence. It was soon discovered that the woman was pregnant, and after seven months she gave birth to a boy who was named William. William 'Billy' Winters!

"Oh God!" she said. "He doesn't know! Billy doesn't know what life was like outside the asylum... because he has never seen the outside of the asylum!"

Daniel was silent as he flipped a few pages and pointed at a paragraph.

Samantha's eyes widened as she read.

Martha Winters had shown psychic potential, but her body was too weak to keep up with the strenuous experiments, and eventually, her heart gave out. Originally, they had meant to give Billy away, but with the new possibility that, like his mother, he would possess psychic abilities, the doctor had instead opted to experiment on him as well. The experiments had gone well, but following the death of his mother, Billy's health had only deteriorated until he, too, had passed during an experiment.

"What... What is this book?" Samantha asked.

Daniel flipped it shut, and she read:

"The Life and Works of Doctor Fredrick von Menschen; A Journal."

Chapter 14:
RECOLLECTION

24th March

Mr. Blackthorne's messenger arrived today. If I was to be honest, I had lost hope long ago that I would see such a day as this. It has been nearly two years since Matthias first approached me, curious about my research. I had published an article relating mental disorders to latent psychic abilities rebelling against the human mind and its inability to accept, much less tolerate, the impossible. Of course, I had presented the details as mere speculations; hence, not a lot of people took me seriously, and those that designed to consider me a madman grasping at the stars, but the warden was an intelligent man who understood not just the things I said, but the things I left unsaid as well. He arranged a meeting and I could tell his interest was genuine, and so I let him take a peek behind the curtains. I showed him the true extent of my research. He was the kind of man who could stand the sight of a little blood, after all.

A simple man with simple yet daring desires, Mr. Blackthorne wanted us to work together even then. but he lacked the capacity to bring anything to the table and so he promised that soon he would be able to provide me with not only the funding and the location but also the test subjects. Today, I have been invited to Ravensbrook. Apparently he's the warden in charge of the new asylum. I could not have predicted such a valuable contribution from Blackthorne. It really is all coming together beautifully.

*****

27th March

I've finally arrived in Ravensbrook, and I must say the descriptions do not do justice. As I write, I'm seated in the back of the car that was sent to pick me up from the train station. The sky is the greyest I have ever seen in the aftermath of a rainstorm that had been coming down since before I arrived at the station. It's certainly not your ideal tourist destination, but I find it oddly comforting. Then again, I've always been fond of all things grey and dull.

*****

28th March

I have settled in, and I am well rested. Today, I received a tour of the asylum, and tomorrow, I get to work.

Warden Blackthorne has been rather thorough; I can't help but be impressed. The asylum is perfect. In the past, I've had to be careful with my test subjects. I've had to hold myself back from taking risks as it was immensely difficult to procure more test subjects— it is fairly easy to pick a homeless bum or two off the streets, but after a while, people begin to notice— but now, I have more subjects than I could ever need to be careful with. In the past, the worry was that someone somewhere would miss them. Now, I have their naive loved ones practically begging me to experiment on them all for the promise of a cure. A cure I have no intention of offering.

The warden has procured me a safe space in the basement where I can operate unseen and unheard. It has yet to be completed, but in a matter of ten months or less, I will have a small area to work with as we continue to expand underground. Not only that, but he has also already compiled a list of prospective patients who show promise. I'm further impressed with how accurate his methods of selection are, considering he did all of it without my help, although I suppose my research did have some influence there.

*****

29th March

Today, I had my first consultation with a patient, and it did not go as planned, in part due to my own carelessness. His name was Jason Black. A twenty-seven-year-old war veteran suffering from post-traumatic stress disorder and insomnia. His family brought him in after, in a manic fit, he had fought with and almost killed his father. A quick evaluation revealed that beyond that, he had a dormant ability to sense his dead comrades, and it plagued his mind.

Unfortunately, the evaluation had put immense strain on his already fragile mind, and he fled the room screaming as he went. The nurses were alerted and soon arrived on the scene, which was more attention than I bargained for, but the warden has assured me that they will pose no concern whatsoever.

I will continue my work as planned and leave the warden to take care of his subordinates. I have little choice, as it will be nearly a year before I can fully utilize the chambers below.

*****

1st April

I can sense that more than a few of the nurses are not too fond of my presence here. It is rather unfortunate that their opinions are not worth the dirt underneath my fingernails. Their frail minds would crumble under the weight of the burden I carry.

In the course of three days, I have assessed four more test subjects. Of the four, three of them tested positive for psychic abilities but only one subject has shown the most promise. I will need to carry out more extensive tests, but I am pleased with what I have found. The subject possesses extrasensory perception to a small degree, allowing her to sense strong motives and intentions. All in all, this has been a productive week. I shudder with excitement at the thought of what I will accomplish one day, one month, one year from now.

*****

11th April

Psychokinesis is an ability I have encountered a few times in my studies— the ability to move objects with one's mind— but in every manifestation I have found, the subject was only capable of moving objects of insignificant mass. The most I had recorded was four pounds moved half a meter to the side before the subject's brain turned to mush and flowed out through his nostrils. That was until today.

A staggering new record of a hundred pounds moved across a twenty-meter gap was achieved with my new test subject. Further still, the subject possesses the ability to move said objects not just through space but also time altogether, making the objects disappear completely from one location and reappear in another— teleportation, if you will. All of this without a drop of brain goo through the nose, although he did pass out about six times. If he survives the next few stages of experimentation, he will make for a valuable tool.

*****

13th June

I remember the first time I put forth my research before a gathering of respectable scientists and investors. I told them what could be done with the mind. I showed them proof. Detailed research with step-by-step documentation of experiments on mice and monkeys. I kept out the human research because I suspected there would be a bunch of weak-stomached bastards among the lot, and I was right. They called me a sadistic lunatic. A madman. They said what I was proposing went against the will of God. I laughed in their faces then, and I laugh even louder now. The work of God is incomplete, and that is where I come in.

Today, I have done what they said could not be done, and all it took was a scalpel, an electric chair, and a few words of encouragement. I have unearthed a power never witnessed before in all my searches. The subject has the ability to invoke fear into the hearts of her victims. I conducted a controlled test with mice, and they were very severely distressed, exhibiting behaviors consistent with outright panic. After a few minutes of exposure to her abilities, they slammed their heads into the bars of their cages until their skulls were cracked open, and the pink of their brains peeked out as blood ran over their tiny little heads and their bodies went limp. It was glorious! I am yet to come up with a name for that but that does not take priority for now.

*****

18th September

I decided to find some use for the patients with no psychic abilities, as it was a shame for them to go to waste just sitting about. I figured they would make perfect, more durable replacements for the mice. The warden was concerned about the attention it would garner from the nurses, but he signed off on it either way.

The warden was right to be concerned, but I do not care. I tested the phobiapathic psychic's powers on the human subject and never before have I heard a scream so... pure! At first, his screams were pleas to end his torture, but soon it morphed into pleas to end his life altogether. When I cranked up the scenario to the max, oh, it was glorious! It was almost as if he wanted to expel his very vocal cords the way he screamed.

Warden Blackthorne eventually intervened and ended my fun because "half of Ravensbrook can hear the fucking screaming!" But I don't care. I'll give the warden tomorrow and maybe the day after for some respite, and then I'll do it again.

Today's poor bastard claimed to see Satan during the experiment. I wonder what the next will see.

*****

24th December

I have come to the limits of what I can do in this little office space, and so I will take my walks and bide my time as I prepare for what is to come. Perhaps I will visit the town and watch the festivities, although it will be hard to appreciate the celebration of a child's birth from two millennia ago when I have done more than any man, living or dead, ever has. The secrets of the unlocked mind are now in my reach, and soon, they will be mine for the taking.

And then I will take some more.

*****

31st December

There are many who think the warden to be a difficult man to understand. From the nurses at the asylum to the patients who still have their sentience intact to even the families who sit at home and pray for the recovery of their loved ones. They all think him to be rather complicated: few in actions, fewer in words, and completely lacking in expressions, but I doubt I have ever met a human being more simple than Matthias Blackthorne. It is for the sake of this understanding that our interests align. I seek knowledge of the unknown corners of the human mind. I would, without remorse, take the human brain apart layer by layer just to understand it— and I have. The warden, on the other hand, is not so curious. I seek knowledge, but Matthias Blackthorne seeks power. Is there anything simpler than that?

*****

1st January

The basement is completed. My work resumes...

Or perhaps it begins.

*****

The chief physician's office had been quiet for nearly an hour as the group stood around the open book, reading through the months with Daniel as the designated page flipper. It was so quiet that the only sound that could be heard was the rustling of pages and James's mouth breathing.

Samantha took her eyes off the page after what felt like forever and caught the flicker of a neglected Billy in her periphery.

She turned her attention to him. He was sulking with his eyes fixated on his bare feet as he drew shapes on the floor with his toe.

"We could be here a whole day," she said. We'll have time to go through the book later, so let's skip forward and find out what we can about—" She jerked her head in Billy's direction.

Daniel nodded.

"Allow me. I've got a faster way," he said. He put his hand on the page and closed his eyes. After a minute, he opened his eyes and flipped confidently until he came to an entry several years ahead. "There."

Samantha reached out to slide the book closer, but he pinned it down.

"You should probably prepare yourself before you read it," he said.

She tugged it free, and he let go.

*****

17th May

Necromancy is a term that exists in many works of literature from myths to works of fiction. It implies, in one form or another, the ability to have command over the souls of the dead and impose your will upon them, usually involving summoning them back to the physical plane, reanimating corpses or even forcing them into constructs. These souls do the necromancer's bidding despite what they want and remain in the necromancer's service until they are banished or until he loses control of them. To reiterate, this was the psychic ability of the subject one-zero-nine, as documented in February last year. The subject's powers have grown to the maximum potential the body can tolerate, and so today, I harvest.

*****

20th May

The harvest was successful. At the small cost of the subject's life, I now possess authority over the dead. I am yet to attune to my new powers, but when I do I shall test it on the deceased Martha Winters. It is only fair that she heralds the arrival of my new powers; after all, they were once hers.

*****

Samantha's teeth were clenched hard as she came to the end of the entry. Not only had the chief physician killed Billy's mother to somehow take her powers from her, but he had also turned her into a slave in death. She was roaming the property just as Billy was, except she was doing so as a malevolent spirit forced into that nature by the cruel doctor.

"What Mark said," Samantha said after a while. "That he may be dead, but this place hasn't forgotten his name. I see now that he meant it very literally."

"You think the chief physician is still... here somehow?" Lila asked

"I don't think it. I know it. I feel it," Samantha said. I had sensed an evil presence since the moment we came down here, but I assumed it was just the history of this place calling out to me. But down here, I know that it's more than that."

"But that's im—"

"Exactly right," Daniel cut in. "The doctor had a plan to find a way to go on to continue his research in the event of his death. He documented this in his final months, and I have a feeling that one way or another, he succeeded."

"You figured that out when you touched the book?" Samantha asked

He nodded. "I haven't read it all, but let's just say I now have the entire thing stored in the back of my mind now."

"So, we're talking about a powerful malevolent spirit who is controlling what could potentially be an army of malevolent spirits?" Lila said.

"Precisely." Daniel nodded.

"And we have to somehow kill him again, but permanently this time," Alexandra said.

"Precisely."

"There's something else that's bothering me," James said. "I don't know if you all have forgotten, but Mark also said that the chief physician would have been very interested in us five if he were still alive. We're just as endangered in this place, if not more so. This evil ghost doctor from fifty years ago could literally murder us, and no one would know. We could have our powers ripped from our bodies and our ghosts' made slaves."

Samantha looked around at all the faces in the room.

"We haven't forgotten, James. I certainly haven't. But I'm not going anywhere."

"She's right. We can't let fear stop us from doing the right thing here," Daniel said. "Don't tell me you're getting cold feet, James."

Samantha expected a typical snappy retort, and she had a feeling Daniel did, too, but James merely smiled.

"You know, before today, I've never really had to think about dying," he said.

"James, don't talk like—" Samantha began.

"No, no," Daniel said. "Let him. He needs to get it out."

"I don't want to be, but I'm scared," James went on. "The weight of all the negative emotions in this place has been growing from the second I came into this place. Now I can barely move."

Samantha felt a pang in her chest.

"Why did you agree to this mission, James?" Daniel said. "What was your personal reason?"

James was silent for a full minute.

"I agreed to this mission because I want to use my gift of empathy to do good," he said. "I've always wanted to help. In this case, that means connecting with the trapped souls and bringing them peace. That's what I want to do. I'm also here because I want to support my friends on this mission. That's... That's my reason."

For a moment, no one said anything, but there were things to say. It was clear on every face.

Samantha decided to go next.

"I act as a bridge between the living and the dead," she said. "I've been this way for as long as I can remember and to be honest, I've never really cared to know why. I just accepted it because I had a lot of ghost friends growing up, and my parents never seemed to think it was odd when I spoke of my imaginary friends." She reached out to hold Billy's hand. "Now, I want justice for the tortured souls of Ravensbrook Asylum."

A strange lightness washed over her as soon as she was done saying her piece like a rock had been lifted off her chest.

"It didn't start out with wanting to help the trapped souls for me," Alexandra began. "Before anything else, before all of you, I wanted to understand and better control my precognition powers. But now, more than anything, I want to fix this."

"Me too," Lila said. "I want to fix... something. I've broken too much."

"I uh..." Daniel scratched his head and looked down at the table. "I just wanted friends, really. Believe me, fighting a horde of evil spirits feels like nothing to me because, for the first time, I feel like I know what it's like to belong somewhere." He leaned back and chuckled. "Wow. I don't think I've ever bared my soul this way to anyone."

"Just as long as we're in this together," James sighed. "What do you say we go kill the bad doctor? For real this time."

Samantha's expression grew grim, and her gaze unfocused.

"You can sense him too, can't you?" she muttered.

He nodded.

From the moment they opened his diary, Samantha had felt the chief physician's sinister presence growing more and more intense. He was close by. Very close.

"I sense him, too," Alexandra said.

Samantha was surprised, even more so when Lila and Daniel nodded. Alexandra could understand; the girl's precognition showed her things that ordinary senses could not pick up, but how could Daniel sense him? Furthermore, how could Lila?

"How is this happening?" Samantha said.

"And how are we so... calm about this?" Daniel said.

Samantha had not noticed it until now. Before, she had been putting on a show, but now she was truly unafraid.

"Guys, I think..." James looked down at his body. There was a strange warm glow around him, and it was spreading out around him to cover the rest of them. "I think I might have something to do with that."

"We're linked!" Lila said.

"Like some kind of psychic connection," Alexandra noted.

"I... I don't know. I've never done anything like this," James said.

Samantha noticed that Billy was no longer standing next to her. He had vanished. She had a feeling it had something to do with the chief physician's intense presence.

"Moving on, do we have an actual plan to kill Doctor von Menschen?" Lila said.

"We've come this far without a plan," Daniel said. "Why change now?"

"He's right, actually," Samantha said.

"Well, I'd feel a little bit better with a plan," Lila said

"I will try to banish his spirit from this plane, and you all will need to keep him busy while I do that," Samantha said. "That's as far as we can go in terms of a plan because there's little else we can do to prepare ourselves to face that monster."

More motivated than ever, Samantha and the gang left the chief physician's office and, in unison, turned their heads toward the door to the right.

The door was unlocked and swung inwards with a push, and then they stepped into the room. It was an open space with about six pillars placed around it.

Unknown to the gang, those few strides into the brightly lit room would mark their last conscious moments before the world they knew turned on its head.

Chapter 15:
Immersive Experience

The sound of a door bursting open saw the figure lying in the single bed rouse to consciousness. The figure went by the name Subject Two-five-one, although once upon a time, she has been called something else. Something she no longer remembered.

She was still trying to blink away the sleep when she heard heavy footsteps storm into the room, moving with unmistakable urgency. She could barely make out their forms, but she could safely assume that they were not friendly. Friendly people did not make a habit of sneaking up on people in the middle of the night.

In three seconds, they had surrounded her, but in that moment of fight or flight, like a cornered animal, she chose to fight. And she took the fight right to them.

She sprang at the first shadowy figure, balled her first, and swung a wide arc, aiming for his head. In her defense, it was uncharacteristic of her to choose violence, and this was to be the first punch she ever threw.

Her fist connected, but as it did, she came to the harsh realization that his head was protected by a sturdy helmet.

"Ow!" she cried out. "Motherf—"

She took a baton to the shoulder, and her entire left arm went dead.

She ducked under the next swing and buried her knee deep in his gut. As he bent over, she pushed past the pain and threw a punch, nailing him right in the head. This time, she was ready for the pain, and so it hurt a little less.

A flash of movement caught her attention, and she turned— grabbing a pillow off the bed as she went— and raised her right arm in time to deflect a blow to the head. The brunt of the force was absorbed by the pillow, and, mostly unaffected, she stepped in and pressed her arm to his neck, shoving him back to the wall with her weight. Before he could recover his balance, she whipped her head back and slammed into his face, breaking his nose.

"Fuck!" he cried out.

Another blow landed on her back, and she sank to one knee, biting down to suppress the pain.

She jerked her elbow backward and caught her attacker in the kidney, but the blow was dulled by his combat gear. Still, it bought her enough time to switch to her other knee, pivoting as she went and punched him right in the jewels.

There was no time to relish in the pain she had caused him because just then, another blow landed on her right shoulder, and she instantly lost all feeling.

Determined to fight till the end, she turned towards her new attacker, prepared to throw herself at him, but she ended up right in the path of a merciless, gloved fist.

A flash of light filled her vision as she fell to the ground, and then they all descended on her, raining blows upon her until she lost consciousness.

*****

Subject Two-five-one opened her eyes to a harsh, bright light shining right in her face.

She blinked profusely as she tried to adjust to the light, but before she could, it was moved to the side, and in its place, she found a pair of glasses staring down at her with a mischievous smile. The rest of the stranger's features were hidden in darkness.

She tried to move but found that both her hands were strapped to her body, and her legs were bound to the chair she was apparently sitting in.

"What...?"

"Ohoho!" he laughed. "You had me worried for a second there, little girl. I thought you were never going to wake up."

The voice sent a shard of ice racing down her spine at lightning speed, and her eyes sprang wide open.

"No," she muttered. "No, no, no, no, no!"

"Oh, but yeeeees," he snickered gleefully. "Yes, yes, yes."

He leaned in closer, and his features came into clear details: a thin layer of flesh spread out over a bony skull. A wiry neck, a tuft of scanty, neglected hair, and, of course, that cold, calculating gaze tucked behind his glasses.

"Doctor von Menschen!" she gasped.

"The one and only," he said. "So, your mental faculties are still intact. Forgive me, but I started without you. The guards brought you in passed out. They said you put up quite a fight, though. Commendable. The warden would probably break you if he found out, but I, for one, love it when they have a little fight in them."

"But... No," she said. "No, this can't be happening. It's not... It's not possible! I can't be here! I... I can't!"

"Ah, except it is, and you can, and you are. I told you I'd get around to you, didn't I?" He laughed lightly. "Perhaps you could use a break to gather your thoughts. You seem a bit out of sorts. Have I been too hard on you?"

Subject Two-five-one could not reply. She looked around the room, and sure enough, she was in the torture room in the asylum basement. And yet she had a strong conviction that her presence there was nothing short of impossible. So how was this possible?

How?

"No, that can't be it," Doctor von Menschen said, answering his own question. "You're a strong-minded one. I admire that. But you should know who is in charge here. You just need your memory..." Just then, Subject Two-five-one noticed the remote in his hand and his finger hovering over a red button. "...jogged."

She was suddenly aware of the weight around her head, pressing against her skull, but before she could say anything— if she even had anything to say— the chief physician pressed the button.

At once, every single thought fled her mind only to be replaced by pain so incredible she could not describe it if she tried.

She gritted her teeth against the pain, but that barely lasted a second before she let out a blood-curdling scream.

*****

A barely conscious Subject Two-five-one was led through the upstairs hallway a half hour later. The hallway was dark save for the moonlight streaming through the window at the end of the hall. Her legs could no longer hold her weight, and so she was carried by two security guards, who each held her by the arm with her feet sweeping the floor.

They took her to a room and tossed her on the bed, then left her to her misery.

The pale glow from the sole tiny window in the room bathed her in its light, putting a more pathetic spin on her situation.

It wasn't long before sleep claimed her.

*****

The hours moved with a strange speed, taking Subject Two-five-one with it, and soon it was morning, and she was standing in a queue at the cafeteria, waiting for breakfast.

Ahead and behind her, patients dressed in identical uniforms lined up. She could not name a single one, and yet she could not help but feel like she had to know them somehow.

As the patient ahead of her moved forward, she moved too without thinking, as if she had done this thousands of times before, and it was now second nature. The feeling that she did not belong in the asylum was fast fading, and in its place, she found a mere wish to be elsewhere.

She tried to think of her life before the asylum and found nothing but a blank space where the memory was supposed to be. All she knew was that she was Subject Two-five-one and she was a patient at Ravensbrook Asylum.

Her fighting will was no longer with her. She was beginning to accept that this was her life. Every dull and grey and miserable inch of it.

She watched with a vacant expression as the last cook dumped a slab of white goo she presumed to be oats on her plate, and then, without much thought, she turned away and walked to an empty table.

As she sat down, Subject Two-five-one looked around the room at the random faces. They all seemed to have the same look in their eyes like even though they were still animate and breathing as living things were, they were very much dead inside. She briefly wondered about a few unique individuals, like the man who sat by the window talking to an empty chair across from him and gesticulating fervently and another man who was fixated on what looked like an intense game of chess, except he was playing all by himself and all the opponent's pieces remained untouched. Next, she looked at the girl seated across the room from her, her head tilted to the side and her mouth hanging open with drool streaming out as a nurse spoon-fed her.

She was not any different from them, was she? With that depressing thought, she let out a melancholic sigh, picked up her plastic spoon, and began to eat her food, tasting none of it— and if it tasted anything like it looked, that was certainly a good thing.

As Subject Two-five-one ate, a nurse came over to her and handed her a couple of rather colorful pills and a cup of water. She stood and waited until she was certain she had swallowed them all, then she moved on to the next patient.

Subject Two-five-one had no idea what the pills were for, but even in her depressive state, she knew not to trust them, and so she had tucked them away under her tongue.

She glanced at her meal again. Whether it was because of the pills, she wasn't sure, but suddenly, everything before her was much less appetizing than before, and that was saying a lot.

Barely containing her disgust, she stood up to dump out her tray in the trash, but she was not paying attention to her surroundings and bumped right into another patient who was also carrying a tray.

Both plastic trays clattered to the ground, spilling food everywhere.

"Oh my God!" the other patient said, bending down to try to salvage what she could. "I am so sorry! I wasn't looking where I was going."

Subject Two-five-one followed her to the ground, feeling just as guilty.

"It was my fault, too," she said. "I wasn't looking eith—"

She and the other patient reached for a fork at the same time, and as their hands touched, the strangest thing happened. A bolt of lightning raced through her arm, coming to an end in the back of her head.

She looked up, taking in the other patient for the first time. She was a girl, not much older than she was, and at that moment, she was starting right back. Her eyes narrowed for a bit before widening in recognition.

"Alex?" she said.

Subject Two-five-one blinked.

Alex? Who was Alex?

Multiple voices, each sounding more familiar than the last, played in her head, repeating the word "Alex."

That was her name! She was Alex!

"How... How do you know my name?" Subject Two-five-one asked.

The girl's brows furrowed, and she looked around like she didn't remember where she was or how she got there.

"What...?" she began. "I... Oh, look at this mess! I'm so sorry!"

She did not say another word as she stood up and walked off in a hurry, leaving Subject Two-five-one— Alex— incredibly confused.

*****

That night, the guards did not come for her, and Alex lay in bed, staring at the ceiling as she replayed the conversation with the girl over and over again.

Who was she? How did she know her name when she herself had somehow forgotten? What was that strange feeling she felt when they touched?

And why did she look so familiar?

She had not had a chance to meet with her for the remainder of the day as she had had too many watchful eyes around at lunch, and at dinner, she was absent altogether.

She tried to remember the girl's name, but although it was right on the tip of her tongue, she just couldn't figure it out. Her mind felt like it was on the verge of shattering, and she did not know if that would be a bad thing or a good thing.

And then those damned pills. What were they? Her thoughts felt clearer than ever, and her focus was sharp, and she had no doubt in her mind that it was because she had refused to take the pills.

But what good was being able to think if she didn't know what to think?

With an infuriated groan, she rolled over and buried her face in her pillow.

Why was there so much she did not know?

Just then, she heard the door across the hall open, and then someone screamed, but the sound was quickly cut off.

Acting against common sense, she got out of bed, skulked over to the door, and pressed her ear to it.

She heard sounds of movement and heavy breathing, and at once, she knew that the victim for the night had been picked out.

Before she could stop herself, she pried open the door and poked her head out.

She could see two guards dragging along a brown-haired boy.

For some reason, even though she could barely make out the boy's identity in the receding light, she felt a strange sense of camaraderie towards him. She had to impose her will over her instincts and retreat into the room, where she tried to pretend she did not know what he was about to endure for the next six hours.

*****

The next day, it was hard for Alex to maintain her usual dull facade because now she had an objective. She had to find that girl again.

She found her in the cafeteria line at lunch and snuck in behind her. The woman behind her was stunned by her intrusion but as she opened her mouth to speak, she decided it wasn't worth the bother and looked away.

The girl gasped as Alex tapped her on the shoulder. She turned around, and in her eyes, there was not a single hint of recognition.

"Hello," she said.

"Do I know you?" Alex asked.

The girl frowned. "I don't... think so? Who are you?"

Black hair, round nose, big, brown eyes. Alex could swear she had seen them before.

"You said my name yesterday," Alex said.

"I did?" She bowed her head in thought. "I'm sorry, but you must be mistaken."

Alex gritted her teeth in frustration, then reached out and grabbed her arm.

A second time, the girl gasped, but this time, her eyes shone with recognition.

"Alex!"

"Shh!" Alex hissed. "Act natural. There's probably eyes everywhere."

"What... What is going on?" she said.

"I was hoping you could tell me. Just find me in the common room, and I'll tell you what I know."

The girl nodded.

"One more thing, and I really hope you remember this because I have a feeling when I let go of you, you'll forget me along with this conversation: whatever you do, do not take the pills they give you. The nurse will stick around until you take it, so you have to fake it somehow."

The girl looked at her with wide eyes and nodded slowly. She seemed frightened and Alex worried if she would have the nerve to follow her instructions.

As she let go of the girl, a confused look took up her face, and then she awkwardly turned away and moved as the line moved.

From her table, no more than five minutes later, Alex watched as a nurse approached the girl and gave her medicine. With bated breath, she watched her swallow the pills, and she watched her drink the water, and as the nurse left the table, she glanced around, then bent over and spat something into her hand.

She looked a bit confused as to why she did it, but she shrugged and put the pills in her pocket.

*****

The girl was already in the common room when Alex got there later in the day. She had secured herself a window seat with an empty chair across from her and a game of checkers between them.

"Mind if I join you?" Alex said.

The girl looked up, and her jaw dropped slightly.

"It's you!" she said. "I have been trying to understand what is going on with me, but every thought in my head before lunch today has been very blurred. I kept seeing you and hearing your voice in my head telling me what to do."

"Yeah," Alex said. "I guess I was right. The pills were keeping your mind dull. Same with me and who knows how many others."

She sat down and moved a piece absentmindedly.

"You said you would tell me what you know."

"I did." Alex nodded. "But I'll be honest, I don't know much." She took a deep breath. "I don't think we're like all these other people."

"How do you mean?" The girl frowned, looking around at the other patients.

"Do you feel troubled in any way at all? Any way that could explain why your family decided to put you here?"

The girl shook her head.

"What was your last memory before this place?" Alex said.

"I was..."

"Who are your parents? What are their names?"

"I... I don't..."

"Where are you from?"

"I..."

"You don't know, do you?"

The girl's confusion had now turned to fear the longer she processed Alex's questions.

"What is happening to me?"

"It's not just you," she said. It's happening to me, too. But I think I can help you remember more."

"How?"

"I'm not sure, but when I touched you, I somehow made you remember me."

"I... I remember the jolt... like lightning straight to my brain."

"I think I could help you remember more if we touch again." Alex placed her hand on the table invitingly. "The choice is yours."

The girl stared at it for a moment.

"I... I want to remember."

She put her hand down on Alex's hand and sucked in her breath expectantly.

A second passed, then another, then another. Nothing happened.

"Are we... Are we doing it wrong?"

"No. I don't think s—"

Alex's head snapped back, and her eyes went blind to the world around her.

The new world she stepped into was blurry and inconstant, changing and shifting as swiftly as she could form thoughts. She saw herself in a familiar-looking house, talking and laughing with an older female who bore a striking resemblance to her. Next, she was in the local gym taking karate lessons with a bunch of fifteen-year-olds. Next she was in the cafe, having a chat with the girl at the counter. Next, she was seated around the table with four strangers. One of them was the girl who now sat across from her.

The world continued to shift, but every time it stopped, there she was with those four strangers whom she was now apparently friends with. She saw them seeking out clues together, and running from danger together, and eating together. These were her friends. And yet she could not remember their names.

Well, that was not entirely true. Now, she knew one name, and as she opened her eyes, she spoke it.

"Sam?" she said.

Chapter 16:
CONFRONTATION

The girl's body responded to the name before her mind did. Her eyes widened, and her pupils dilated.

"That's... That's me! I'm Sam!" She could barely contain herself.

"If I've found you here, then it's safe to assume the others are here too." Alex wondered aloud.

"Others? What others?"

"There are five of us who don't belong here. I remember your name, but I don't remember the others. I don't even remember their faces, but they're definitely here, and I think I might've sort of seen one last night."

"But how do you know all this?"

"I... I think I have some sort of psychic ability," she said.

Sam laughed nervously. "What?"

"And so do you."

"I... have superpowers? Yeah, right."

"Consider the situation. Why would I joke about something like that right now?"

"Well, if what you're saying is true, what powers do I have?"

"You... I don't know just yet."

"What?" She grabbed Alex's hand tighter. "Come on. Try harder!"

Before Alex could protest, she was cast back into the visions again, except this time, it focused on Sam alone. She saw Sam speaking to no one in particular until one scene where she could see what she was talking to. It was a translucent man.

"I uh... I think you talk to ghosts," Alex said.

"I what?"

"I see you talking, but I don't see who you're talking to, except for one time when I saw what can only be a ghost."

"You're kidding."

"Again, this would be the most inappropriate time to kid."

"But that's crazy, and looking at where we are, that's saying something."

"I know what I saw, Sam."

"Alright then, how do I use it?"

"I have no clue."

"That's not helpful."

"Hey, it's your superpower; figure it out."

"So, what do we do about the others?" Sam asked. You said you couldn't remember their faces.

"Yeah, but I have a lead."

*****

Later that night, Alex lay awake listening. She could not tell the time as there were hardly any clocks to be found within the asylum, but she could tell from how dark it was out that much time had passed. Soon, she heard the sound she was waiting for.

It was a nigh imperceptible shuffling as guards skulked by, and the only reason she heard it was because she was listening for it.

She waited for them to enter a room. She waited through the sound of quick and brutal subduing. She waited for the sweeping sound of them dragging their victim away.

When the sound had faded away, she snuck out of the room, checked to make sure the coast was clear, then went ahead and entered the room across from hers without knocking.

The occupant of the room stirred as she shut the door behind her.

"Wha..?" he blurted.

He did not get to say more as she put her hand over his mouth and held her finger to her lips.

"Hi," she said. I'm your neighbor from across the hall, and I'm not going to hurt you, so I need you to stay quiet. Otherwise, you'll bring attention to us and get us in major trouble. I don't plan to take too much of your time. Nod if you plan to cooperate."

He nodded.

"Good." She let go of him and backed away. "I'm Alex. Hi "

"Hello."

"What is your name?"

"I'm Subject Two-five-four."

"That's not your name. What's your real name?" She waited a bit and got no response. "You don't know, do you?"

"I don't have a real name."

"I doubt that's true," she said. "Let's find out what it is."

She touched him again, but this time with intention. As her hand made contact with his arm, she went through the same scenes she had gone through with Sam, except this time in more detail. He was more than just a blurry face constantly out of focus, and he did, in fact, have a name. It was...

"Daniel," she said.

Then came the look of recognition.

"Alex?" He looked around. "What's... What is happening?"

"Still in the process of figuring that out, but none of this is real."

"No, but I remember being in the basement. The chief physician was there. He tortured me. A lot. That was... That was real."

"That wasn't..." Alex wanted to say the torture wasn't real either, but she did not believe that. Nothing had felt more real in this place than the pain. "What do you remember from before here? From before the torture?"

"The last thing I remember before that was... the chief physician's office. We were there. You and me and...three others?"

As he spoke, the memories came to her, gaining more clarity as more time passed.

"One of them is Sam. Still no clue on the other two yet."

"Sam..." Alex could tell he was struggling to remember. Judging by the defeated sigh, he had failed. "So, your powers are working?"

Alex raised a brow in surprise. "That's more than Sam recalled when I touched her."

"Maybe your powers are getting stronger, too."

"Looks that way. The longer I go without those damn pills, the more I can remember of the real world."

"Speaking of. How do we get back there?"

"I don't have all the answers yet, but at least you're starting to remember," she said. "For now, our mission is to find the last two, then we can work on leaving."

"I think I can help with that."

"How?"

"My power. I have the ability to see the past through any object I touch."

"You know about your power already?" Alex said. "Sam doesn't even believe she has powers."

He put his hand on his bed, and after a moment, he paused with a perplexed look on his face.

"It's... not working."

"What?"

"I can't see anything!" He patted the bed multiple times and even grabbed the sleeve of her shirt. "Nothing!"

"Maybe it's because this isn't the physical world. Nothing you're touching is real."

"Then why are your powers working?"

"Because I'm using it on you, and you're real."

"What do we do about Doctor von Menschen?"

"Nothing until we have our memories and our numbers back. We'll meet up tomorrow on the service staircase right after lunch. See if any memories are jogged before then."

After warning him about the pills, she left the room and sneaked back into hers.

*****

The next day, at both breakfast and lunch times, Alex tried to find the fourth and fifth members of their team, focusing on each and every face, but no one stuck out to her.

To her surprise, however, when she went to meet up with Sam and Daniel, Daniel had yet to arrive, but there was another person with Sam. It was a boy with a tall and slender build and soft brown eyes.

"Did I not stress enough how important secrecy is?" Alex said.

"You did," Sam said. "But I think he's our fourth."

"You think?"

"He came up to me in the cafeteria and said he trusted me but had no idea why."

Alex's brow rose.

"You too," the boy said. "I... I trust you. You're my friend, aren't you?"

He tried to approach, but Alex held up a warning finger.

"Easy there, tiger." She held out her hand. "Give me your hand."

Before he could comply, the door opened as Daniel joined them.

"Hey, Sam," he said.

Sam squinted at him. "Danny?"

"Daniel," he corrected. His eyes flitted to the other young man. "Who is he supposed to be?"

"That's what I'm about to find out. Sam thinks he's one of us."

"No way in he—"

His voice faded away as she touched the strange boy's hand.

Like with Daniel, it was like unlocking a new character in a game she had played before.

When she stopped, he turned over the railing and retched.

"Yep. One of us," Alex said.

Daniel watched him for a moment. "Are you sure?"

"I'm sure your memories of him are starting to return."

"They are." He sighed wistfully. "Doesn't mean I have to accept them."

"Good to have you back, James." Sam patted him on the back, inadvertently causing him to hurl some more.

As they waited for him to recover, Alex had a thought.

"Anyone else notice that with each member of the gang we find, our collective memory expands?"

"Huh?" James wiped his mouth as he joined the conversation.

"Not you, James. You're new."

"Right "

"So, if we find the last person, we might figure out how to get out of this place?" Daniel said.

As he spoke, distorted images of a young girl filled her mind.

"Short, red hair," she muttered.

"What?"

"I sort of see her. The last person. I see short red hair."

"Now that you mention it, I see freckles," Sam said. "On her face and her shoulders, too."

"Come on, guys. Think," Alex said. "We all remember pieces of her. Let's put them together."

"Bright, piercing green eyes," Daniel said. "She's younger than everyone here."

"She's got a pointy nose," James said. "Is that helpful?"

Alex shut her eyes in concentration.

Freckles... Pointy nose... Green eyes... Teenager...

She had seen someone who matched all these features. But where?

"Wait a minute!" It was the drooling girl in the cafeteria. "I know who she is!"

"Well?"

"Do any of you remember a girl in a wheelchair? She seemed completely catatonic."

"Yeah, I remember," Sam said. "That's her?"

"I'm very sure it is."

"But... What could have happened to her?" James said. "None of us were in any state similar to that, were we?"

"In order to find out, we should find her."

"Her room is right across from mine," Sam said.

"Lead the way!" Alex said. Over her shoulder, she added, "You two stay behind."

"Screw that!" Daniel said.

"Agreed," James chipped in.

With Sam in the lead, the four of them hurried back to the wards. They came to a stop two doors away from Alex's room.

"That's her," Sam said.

Alex pushed open the door, and there was the red-haired girl sitting in her wheelchair, facing the door as if she had been expecting them. Except she wasn't the one expecting them. The man who sat beside her with a big smile on his face was.

"Oh, look. You made it!" the chief physician said dryly. "We've been expecting you."

Guards arrived on the scene quicker than Alex could think up a reply, and they were quickly surrounded.

Alex readied herself for a fight, but they must have learned from the last time because the next thing she felt was a blow to the back of her head.

She fell to the ground, and her vision faded to black.

*****

When Alex came to, she immediately realized she was in the basement, but in a different part. She was lying flat in a hospital bed, and her eyes were fixed on the ceiling. She tried to move but found, unsurprisingly, that her hands and feet were cuffed to the bed.

"Alex?" someone called out from beside her.

She turned. It was Sam.
"Sam!" she said. "Are you okay?"

"Yeah. Daniel's next to me, and James is on his other side."

On Alex's right side, the other girl lay motionless. If her eyes were not wide open, it would have been easy to think she was asleep or even dead.

Alex lifted her head and looked around. The five of them were in a small room with the door directly opposite to them.

"How long have you been awake?" Alex said.

"About ten minutes now."

"And the doctor?"

"He wasn't here when I woke up."

"If anyone's got a plan, we should probably hurry up," James said.

No one responded.

"Guys?" he said. "Daniel?"

"What are you calling me for? What good would being able to see the past do for us?"

"Sam?"

Alex heard grunting and turned. She had her eyes shut in concentration like she was constipated.

"That's not what it looks like when you use your powers, Sam," Daniel said.

"Oh, shut up!"

"Alex?" James said.

Alex's mouth opened and closed like a beached fish, but she could not form words.

She turned back to the third girl. She was still a blur in her memory, but she could remember being in awe of her powers, whatever they were.

"Hey," she said. "Listen, I don't know what you've got going on, but I feel we need your help."

She waited for a sign but got nothing.

"Come on, please," Alex said.

"Alex..." James said.

"If I could just..." She struggled against the bonds to no avail. "If I could just reach her somehow."

"Alex!"

"What?" she snapped.

"Her name," James said.

"What?"

"Her name. Call her by her name. Remind her that she's a person."

She tried to think of her name, but there was a big blank.

"I don't know her name!" she said. "Anyone?"

"Not a freaking clue," James said.

"What if we just throw names at her until something sticks?" Sam said.

"What?"

Sam ignored the question and started blurting off names.

"Daisy. Theresa. Patricia. Quinn. Bianca. Lucy—"

"L!" James called out.

"What?" Sam said.

"First letter. L!"

"You sure?"

"Absolutely!"

Alex still had her eyes on the girl and saw her eyes close.

"Oh my God! Keep going!"

"Lori. Lana. Lexi. Liza—"

"L-I!" Daniel said.

"Are you—"

The door opened, and the doctor stepped in.

"I trust you've all said your goodbyes." He smiled. "None of you will be making it out of here alive."

He stepped aside, and three guards filed in. One was pushing a trolley laden with medical equipment, a bone saw, and a drill. The last two came dragging in a big machine that was clearly meant for some form of torture.

They came to a halt between Alex and Sam.

"You've been a nuisance," the doctor said, looking right at Alex. "You go first."

"Guys!" Alex called out. "I don't... I don't want to die!"

"What you want doesn't matter, unfortunately," he said. "We're gathered here for what I want." He gestured to the guard with the trolley. "You may begin."

He nodded, picked up the saw, and approached Alex.

Alex turned away from him in fright.

"Come on. Please!" Alex pleaded. "Wake up!"

The girl did not respond and the saw inched towards her skull.

Alex shut her eyes as the teeth of the saw bit into her flesh, muttering a prayer.

"Lila!" Daniel yelled.

Alex's eyes snapped open to find Lila staring at the ceiling once again, but it lasted half a second before her eyes darted over to the guard.

As she looked at him, she saw that he had frozen in place. He was lifted off his feet and tossed at the far wall.

There was a sickening sound of bone breaking upon impact; then, he fell to the ground in a crumpled heap.

The cuffs fell away from Lila, and she hopped off the bed.

"Lila, get us out of these cuffs," Alex said. "We can help."

"I've got this," Lila said.

The two guards left tried to attack, but she flicked her wrist and sent them flying into a wall with no more difficulty.

Doctor von Menschen thrust both hands, and Lila was pushed back several paces, but she looked more insulted than hurt.

She raised one hand and pushed.
The door burst open as the chief physician was unceremoniously thrown out of the room.

"Holy hell!" James said.

Lila glanced in their direction, and their shackles came loose. She did not wait around for them as she stepped out after the doctor.

"Remind me never to get on her bad side," Sam said.

"I'd say the same, but it's already too late for me," Daniel said.

They got out of bed and ran after Lila. To their surprise, they found her down on her hands and knees.

"Lila!"

They rushed to her, but before they could get close, the doctor shifted his gaze to them.

In one instant, it felt as though the gravity in the room had been doubled or even tripled. Against their will, they were forced to the floor.

"You might be powerful, but this is my world, and in my world, I have the ultimate power," he said.

Alex tried to rise, but even remaining on her hands and knees was too much. She gave up the physical effort and let her mind work. This was an illusion, after all.

Wait! That's it!

No matter how real the pain felt, it was all an illusion. And all she had to do was open her eyes.

"Your... world..." Alex muttered, "is... an illusion. You... are nothing... but a man... behind a curtain... of lies." She pushed off the ground again, and as she did, the weight on her back lessened. "And I see right through your lies."

The doctor doubled his efforts, and James and Sam fell to the ground, but Alex was unaffected. She rose to full height.

"James, link us! Now!"

"I can't! It's too much!"

"You can. This isn't real. Focus."

"It's not real... it's not real... it's not real," he repeated to himself.

Soon, a calming wave began to wash over them, and one by one, they stumbled to their feet.

"No! No, no, no, this can't be happening!" Doctor von Menschen screamed. "You should not have this much power in—ack!"

His words were cut off as Lila picked him up by the throat. She lifted him to the ceiling, where he clutched helplessly at his neck.

"Consider your license...revoked!"

She pulled her hands apart in a tearing motion, and with a deafening scream, he exploded into nothing.

At once, the world began to shudder and fade away until the illusion was gone, and they were back in the real basement, lying on the dusty floor.

They got up and looked around.

The room was strange. It was just an empty space with pillars all around. Between each pillar, there was a creepy statue of a kneeling knight that looked just like the ones from the chessboard earlier.

This was the room they had been about to enter after leaving the chief physician's office.

"The illusion must have hit us as soon as we entered," Alexandra said.

Doctor von Menschen was in the room with them; now a semi-transparent, green-tinted specter, crawling on the floor, seething and blubbering.

"What's he got to be pissed off about?" Daniel said. "We're the ones who got tortured!"

"My forces!" Doctor von Menschen slammed his hand into the floor. "Arise! Come to my aid!"

Lines of green flames spiderwebbed their way around the room, each one heading for a stone knight.

"Oh no," Alexandra said.

"What's happening?" Lila asked.

There was no need to answer because as soon as the green energy made contact, the knights shuddered aggressively, then rose to full height. From the holes in their visors, menacing pairs of green orbs shone back at them.

"Tear them limb from limb!" Doctor von Menschen said. "Show no mercy!"

"Guys, we should leave this place," James said. "Right now!"

"Absolutely not," Samantha said.

"Are you crazy?" he said. "He's got the advantage here. We're outnumbered, and his powers probably surpass ours."

"Open your eyes and look closer, James. He isn't taking his sweet time getting up because he's trying to be nice. He's weakened, too. Probably even more than we are. The illusion and whatever he did to us must have taken a toll on him as well as us. We can finish this. We have to finish this. Here. And now."

She pushed off the floor and took off sprinting towards him.

"Die!" Doctor von Menschen screeched.

With a sweeping motion, he broke off a piece of the pillar and chucked it at her, but before it could hit her, it pivoted and flew to the side.

Alexandra glanced to the side and saw Lila's hands in the air.

She looked around and saw the stone knights closing in on them from all sides.

"What do you want us to do?" Alexandra called out.

"Back me up!" Samantha yelled. "If he dies, they die too!"

"James, with me!" Alexandra said. "Daniel, watch Lila's back! Move!"

As they ran after her, two more boulders came flying, but they were stopped and crushed in thin air.

"Watch her back how exact—" Daniel yelled. "Lila, watch out!"

Worried, Alexandra glanced over her shoulder. Two knights were bearing down on Lila and Daniel, but Lila was one top of the situation.

She thrust out both hands, and they flew back.

"That's how!" Alexandra called out before turning to focus on the task ahead.

Doctor von Menschen was on his feet now, but he looked far from menacing.

"No!" he said. "Stay back! Get away from me!"

Samantha ducked and rolled as yet another came for her head, which was fortunate because Lila was too preoccupied to help. She got back upright within arm's range and lunged at the chief physician, closing the remaining distance.

She grabbed his head with both hands and held on tight.

"Doctor Fredrick von Menschen," Samantha said. "For your sins against God and against man; against the living and against the dead, I will exorcise you from this world. Permanently!"

The air around them grew tense with psychic energy as Samantha dug deep into the well from which she drew her powers. Using her authority as a medium, she linked herself to him.

Alexandra could tell she was depleted from their time in the illusion— they all were— but it was clear she was determined to end this.

The chief physician retaliated by grabbing her in turn.

"You arrogant child!" He spat. "You don't have the power to take me on!"

"No. Not alone, I don't." Alexandra and James were behind her now. "But I am not alone!"

Alexandra instinctively extended her hand to James. If she had been asked what the plan was, she would have said she did not know, and she didn't, but her instincts were clearer than they'd ever been, and she let them guide her.

"Whatever you feel," she whispered, "stay calm and trust me. You can't have any doubts."

James nodded and when she placed her hand on her shoulder, he took off his gloves and mimicked her. Without needing to be told, he established a psychic link between the three of them. With physical contact, the link was stronger than before. When Sam breathed, it felt like the air was flowing through Alexandra's lungs. She felt the sweat beading across James' forehead. She knew they could hear the beating of her own heart. Now, they were three as one.

There was a sharp tug as Samantha drew on their strength along with hers and poured her powers into the doctor's incorporeal form.

He let out a loud wail and his form began to distort.

"I will not lose! I will not lose!"

He pushed back with renewed vigor and pain like nothing before flared through their whole bodies, like their own skins were threatening to peel off of their bodies and their tissues and bones right along with them.

Cracks appeared on their skins, glowing green with the doctor's aura. He was trying to do to them what Samantha was trying to do to him. He was trying to literally obliterate them from existence.

Somehow they held on, even though she could sense inklings of fear and doubt among them. They were determined.

"Stay calm, James!" Alexandra reminded. "Stay calm!"

But she could sense that the reminder wasn't necessary. He was fully in control. Perhaps because their pain was shared, it was easy to bear. Even then, there was only so much three bodies could take.

The doubt continued to rise in triples as each negative thought propagated another, but just when Alex began to fear that James, who was most vulnerable to negative energy, would let go, she felt a hand rest on her shoulder.

She looked up, and there was Lila, and next to her was Daniel.

"Need a hand?" Daniel said.

She felt James' link spread to incorporate them.

Samantha's body began to glow, a bright blue glow that rivaled the doctor's green aura and eventually overwhelmed it.

"Your evil ends here, Doctor!" Samantha said.

Blueish cracks were starting to bloom through the doctor's ghostly body, but he remained as defiant as ever.

"You think you've won?" he said. "I was trying to take your powers from you; that's why you had a chance to fight back. Now, you're going to wish I had killed you."

"We're not scared of you," Alex said. "We beat you."

He opened his mouth as if he wanted to say more, but his face froze in a mix of pain and horror as reality set in.

"Your services in this place are no longer required," Samantha said calmly. "Consider your employment terminated."

The doctor let out a screech like nothing a human could make, and then, with a violent burst of blue and green, he exploded.

They were thrown back to the floor; they watched as his remains, scattered about the room, turned to dust.

Chapter 17:
Havoc Unleashed

Lila was the first one back on her feet.

Before that, she had opened her eyes to the dull grey ceiling of the basement and, after a glance at her watch, quickly came to terms with her surroundings and the fact that the past hour or so had indeed happened. Then she thought back to home, and about what she would have been doing instead of lying on the dusty floor in the basement of an abandoned asylum.

It was a Saturday night. Once upon a time, that meant game night in the Sakarov house. They would have chips and her father would make his infamous, and tastefully questionable, secret-recipe dip to go with it— it was warm crab parmesan with enough garlic to ward off any vampire within a mile of Ravensbrook and enough Tabasco sauce to make Satan himself sweat, and everyone knew but they pretended not to preserve his ego. It was also one of the few things he knew how to do in a kitchen without setting off the smoke alarm. Her mother was usually the games master as she was the only one they could trust not to be swayed. Her sister would pretend to be too old for the family game night, but as soon as the points started stacking up, she got heavily invested.

Such a night had not happened since the accident.

It was when she came upon that depressing thought that she had risen from the floor and shaken off the memories along with the dust on her clothes.

She found Samantha and Alexandra out cold with James not too far off.

The only other person still fully conscious was Daniel and he joined her upright momentarily.

The stone statues had been reduced to rubble, and any trace of the green energy that had possessed them was long gone.

"You okay?" Daniel asked in a small voice.

She nodded.

"Yeah. Better than they are, that's for sure."

They both happened to look at Samantha at the same time.

"She was incredible, wasn't she?" he said.

"She was. Brave and powerful. To take on and defeat a malevolent spirit like Doctor von Menschen. That can't have been easy."

"Don't sell yourself short," Daniel said. "Back in the illusion, you handed him his own ass."

"Hardly." Lila scoffed. "I got, what, two shots in before I got put on my ass? If not for Alex, we would have..."

"Died?" Daniel finished. "Yeah probably. But you landed the blow that freed us from the illusion."

She said nothing in the way of a response. Instead, she shifted her focus to Alex.

"Alex looks just as spent as Sam. I mean, James is starting to wake up, but she's totally out of it. I wonder if it's because she repelled the effects of the illusion during that battle."

"Alex did more than that. She was the first one to wake up in the illusion. I can't imagine being all alone in a place like that. One by one, she found us and somehow made us remember who we were."

"Not me," Lila noted. "The first real memory I have of the illusion was your voice. You called my name. You made me remember."

"Yeah, we were trying to guess your name to wake him up. It was James' idea."

She raised a brow, clearly requesting for more of an explanation.

"Each of us awoke with fragmented memories. The more of us she found, the more the memories expanded, but even till we found you, none of us could tell what your name was."

"So that was a lucky guess?"

He shrugged. "It was my only guess. Then again, Sam and James got the first two letters so I can't take too much credit."

Lila nodded absentmindedly.

"How long do you think it'll be before they awake?" Daniel said.

"I have no clue. All I did was support, and I felt my energy being siphoned by the bucket."

"Yeah. Between that and the battle in the illusion, I'm starting to think I got the better end of this deal with my powers."

Lila looked at the spot where they had last seen the chief physician.

"Is he...dead?" Lila said, "Deader than before, I mean."

"Yeah," Daniel said.

"This better not be like those video games where music comes on and the boss revives with an extra health bar and a whole new power set we have to adapt to because I don't have much fight left in me."

Daniel chuckled. There was little humor in it but it was clear he understood the reference.

"Sam's in the best place to answer," he said, "but I felt it when he died. It was like something about this place had changed."

"We beat an evil ghost psychic."

"We did. But I can't help but feel... I don't know. Let down? I expected the air to feel..."

"Lighter?"

"Yeah," he said. "Instead, there's this sense of foreboding that I can't shake."

"It'll pass," Lila reassured. "We won, didn't we?"

"Yeah... Yeah, we did."

So why didn't either of them believe it?

*****

James woke up a few minutes later, and within the next half hour, Alexandra and Samantha did too, respectively.

While they replenished their energies with snack bars and energy drinks, Samantha confirmed that Doctor von Menschen was indeed dead and gone, but she said it with a strange expression that led Lila to say,

"Why am I anticipating a 'but'?"

"The chief physician was definitely exorcised. There's no doubt about that," Samantha said. "The feel of his aura is burned into my mind, and I can sense the absence of it."

"But?" Lila pressed.

"But it feels like something is slowly filling the void that the doctor left behind, and it's already making my skin crawl."

"I don't understand," James said. "We did what we came to do, didn't we? We vanquished the evil doctor and freed the tormented souls of the inmates. What else is there?"

"I don't know, but whatever it is, it definitely has something to do with the doctor's absence."

"Don't tell me killing the doctor was a bad call," Lila said.

Samantha's answer came after a lengthy delay:

"I... don't know."

"While we're working on that, maybe we should get above ground. It could just be the residual negative energy from this place," James said.

They came to an agreement, and so began the trek back up to the surface.

It was almost disappointing to find that the rest of the basement still maintained its dreary visage and the unmistakable haunt of evil still lingered in the air. Perhaps Lila had raised her expectations too high, but it wasn't like she had been hoping for rainbows and sunshine. Just a little something different.

To her side, the others very clearly shared her disappointment, and not a single one of them seemed to be relishing their hard-fought victory.

What was it all for then?

As they got to the outer space with the hospital beds, Daniel asked Samantha if she could perhaps ask one of the ghosts what was going on, but she was still far too drained to use her powers and, so she could not sense them.

After that, the basement returned to quiet, and the only sounds that could be heard until they left came from their sluggish footsteps and eventually, the ding and then the groaning of the elevator.

Nothing about the top floor was different either, except for the fact that night had fallen while they were down in the basement— perhaps during their time trapped in the chief physician's illusion.. The hollow emptiness still had a depressing vibe, and the shadows looked like they wanted to reach out and grab them, but after spending what felt like weeks in the hellish— and considering the state of the real thing that was saying a lot— version of the asylum, they were unmoved.

"What's the plan now?" Daniel asked as they got to the stairs. "Do we head home and sleep?"

"Should we be walking through town at this hour? Is that wise?" James said.

"Wise?" Daniel said. "What, you're worried the streets will be unsafe? Look at where we are and look at what we've done."

"Try telling that to my mom."

"So, you really do have a curfew." Daniel laughed teasingly.

James did not respond. He was too tired to fight.

Lila looked to Alexandra for a decision and realized everyone else was doing the same.

"I don't..." She sighed. "I don't know. But a good night's rest will be good for everyone, and if I'm to get a proper rest, it'll be in my bed. We can all crash at my place for the night."

"Sounds like a plan," James said.

"Amen to that," Samantha muttered.

Nothing felt right. The chief physician had admitted that he had been trying to siphon off their powers, which, coupled with the energy it took to defeat him, explained the physical and mental exhaustion. But was that the reason the team morale had suffered a blow?

As they entered, the moon's light shone generously into the lobby through the window and half-open door, so much so that flashlights were unnecessary. Beyond the entryway, the front yard, with its tall grasses and neglected trees, took on a pale yet haunting appearance.

When they tried to cross the threshold out of the building, the strangest thing happened, and it happened to Daniel, who was two paces ahead of the rest of them. As he walked through the doorway, he stopped dead in his tracks for half a second, and then, with a pained grunt, he was thrown back several steps.

"Ow! What the fuck?" he said.

"What?" Lila said.

"It zapped me! And it fucking hurt!"

"What zapped you? The door?"

"No." He frowned. "The doorway. It's like there's something blocking the way out."

Alexandra reached out with a finger and poked at the air in front of her, and with a hiss, she retracted her finger.

"What the hell!" she said. "There's a barrier up."

"A barrier?" Samantha said. "Since when?"

"I don't know, but it's definitely a new development. James and I went out to fetch firewood before and nothing like this happened."

Lila gestured for them to step back, and then, summoning her abilities, she reached out toward the space telekinetically. She made contact with some invisible barrier and, increasing her output, she tried to push through it. Two bluish-black spots appeared in thin air where she pushed, in the shape of her hands, but it would not budge. When she stopped, they faded away.

"I can't break through it," she announced.

"That dark aura just now," Daniel said. "Something or someone is doing this. Someone doesn't want us to leave. But who could it—"

All of sudden, Samantha let out a groan and clutched at the sides of her head.

"Sam!" Daniel said.

"What is it? What's wrong?" Alexandra asked.

Samantha opened her mouth to respond, but all that came out was a sharp cry before she sank to the floor.

"Sam!" Alexandra yelled, following her to the ground.

She had barely put her arms around her when James' knees gave out.

"What the..." Daniel said.

He did not scream or gasp; in fact, he made no sound at all, but as he knelt there, his body shuddered like he was sporting a fever. His eyes were unfocused and glazed over.

"James!" Lila called.

She started towards him, but Daniel stopped her with a look and checked on him in her place. Lila understood the meaning behind the look. He was asking her to stay vigilant because she was the only fully conscious one with offensive abilities.

Stepping up to the task, she moved to put herself between them and the rest of the lobby.

A loud bang startled them, and Lila's hands went up, but it was a window swinging violently in the wind.

Another window followed suit, then another, and another, until there was not a single stationary window. Even the doors joined in the chaos, and soon, the entire asylum sounded like a low-budget remake of *Drumlines*.

"No wind," Alexandra noted.

"What?" Lila glanced back.

"There's... There's no wind."

Lila stopped to think about it. They were standing right in front of the door and she did not feel so much as a breeze.

There was a flash of dark blue as something streaked by. It was too fast for her to catch.

"...The fuck?"

"Do you see something?" Daniel said.

"I... I'm not sure."

The next time it appeared; however, she was expecting it.

It flew past her at impossible speed and she moved her hand to follow it. Like a fisherman with a pole, she felt a tug at the end of her line and reeled her target in.

"Not so fast, you weaselly bastard," she said.

The entity thrashed about in her grasp but it could not escape.

She pulled it in until it was less than two meters away.

Surprisingly, it bore no physical difference from the malevolent spirits from before. It was decayed and ugly and generally vile. The only difference, in fact, was the new aura that surrounded it. Well, that and the fact that it was easily five times stronger than the previous spirits.

"A malevolent spirit?" Alexandra said.

"Yes, but there's a significant power increase," Lila said.

"Hang on, where's that shadow coming from?"

"What shadow?"

The words were barely spoken when she noticed a perfect black circle in the center of the lobby. And then with a rush of wind and the wailing of a thousand souls, it erupted, letting loose an army of malevolent spirits.

They flew around forming a terrifying black tornado rising as high as the vaulted ceiling.

Taken by surprise, Lila lost her grip on the spirit she had caught and it disappeared into the tornado of ghosts.

"Well, that's... not good," Daniel said.

"You got any more pearls of wisdom, Captain Obvious?" Lila said.

"Something's... Something's coming!" Samantha blurted just then.

"Yeah no shit," Lila snapped. "We see them!"

"No, you don't understand. It's him! The doctor was not the one keeping the spirits trapped here; he was working for him. Now that the doctor is gone, he's coming."

"Him?" Curiosity overtaking fright, Lila turned. "Him who?"

Through the ghostly wailing, she heard what could only be the sound of cover shoes stepping on tiles.

"I believe she would be referring to me," a new voice; gravelly and low yet resonating, joined the conversation.

Lila looked forward, and her breath hitched in her throat. It felt like the temperature in the room had dropped all of a sudden, and she was almost surprised that when she finally exhaled, her breath did not mist in the air.

Across the lobby from them, there stood a man; except that even at a glance one could see that it was no ordinary man— and that was even before you got to the fact that he was see-through and the imposing blue-black aura that outlined him; bending the light of the moon around it like a black hole. His eyes were two marble orbs in their sockets; cold and unfeeling. His face was severe and intimidating without even trying. He was a tall man, standing at six foot six, and his shoulders were so broad that he looked like the stereotypical corporate type of comic book villain in the suit he wore.

He made as if to sit where there was no chair, but as he lowered himself, a high-back chair appeared underneath him out of nowhere.

The shadow on the floor was gone now, but the ghosts continued to zip around the room overhead, flying through solid walls as though they were nothing.

He propped one arm up and rested his chin on his fist.

"From the moment you set foot in my asylum, I took notice of you," he said. "And then, when you fended off Fredrick's minions and got through his obstacles, you had my curiosity. But you did not stop there, did you? You went on to destroy my dear friend, the doctor, and for that, I must congratulate you. Because now, you have earned my attention. Allow me to introduce myself. My name is —"

"Matthias Blackthorne," Lila whispered. She instantly recognized him from the picture in the library book. He had not aged a day in fifty years, after all. "The warden of Ravensbrook Asylum."

The warden's brow rose, and his facial expression took on the form of mild amusement as he cracked a smile, but in a way that did not guarantee that they would still be alive in a minute.

"Have the children of this age become so impertinent?" he said. "How rude of you to interrupt me. Granted, I am about to kill you one way or another, but we must not get so far ahead of ourselves that we forget such important things as manners."

"Manners?" Alexandra spat. "You're a monster."

The warden's smile did not waver.

"A monster, you say?" he said. "And here I was polite enough to strike up a conversation with you before getting to the business of killing you."

Lila stared him down, feigning confidence that she did not feel.

"Bring it on, old man."

Chapter 18:
Trapped Within

From the moment Samantha had sensed the chief physician's presence, she could tell that she was outmatched. The only reason she had managed to beat him was she had the numbers on her side, but otherwise, his psychic prowess was levels beyond hers and that of the others.

And then there was Warden Blackthorne.

It was hard to imagine that the apparition before them had once been flesh and blood. He radiated so much negative energy that it could be felt long before he manifested himself.

Samantha was easily the most vulnerable to the effects of his powers too. He was a ghost first, in spite of how powerful he was, and so as a medium, she was connected to him in a way she was not too fond of right then.

The sheer force of his powers had hit her with the gentleness of a freight train, bombarding her head from all directions like she was being crushed. And it was not just a mental barrage. Blood streamed from her nostrils and mouth as a result.

James suffered too, except in his case, he was merely susceptible to negative energy, and the warden was nothing but a bundle of negative energy barely held together.

Surprisingly, it was James who first got over the aura effects, and when he did, he used his powers like before and spread a calm around them.

Samantha's headache subsided, and her thoughts became clearer once more. With Alexandra's help, she returned to a fully vertical position. That was when she noticed Daniel's hand on James' arm, and then James' recovery made sense.

James was susceptible to the emotions of others, good or bad, and even though the warden was pure evil, Daniel beat him by proximity. He had somehow managed to maintain a calm line of thought in the face of imminent threat while maintaining physical contact and that had helped James snap out of it long enough to mount a shield around them.

Overhead, the malevolent spirits continued to zip around like they had somewhere important to be but had no sense of direction. The wailing had died down to moaning in the background as if they were merely setting the mood for the warden.

"The doctor was right, as usual," the warden smirked. He predicted your arrival a long time ago, you see. Decades passed, and even I started to question his faith, but here you are. This meeting is fifty years in the making."

"What? You were waiting for us?" Samantha said. "You really expect us to believe that load of crap."

"Not you five particularly, no." He shook his head and then fixed his eyes on Samantha. "And especially not you, ghost whisperer. You're just additional baggage, like dirt that sticks to the carrots taken from the garden. I couldn't care less about you or your paltry skills if I tried. But as far as the rest of you are concerned, you were very much meant to come here. Or should I say, psychics of your level and of your skill set were meant to come here, and it just so happens to be you four."

Samantha did not know how to interpret the warden's words. Was she supposed to take offense at the fact that he did not want her or was she supposed to be thankful? What would happen if she tried to walk out the door? Why did it matter that the big bad villain had practically called her useless?

Disgusted at herself, she shook off the thoughts. This was his way of trying to get in her head and she was letting him. It was a fairly common strategy: divide and conquer.

"That's not possible," Lila said. "There's no way you brought us here. There's no way you brought us together."

Warden Blackthorne shrugged and raised a lazy finger to point at her.

"Let's see..." he said. "A telekinetic unlike any before her." He moved his finger to Daniel. "A gleaner who looks through time with the brightest eyes." He moved on to James. "A highly sensitive empath with the ability to connect with other humans through cognition, and a clairvoyant to bring them all together."

His finger lingered on Alexandra before he gently lowered it.

"Doctor von Menschen put out the lure. He appealed to your sympathy with all those little visions you had. He planted the seeds in your mind and let them germinate on their own, knowing that you would nurture them."

Alexandra frowned. "No. No, that's not right."

"Ah but it is," he said. "Every obstacle you faced and conquered, every secret you learned, has brought you to this very moment. It all brought you to me."

"The chief physician is dead!" Daniel said. "We foiled your plan already!"

"I'm well aware of Doctor von Menschen's demise," he said, unfazed. "I felt his presence disappear into the night, kicking and screaming till the bitter end." His eyes flitted to Samantha without warning. "I suppose I have you to blame for that." He sighed deeply, which was an odd sight considering that he had no need to draw breath. "The chief physician and I wanted different things. That was part of the reason that our alliance worked out without a hitch. Believe it or not, Doctor von Menschen did not want power. Not for himself at least. The chief physician wanted knowledge. He had an itch for psychic abilities and with my resources, he was able to scratch that itch. Had he not met an untimely demise he would have scratched away until he was old and grey. Me? I wanted power. In exchange for the resources I offered him, the chief physician worked on a way that I could absorb the powers of his best subjects.

"He was more than happy to do it, but of course, there were risks. He predicted from his tests and research that I would be able to take on a psychic ability or two before my body would begin to reject them and shut down, and then I would run mad, but as it so turned out I was the most viable candidate the doctor had ever met. I surpassed his expectations significantly, and he continued my experiments even in death. But it turned out that my powers were too volatile without a body to hold them together, and as I could not leave the place of my death I was at risk of destroying everything here, including the dead. I had to be contained to keep my powers in check. Doctor von Menschen made sure of it. By killing Doctor von Menschen, you have freed me from my containment, but you have also brought me something I need: your lives. With you four as the missing pieces of my plan, I will finish his final work: resurrection."

Samantha's eyes widened in horror. As a ghost bound to the asylum, the warden's powers were already off the charts. She shuddered to think of what he would become if he could roam Ravensbrook as flesh and blood.

"But first you will entertain me," he said. "It had been a long time since I enjoyed a spot of entertainment, and I would like to see your powers in action with my own eyes... before I rip them from your cold, lifeless bodies." His body began to dissipate until he was nothing but a pair of floating blue eyes. "Be sure to put on a good show."

Like a wisp of smoke, his eyes vanished, and as soon as he could no longer be seen, the spirits ceased their movements, and all eyes turned to face them.

Alexandra's head whipped back and forth as she assessed the situation. The ghosts had cut off every other exit out of the lobby, and the one behind them was more wall than the actual walls.

"This is a trap," Alexandra said. "There's nowhere to run and nowhere to hide. We have no choice but to fight."

They all knew that there was not much of a fight here. The only choice before them was a painful defeat.

"Well, I'm not going down easy," Daniel said.

"Ditto," James said.

"So, we're like colossally screwed, we realize this, right?" Samantha said.

"What?" Daniel said flatly. "Five against, what, five hundred? A thousand? That's light work."

A cacophony of wailing and howling preceded the assault. In tens and twenties, they swooped down towards them like a multitude of birds of prey.

Reacting quickly, Lila's hands went up in defense. The ghosts slammed into a telekinetic force field and rebounded, scattering about. But their recovery was swift, and as quickly as they were repelled, they bounced back and attacked again. They scratched and clawed and bit at the air in front of them, a blazing hunger in their eyes.

"I'm buying time here. I can't keep it up forever. You guys better come up with a plan!" Lila yelled. Her arms buckled under the barrage. "And you better do it fast!"

"There is no plan!" Alexandra said.

"What?" Lila said.

"They have us pinned down, and three of us can't even do anything to hurt them!"

"Sam?" The urgency in Lila's voice had risen a notch. "You destroyed the doctor. These are the regular malevolent spirits, right? This should be easier for you."

"These ghosts aren't like the ones we faced before. I'm sure you can feel it, too," Samantha said. "They're backed by the warden, who is more powerful than the doctor ever was, and I'm not at full strength just yet. I can't just deal with them."

"Samantha, you and I are the only ones who can hurt them, so you better rethink and give me some good news before this shield breaks."

A light bulb lit up in Samantha's head.

"Wait a minute!"

"That better be a good news 'wait a minute' because I can't take any more bad news."

"You said only you and I can hurt them."

"Yeah?"

"What if that wasn't the case?"

"What are you talking about?"

"I can't destroy them in their numbers, but perhaps I don't have to," she said. "All I have to do is weaken them."

"You can do that?"

"I have power over ghosts, and within a small space, my authority can be manifested in a more powerful form," she said. "Care to try it out?"

"My muscles are crying out in pain right now. I'll try anything!"

"Find a weapon you can make a good dent with," Samantha said, speaking to Daniel, Alexandra, and James.

While they did as she instructed, she took a deep breath, and as she exhaled, she visualized her authority as a mediator of the dead expanding out of her to cover about as much space as Lila's shield extended.

"Lila," she said. "Create an opening. Limit their entry points."

"Got it."

"Everyone else, swing and swing hard."

"Gotcha," Daniel said.

"Whenever you're ready, Lila."

A ghost broke through the telekinetic shield almost as soon as Samantha was done speaking, startling her, but Daniel was ready.

Like a baseball batter, he stepped in and swung the plank he had pulled out of the barricaded window behind him.

With a nasty crunch, the piece of wood made an impact, bashing the ghost's head in for half a second before it went up in a poof of black smoke.

"Nice!" Daniel said.

Two more ghosts came through the opening and just as efficiently, James and Alexandra got rid of them.

"Great," Lila said. "Three down, nine hundred and ninety-seven to go."

"You got a better idea?" Samantha said.

"Yeah," Lila said.

She clenched her fists, and a row of ghosts exploded; then she shoved the whole horde back, scattering them all around the room.

"Lila!" Alexandra scolded.

"Why don't you try holding back this many ghosts? See how you like it!" Lila snapped. "You wanted a plan? Here's my plan: attack!"

They recovered quickly and moved into stance while the monsters regrouped. Each of them took up a segment of the room with Lila taking up the greatest portion, and then they attacked.

Samantha swung her bare hands this way and that, tearing through the enemies. She had no need for weapons because the moment the ghosts touched her, they shattered in a spray of black.

It did not take long for her to get lost in the motions, fending off the impossibly overwhelming forces and hoping that somewhere out of her field of vision, her friends were holding their own.

And for a while, that hope held true, but then a blur passed by her, and with a grunt, someone was thrown against the doorway.

"Lila!" James said.

Lila?

A panic shot through Samantha's body. If Lila was down, there would be a huge hole in their defense, and none of them was capable of compensating.

Her head whipped around automatically to seek her out, but instead, she got to watch Daniel take a mean uppercut that sent him flying through the air before he crashed into the wall.

That split second of distraction was all it took for a couple of ghosts to sneak past her guard.

Sharp claws tore at her face. Another set caught her in the midsection. She was blinded and in pain when the third attack came, and it was a blow right to her chest that knocked her off her feet.

From the floor, she barely registered the sound of her remaining teammates being taken down. She opened her eyes and looked past the stinging pain and the blood dripping down her face to find the ghosts ready to finish the job.

Mere inches away from her face, they paused, suspended in mid-air.

Next to her, Lila's eyes were only half open. She was bleeding from the corner of her mouth, and her hand had four deep gashes running along it, but she held the hand up. It was the only thing keeping the ghosts at bay.

But it was clear the fight was gone from her. It was a matter of seconds before her eyes closed, and then they would be ripped to shreds. Even now, they rattled the invisible forces that held them back with their wild thrashing.

The look in Lila's eyes threatened to break Samantha's resolve. Lila was barely an adult. The mouth on her, combined with the magnitude of her powers, made it easy to forget, but she was young, too young to be holding all their lives in her hands. She looked defeated, and she looked ashamed like she had somehow disappointed them.

"Guys, I'm... I'm sorry," Lila said, her voice breaking with raw emotion. "I... I can't hold on much longer..."

"Don't," Daniel said. "You don't have to apologize for anything."

"You did good, Lila," Samantha said. "You did good."

"You really kept us alive this long," James said. "We should be apologizing to you for not doing more."

Alexandra did not speak. She could barely raise her head to look on as blood dripped from a cut to her forehead.

Whether it was James' empathy link connecting them, Samantha could not say, but she knew what they were all thinking. This was really it. No more tricks up their sleeves. No more moves.

This was the end.

Lila's hand began to drop. She fought hard to hold it up but it was a battle long lost.

Samantha accepted her fate and was about to close her eyes in anticipation of the end when she sensed a familiar presence nearby. She looked around with renewed hope, but the source was nowhere to be found, and it was already too late because Lila's hand hit the ground, and the force field fizzled out.

She forgot to close her eyes, however, and it was fortunate that she did because she saw what happened next.

A light blue aura manifested in the form of a small human, then it turned into bright white and exploded away from them.

The angry wailing turned into confused and pained screeching as several rows of malevolent ghosts froze in mid-air and fell to the ground, where they shattered.

The movements of those who were not immediately destroyed turned frenzied and directionless as they flew about trying to get rid of the ice somehow, but of the lot that were touched by the ice, none survived as the ice grew to encase their entire forms. The rest retreated, clearly wary of the newcomer.

To ensure they stayed back, she made a wall of ice around them.

The figure responsible for the fiery assault reverted to a blue form and went on to manifest the rest of their features. It was the very same young girl they had met the day before.

"Hello again, friends," she said, smiling sheepishly. "It is good to see you all again."

"Sylvia?" Alexandra said.

"You see her?" Samantha questioned.

"Quite a lot has changed since we last communicated, Medium," Sylvia Grace said.

"But... how? And how did you do that?"

"For a ghost, purpose is everything," Sylvia explained. "The malevolent spirits you've faced are powerful not because they are evil but because they have a purpose. Before you five came to this place, I was a wandering spirit, trapped and powerless, doomed to endure my suffering while I waited for an end to it. For as long as I can remember, I had no purpose, and as such, I had no power here. That has changed. You gave me purpose, a reason to fight for what I wanted, and therefore, you have given me power. The power that I will now lend to your cause."

"And how—"

"There will be time later to answer whatever questions you might have," she cut in, "but for now, all you need to know for now is that I have come to aid you in your quest, and I brought some friends."

On cue, two ghosts appeared on either side of her. One was Mark Waters, and the other was the boy ghost Billy Winters.

"You two?" Samantha said.

Billy waved shyly, and Mark nodded in greeting.

"We meet again," Mark said.

"Any chance you got more on the way?" Daniel asked. "Three ghosts against an army isn't exactly encouraging."

"We will suffice," Mark said. "Trust us."

"We don't exactly have much choice here, do we?" Daniel chuckled derisively.

"It won't be long before they attack again," Mark said. "We're here to help, but we cannot do it alone."

"You need bodies to possess," Samantha said.

He nodded. "We will burn up faster without a host vessel."

"But the host vessel will burn up from the possession."

"Normally, that would be the case, but not if we remain passive."

"Like a backseat driver?"

"Precisely. You stay in control while we lend you our power and advise you on how to use it."

"Well, Lila is out cold, and James dislocated his shoulder when he fell," Daniel said. "I don't know about you and Alex, but I can barely move myself."

"Don't worry about that," Mark said. "All you have to do is let us in."

Daniel and Alexandra looked at Samantha. The decision was hers.

Samantha nodded. "Do what you have to do."

Billy flew up in the air and then dived into Alexandra's body.

Her body shuddered, and for a moment, her eyes glowed blue.

Alexandra laughed nervously. "Okay, this feels very strange."

She cocked her head to the side as though listening to something; then, she reached out to touch James' shoulder.

At first, nothing happened, but then her hands began to glow.

"What's happening?" James said. "What are you doing?" He winced in discomfort. "Hey, hold on! Ow! Ow!" His shoulder snapped back into place, and he screamed. "Ahhh! Fuck. Fuck. Fffuhh—wait a minute."

He blinked in confusion, then flexed the shoulder.

"I'm healed?" He chuckled. "I'm healed!"

Alexandra went on to heal Samantha's injuries, and while James was still processing his miraculous recovery, Mark jammed his hand through his chest.

"Jesus Christ!" James's face went pale. "That's a freaking hand in my chest!"

"Calm down, James!" Mark urged. "This will be painful if you fight it."

"Calm down? Ever heard of personal space!"

"Relax and take a deep breath. It will be over before you know it," Samantha said. "The wall protecting us won't last much longer."

"Hey, I didn't consent to— oh fuuuck!"

The rest of Mark continued to get sucked in until he was completely absorbed, and then like Alexandra, his eyes glowed, but unlike her, he collapsed, exhausted.

"That's what you get for fighting it, you idiot," Samantha said.

She wiped the blood off her face to reveal her newly mended skin underneath it, then nodded her appreciation to Alexandra.

"Why the hell did I get picked for this?" James mumbled.

"I'm guessing because Lila and I can actually do damage to these things, so that leaves you three," Samantha said. To Sylvia, she said, "Did I get that right?"

Sylvia nodded, then turned to Daniel.

"Are you ready?"

He nodded.

He shared the same fate as Alexandra and James as Sylvia's ghostly form disappeared into his body.

Alexandra was now crouched over Lila with both hands on her chest.

"This will take a while," she said. "She's really hurt."

"You do what you have to do," Daniel said. "We've got this."

"Hang on a sec, I have no idea what my guy's thing is," James said.

No sooner had he spoken than a light blue aura enveloped him. The aura shaped itself about him and hardened into a solid light construct. When the transformation was done, James stood dressed in medieval armor made of light, complete with a sheathed sword at his side.

"Now that is awesome!" James said.

He drew his sword and, bursting right through the melting ice wall, he charged the ghosts, all the while screaming at the top of his lungs.

With each swing, he tore through multiple ghosts. His moves were efficient and deadly, and nothing like James in full control of his body would have been capable of.

Daniel held out his hand, and in an instant, a floating snowflake manifested in his palm. He did the same with the other hand, and then, as the last of the wall of ice melted out, he rushed forward.

He sent ice shards flying left and right, freezing them one cluster at a time.

But the ghosts had learned from before. They adapted quickly and scattered about. They began to fly around, making themselves harder targets to hit.

Unfazed, Daniel folded his fists, and the ice extinguished, and then, to Samantha's surprise, both hands erupted in flames. As he released his fingers, bolts of fire shot out in different directions. Upon impact, the ghosts burst into flames and spiraled to the ground, where they melted into nothing.

Samantha checked on Alexandra and Lila and found Lila conscious and seated while Alexandra continued to heal her wounds.

It seemed that things were being taken care of nicely on both ends, and Samantha had little to do but watch.

Chapter 19:
DARKNESS FALLING

As the moon hid behind a cluster of clouds, the five of them stood victorious over the ashes and water puddles. Although they were covered in blood, their wounds were healed now.

One by one, the three benevolent ghosts materialized out of the hosts and came to stand before them.

"You guys really helped us out back there," Daniel said. "We owe you our lives. Thank you."

"Yeah. I really thought we were goners," Alexandra said.

Mark smiled warmly and shook his head.

"You've got it all wrong," he said. "It is we who are grateful to you. For fifty years, we have called out for help. Few heard us before you, but no one answered. You five did, and you gave us something we haven't had in decades. You defeated the chief physician, the man who tortured us and killed us for years. You gave us hope and a reason to fight against our enemies. Thank you for that."

"Yeah, well, we still have the warden to beat," Samantha said.

"And we have every faith in you," Sylvia said. "You can do it."

"Any chance you three could team up with us for that particular fight?" Daniel said.

Sylvia shook her head.

"I'm sorry, but we cannot," she said. "We have done what we can. If we went up against the warden, he would bend our minds to his will and turn us against you."

"Plus, we don't have a lot of energy left," Mark added.

"It is alright," Samantha said. "You have done plenty. You helped us back to full strength."

Mark nodded.

"Good luck," he said.

One by one, the ghosts began to disappear.

Billy was the last to go, and as Samantha looked at him, she felt a pang of guilt. They had yet to find his mom, and she had been mean to him, yet he had chosen to help them.

She started to say something, but Alexandra put her hand on her shoulder and shook her head. Instead, she quietly watched him fade away.

"So, what now?" James asked.

"Hey!" Alexandra yelled out. "We beat your minions! You're up next!"

The sound of clapping echoed through the room as the warden reappeared.

"That was certainly entertaining," he said. "But you had some help with that challenge, didn't you?"

"What's it to you?" Daniel said.

"Quite a lot, actually," he said. "You see, I wanted to see your own abilities, not those of a bunch of failed experiments."

"Those failed experiments defeated your army!" Samantha said.

The warden's expression hardened, and his nose turned up in apparent disgust.

"I have no qualms ripping your head from your shoulders, Medium," Warden Blackthorne said. "You are far more expendable than your friends, as I have no use for you. You would be wise to choose your words wisely."

"Go to hell!" Samantha said.

The warden lifted a finger, and immediately, Lila and Daniel stepped in front of Samantha while James and Alexandra guarded her sides.

He cracked a smile and lowered his finger.

"How sweet of you," he said. "Your camaraderie matters little, however, because each of you will be undertaking your next challenge... alone."

He exploded into a black smoke cloud that quickly filled the entire lobby.

*****

Lila had no memory of blacking out, but when her consciousness returned, she was far away from the asylum in a place she knew more than any other: home.

She was seated in the living room. The television was on, and her favorite show was playing, but her eyes were fixed on the wall. She tried to turn her eyes elsewhere to look around the room, but that was impossible. She could not impose her will on her limbs. It was as if she were merely a guest in her own body. But she could hear, and she heard the heavy pitter-patter of raindrops beating on the roof and on the tarmac outside.

Lila also noticed that, for some reason, she was frightened. She was usually timid whenever her mother was home and tried to stay off her radar, but this was more than that. It was a very familiar feeling, too, but she could not yet understand why.

While Lila had yet to figure out what was happening, she was certain that this was no ordinary illusion. For one, she was very aware that the world she was in wasn't real. She remembered her friends and the warden and the asylum.

But there was something personal about the illusion, too, and it was not just because she was in a recreation of her own home. If she had to guess, she was in a memory, and it was not a recent memory either. She could tell at a glance because the walls were lavender, and the last time they had been so was shortly after her father moved out. Her mother had gone into a mad frenzy and set about changing things all around the house like she was trying to erase any memory of him.

As though to solidify her conclusion, she heard footsteps and turned to see her sister *walk* into the room.

She wanted to call out her name and hug her, but instead, her head turned away, and she returned to staring at the wall.

"Lila, I am so sorry!" Bobby said. "I tried to explain that it was my fault, but she wouldn't listen."

Lila felt as though a bucket of cold water had been poured over her back. This was her memory, alright. It was the memory of the worst day of her life.

Lila's mother had never approved of her powers and forbade her from ever using them, claiming they were evil. Less than an hour ago, she had walked in on her using the very same powers to make her sister float around the room, and she had been furious.

She then sent Lila out to wait for her in the living room, shut the door after her, and then proceeded to yell at Bobby.

Just as she knew the past, Lila also knew what was about to happen next, and without meaning to, she counted down the seconds in her mind until...

"Lila Sakarov!" her mother bellowed from the other room.

The young and terrified Lila jumped out of her chair and backed away as her mother walked into the room.

Lila remained wary of her mother to this day, but as she had grown taller since she wasn't used to seeing her mother tower over her. It was refreshingly frightening, especially coupled with the fiery look that burned in her eyes.

"Mom, I... I..."

"How many times have I warned you against using your devilish magic in this house?"

"It's not devilish magic. It's—"

"Shut up!"

"Mom, I've told you already; it was my fault!" Bobby tried to chip in. "I asked her to do it."

"You stay the hell out of this, Bobby!"

"Mom, I'm sorry," Lila said. "It was just a little fun—"

"A little fun?" her mother snapped. "You used your devil magic on your sister for fun?"

"It's not..."

"You dropped your sister from the ceiling for *fun*?"

The moment Lila had seen her mother standing in the doorway, her mind went blank and she let go of Bobby. Luckily, she had been hovering over the bed and landed with minimal discomfort, but the way her mother had seen it, she might as well have pile-driven her through the ground.

"I didn't—"

"I should have done something about this long ago," she went on. "Oh, I blame myself for this nonsense. As a matter of fact, I blame your father. I told him we should take you to see a priest and get the demons out of you, but he said no. Look at this now. You just tried to kill your sister!"

"I didn't try to kill her. I—"

"I don't want to hear another word of this. You will go to your room and stay there until dinnertime, and then tomorrow, I will take you to see Father Fletcher."

"I'm not going to see the priest!" Lila yelled.

"Are you talking back to me?" her mother said. "Have you lost your entire mind?"

"Why won't you listen to me?"

"You possessed spawn of the devil!"

She grabbed Lila harshly by the wrist, but Lila tugged her arm free and backed away.

"I am not possessed!" Lila said. "And it's not devil magic. I have superpowers, like the X-Men!"

Lila— the older one— knew what was coming next and mentally prepared herself, but nothing could have prepared younger Lila for it.

Her mother's hand moved faster than her eyes could follow, and the next moment, her face felt like it had been lit on fire.

Lila was stunned and blinded as she held her smarting face.

Her mother's chest was heaving now. "For the last time, get in your room! And this time, no dinner for you, you disrespectful child!"

Lila took one step back and then another, and then she turned and walked out of the house.

"Lila!" Bobby called out to her.

Lila did not stop on the front porch. She walked out, past the driveway, and into the street. The rain was coming down in buckets. Coupled with the merciless wind, it felt like she was being pelted by small rocks.

She heard the door open and shut and heard footsteps follow her into the rain.

"Lila, stop! Please!" Bobby called after her.

"Go back in the house, Bobby!" Lila retorted.

"You have nowhere to go, and it's freaking raining. She didn't mean to react like that, Lila. You know she doesn't mean those things. Please, come back inside."

Lila turned around. Bobby was standing in the shade of the neighbor's tree as its long, thick branches grew into their front yard.

"Leave me alone!"

"Lila, please," Bobby pleaded. "Just come in the house and apologize."

"So, you think she's right?" Lila said. "You think that I'm demon-possessed? That my powers are evil?"

"No, but you know how she is. Just tell her what she wants to hear. I'm sure she won't even remember all that talk about the priest in the morning."

"No. I'm not going back in there until... until Dad gets home."

"Lila, Dad's not coming home tonight."

"Then I'll come back in the morning."

"Don't be ridiculous. You'll catch a cold out here, and you know how you get when you're sick."

"Leave me alone, Bobby." She resumed walking away.

"Lila, come on!"

"I said, leave me alone!" Lila yelled, facing her sister once more.

Acting impulsively, she sent out a telekinetic blast, aiming for one of the branches in the tree.

Her intention was to scare her sister off, but in her anger, she lost control of her powers. She watched in horror as her sister was lifted into the air and thrown backward, screaming in terror.

Her body broke the porch railing and hit the side of the house at an awkward angle before she fell to the ground in a crumpled heap.

"Bobby!" she screamed.

She ran towards her sister but stopped as the front door opened and her mother stepped out of the house.

"Bobby, get back in the house right now!" she was saying.

First, she looked at Lila with visible disgust; then she noticed the body, and disgust became dread.

"Bobby?" she said. "Oh my God!"

She dropped to her knees and picked Bobby off the ground.

"Bobby, wake up!"

Lila tried to go closer, but her mother heard her coming and fixed a warning glare at her.

"Mom, I..." Lila said.

"Don't you call me that, and don't you dare come in this house!"

She carried Bobby into the house, and Lila was left standing in the rain.

"Mommy!" Lila said, her voice breaking. "Mommy, please!"

The weight of her sins bore down heavily on her, and Lila's legs gave out. As she fell to the ground, her gaze was drawn to the fallen branch, the intended object of her anger.

"What have I done?" she muttered. "What have I done?"

Lila shut her eyes and tried to will herself back to reality, all to no avail. She did not want to be there. She did not want to feel all those feelings again. She did not want to be the monster who crippled her sister.

She wanted to die.

She deserved to die.

The porch light went off, and then the streetlamps fizzled out one by one until Lila was plunged into absolute darkness.

Control of her body returned to her, and Lila looked around, but there was nothing to see. Until there was.

Her mother's head popped into view from the darkness right in front of her.

"Devil spawn!" she screamed.

Lila scrambled away in terror, but as she came to a stop, another face popped up from the side.

"You evil child!" The face and the voice were her father's.

"Daddy, wait, no I—"

He disappeared like a candle being blown out, except the smoke reformed into a new face.

"Monster!" Bobby said. "I hate you!"

"Hate you!" her mother echoed as she made a reappearance.

"You destroyed your own family," her father's face said. "What kind of monster would do that?"

"I didn't mean to. You have to understand, I—"

The face morphed into Father Fletcher.

"God hates you, Lila Sakarov," he said. "Do you know why? It's because you're a monster. A vile creature. An abomination."

"Abomination!" Her mother appeared once again. "Demon-possessed child!"

"Stop saying that!" Lila screamed. "Stop saying that!"

She shut her eyes and covered her ears to try and blot out their voices. To her surprise, it worked.

When she eventually opened her eyes, though, her sister's face was waiting for her like they were playing peek-a-boo.

"You took my life away from me!" she said. "You ruined my future! I hate you so much! Mom was right. You really are a monster."

One by one, the others popped up, and they echoed the word "monster" over and over again. They threw in a few choice words like "evil creature" and "devil spawn," too, as they hovered in front of Lila's face wherever she looked.

"I'm sorry!" Lila cried. "I'm sorry. Please stop!"

But the voices did not stop. They rang in her ears and bounced around the walls of her mind. They were hell-bent on making sure she understood just how evil she and her powers were.

She sat on the floor, hugging her knees to her chest as she rocked back and forth.

Suddenly, the lights came on again, dispelling all the phantom heads at once, and Lila was back on the street. The rain was still falling, and the wind raged on, but she felt none of it.

She rose to her feet, confused.

This was not a part of the memory. In her memory, she remained there, kneeling in the rain, until the ambulance showed up, and it was only at the paramedic's insistence that she finally went inside, but not before she watched them take her sister away in a stretcher with a neck brace around her neck.

So, if this wasn't a memory, what was this?

"It's not your fault," someone said.

She heard a familiar rhythmic squeaking and turned to find a wheelchair-bound Bobby wheeling herself over.

Lila almost laughed, although there was not an ounce of humor in her body.

"What?" she said.

Bobby wheeled past her and turned to face her.

"I said it is not your fault."

This time, Lila did laugh.

"How can you say such a thing?"

Bobby cocked her head to the side.

"Lila..." she said.

"No!" Lila said. "How can you say that? You know what I did! I hurt you! You know better than anyone that what happened that night was my fault! Why are you lying to me?"

"You're asking the wrong question, Lila," Bobby said. The real question here is why you are lying to yourself."

"What?"

Bobby turned her wheelchair to face the house.

"Lila, come here for a moment," she said.

Lila did as she asked.

She was about to question her when the front door opened, and younger Lila came storming out.

They watched her stomp into the street, and on cue, Bobby came running after her.

Lila watched the exchange halfheartedly, anticipating that tragic moment.

"Lila." Bobby nudged her. "Pay close attention."

Lila rolled her eyes at the assumption that she did not already know what happened next, but she focused on the younger versions of them.

"Lila, Dad's not coming home tonight," Younger Bobby was saying.

Perhaps it was because this was a memory, but Lila could hear them just fine despite the howling wind.

"Then I'll come back in the morning."

"Don't be ridiculous. You'll catch a cold out here, and you know how you get when you're sick."

"Leave me alone, Bobby."

Lila watched her younger self walking away and wondered what would have happened if Bobby had not called out to her once more. She had nowhere to go. She barely knew anywhere, and even if she did, the weather was terrible.

"Lila, come on!" Younger Bobby pleaded.

"I said, leave me alone!" Younger Lila yelled.

She turned around as she did, but surprisingly, her hands stayed at her sides. It was like watching an actor miss a cue.

"What the...?" Older Lila said.

"Shh." Older Bobby held a finger to her lips then she pointed.

Just then, there was a loud crack and they all looked up to watch as a large branch snapped off the tree and plummeted towards Bobby.

"Bobby!"

It was both Lilas that screamed but the younger one acted. Her hands went up instinctively to push her sister out of harm's way, but in her panic, she overdid it and young Bobby went sailing through the air.

This part fell in line with Lila's memory and the rest of it went by in a blur until the street was empty again.

Lila's throat was dry and her vision was hazy with tears unshed.

"What..." Her voice cracked. "Um... What was that?

"That was the night of the accident, Lila."

"N-no," Lila said. "That's not how it happened. I—"

Bobby reached out and grabbed her hand.

"You lied to yourself, Lila," she said. "Mom's words were deeply ingrained in your mind, so much so that you perceived yourself as a monster and built this fake memory to fit into the narrative you found convenient. You saved your sister from certain death and accidentally hurt her in the process, but your intentions were good. You never lost control. Lila, this is the truth. The real truth. It is high time you see it for yourself and forgive yourself. Because Bobby has forgiven you."

More than anything, Lila wanted to believe the words she was hearing, but she thought about the arguments and about her father's absence. She was still responsible for that.

"But... Dad left because of me," she said. "Because he could no longer stand having a daughter like me."

"Lila, you're not the reason that he left. Your mother is."

"What?"

"Mom and Dad fought a lot. Many of those times, it was because of the way she treated you and talked about you and your powers. He saw you as a blessing. He loved you with all his heart, powers and all. Even after the accident, his love for you didn't change. Perhaps he didn't show it enough because he was away often, but it is true. Mom hated that because when she tried to take you to Father Fletcher, he stood against it. He also stood against having you see a shrink or a doctor or getting the government involved; and yes, these are actual ideas she had. Eventually, he filed for divorce, hoping he could take you l from him, but she won custody."

Lila was quiet for a while, but tears streamed down her face ceaselessly.

"I... I..." she stammered. "I'm not a monster?"

Bobby shook her head. "No, Lila. You're not a monster. You were never a monster or anything else Mom called you, for that matter. You're a good sister, a good daughter, an amazing friend, and a powerful psychic. Open your eyes, Lila."

"I'm not a monster..." she breathed in relief. "I'm not a monster."

She fell on her knees and wrapped her arms around her sister.

Everything turned smoky and like dust being sucked into a vacuum, the illusory world receded from her as the asylum reformed around her, but the arms around her remained, as did the shoulder she rested against.

Curious, she pulled away.

"Bobby?" she said.

It wasn't Bobby.

Daniel grinned back at her sheepishly.

"Sorry to disappoint you," he said.

"You... In the illusion, you were the one?"

"I'm not entirely sure what 'the one' entails, but I was here talking to you."

"How?"

"I figured out that the illusion was fueled by negative influence and meant to show us visions of experiences that haunt our past, and I knew the one experience that haunted yours," he said. "Plus, you were mumbling a bit."

"So... the version of the accident I saw. Was that some lie you somehow conjured up to get me to snap out of it?" Her heart was on the verge of breaking. All it would take to send her over the edge was a 'yes' from him.

"No," he said. "That was the real thing. One hundred percent."

"But how did you know when I didn't?"

"That day in the cafe, I saw your past when I touched your sweater. I saw the accident as it happened, not as you saw it. It is impossible for my vision to be false."

"Oh, Daniel!" She hugged him again. "You have no idea how much this means to me."

"Any chance it makes up for everything else you hate me for?"

"Absolutely!"

She felt him smile as his cheek pressed against hers. "Great."

Around them, she found the others lying on the floor.

Something occurred to Lila, and she looked at him again.

"Wait, they're all trapped in illusions too?"

"Yeah," Daniel said. "Haunting memories and fears."

"So, how are you standing here, awake?"

"I dealt with my past a long time ago, Lila. Never again."

Chapter 20:
Evil Company, Good Manners

A few feet away from Lila, Alexandra found herself trapped in a significantly different illusion from that of Lila's, but like Lila's, this one found the very thing she dreaded and began to gnaw at it.

There were no unresolved traumas or haunting memories in Alexandra's past. She had been born into a loving, moderate-sized family and hardly ever knew want. Her mother was a college lecturer in a town thirty minutes outside of Ravensbrook, and her father was a football coach at her high school with a hobby as an inventor, but that had changed a few years back when a big company had taken interest in her father's invention: a self-watering plant system that could tell when plants were thirsty and automatically water them. Her father had had to move to the new town to work on the project, and her mother had gone with him to support him— she had recently even gotten a job as a secretary at a law firm.

Alexandra's oldest brother Stanley started out as a hothead jock with dreams of playing professional football, that was until he discovered his love for acting. He was currently working on a long-running series in Chicago. At first, he had been offered a small role, but recently, he informed them that he had been promoted to a series regular due to the attention from fans. The immediate younger sibling was Amanda. Amanda was Alexandra's only sister and so despite the age gap, they were close. So close that after leaving town to study literature in the university of her choice, and almost getting married to her college sweetheart, she returned home to take care of Alexandra after their parents moved away. The younger brother Tim was the jock who stayed on the field and was currently trying out for a small-time football club in Chicago while he bunked with Stanley.

All in all, Alexandra's life was great. It was not perfect, but she loved it. And it was precisely for this reason that her vision began with her standing in a foggy open field in the middle of nowhere, surrounded by the battered and bloodied corpses of her family members.

Alexandra was rooted to the spot, her body frozen solid while her mind panicked and her heartbeat clocked at a hundred and twenty per minute.

The fog began to recede as she looked on and with each square inch revealed, she added a new body to the list. There was James, then Lila, then Samantha, then Daniel, and it did not stop there. Next came Wesley from the cafe, then Bethany from the library, then Ricky from chess club, and on and on until she could no longer even put a name to the faces.

"Oh my God," she gasped, finding her voice at last.

While she was still struggling to process what was happening, a bright light shone through the horizon. She looked at it and, to her horror, found a missile nosediving towards the field.

Just before impact, she felt a tug in her stomach, and then she was pulled through space.

When the sensation ceased, she was sitting in the living room of her home. Her parents and siblings were present, talking and laughing as they often did before everyone moved away. Amanda and Tim were playing a game on the television while Stanley and their father discussed football. Their mother sat next to Alexandra, contentedly watching them get loud.

Alexandra wanted to laugh along with them, but she couldn't. A sense of foreboding lingered in her heart like something bad was about to happen.

She was still wrestling with the feeling when the door burst open, and men with guns stormed the house. Without so much as an explanation, they took aim with their guns and sprayed bullets all about the room.

By the time the gunfire ceased, Alexandra realized that she was the only one spared, but she might as well have been shot in the chest with the pain
she felt in her heart. Once again, she was standing in the middle of a massacre with her loved ones as the victims.

As if someone hit reset, the scene went back to the beginning. They were alive again, playing their games and discussing football like nothing had happened.

"Hey, something bad is about to happen," Alexandra called out.

But no one heard her. No one was listening.

"Everyone, we need to leave. Or hide. Something! And I mean now."

Again, she was ignored.

"Hey, guys!" she yelled.

This time, she got their attention.

"What is it, Alex?" Amanda asked.

"I said something bad is about to ha—"

The door burst open. The men rushed in, shots were fired, and her family died.

And then the scene reset.

"No, no, no!" Alexandra cried. "Not again! Not again!"

More talking. More laughing.

"Guys, we have to leave!" Alexandra yelled.

They stopped and looked at her.

"What is it, Alex?" Amanda asked again.

"We have to leave. Some bad men are coming to kill you. We have to leave!"

They stared blankly at her, then they laughed.

"Jeez, Alex. Have you been playing too many video games lately?" Stanley said.

They returned to what they were doing, ignoring her even as she continued to plead with them to take her seriously.

A third time, the men came and killed them.

As it had happened twice before, she saw it coming, but that did not mean she was prepared for it. She shut her eyes and with every gunshot, she flinched. When the shooting stopped, she had tears running down her face.

"Please," she said. "No more."

But the scene reset and the laughing resumed.

Like the thunder after lightning, the shooting came swiftly and surely.

This was Alexandra's greatest fear manifested on repeat: seeing a tragic future that she could not prevent.

*****

Of the five of them, Samantha was probably the luckiest when it came to her powers. Not only had mediumship been heard of in her family, but it was also, to some extent, hereditary. Her mother did not have the power, and neither did her grandma, but one of her distant aunties did, so her great-grandma and those who didn't have powers still had stories to tell her.

When Samantha was much younger, she heard a story that stuck with her. It was the story of a particular medium who had her body taken over by a legion of ghosts. To her, that was the most terrifying thing she had ever heard, and to this day, that held true. And so, when Samantha opened her eyes to the illusion, there she stood, stuck in place like a scarecrow in a cornfield, alive and aware, and yet unable to move or speak as malevolent ghosts ripped her open from the inside out in their battle for control.

*****

Back in the waking world, Lila and Daniel were trying to figure out how to wake the others as they knelt over their sleeping motionless bodies.

"What do you mean you don't know how to free the others?" Lila said.

"I mean, I got lucky with you. I knew what you were afraid of, and I knew how to guide you out of it. I don't have any idea what the others fear."

"How hard could it be to guess?"

"Why don't you take a shot at it and let me know?"

Lila did not have a reply there. Her eyes moved from one unconscious figure to the next.

"I say we should start with James," she said.

"Why?"

"For one, if anyone can figure out what the others are afraid of, it's him," she said.

"And who's gonna tell us what he's afraid of?"

"That brings us to point two, I think I know," she said.

"You do?"

She inched closer to James.

"James is sensitive to the emotions of others, and sometimes that can be overwhelming. I imagine he would be afraid of that."

"So how do you propose we help him? And that's if you're right."

"I haven't quite gotten to that part yet." She picked up his head and placed it in her lap.

To both their surprises, James snorted, smacked his lips, and rolled over. Lila and Daniel locked eyes.

"Are you sure he's trapped in a nightmare?" Daniel asked.

"Actually, I think he's... asleep," Lila said.

"Asleep?"

Lila shoved him off her leg; as he hit the floor, he let out a loud snore.

"This bastard," Lila swore.

"How is this possible?"

"I say we ask him."

She slapped James right across the face, and he sat bolt upright.

"It's Warden Blackthorne!" he said, looking around wildly. When he recognized them, he relaxed. "Oh. It's you guys. What happened?"

"You were asleep!" Lila accused.

"Was I?" He scratched his head. "I guess I was."

"How?"

"How did I fall asleep?"

"Yes! The warden's powers put us through haunting visions, and all it did to you was put you to sleep? You, of all people? I thought you were sensitive to emotional attacks."

"Yes,,.." James said. "Typically, that is the case, but this wasn't an ordinary emotional attack. His power causes us to attack ourselves with our own fears."

"What? Is this the part where you say you don't have fears?"

"Oh, I do. Several. But no one here has a greater mastery over their emotions than I do. I might not have conquered my fears, but I understand and respect them. I dealt with the illusion fairly easily, but the effort knocked me out."

Lila and Daniel nodded simultaneously.

"How much of that did you understand?" Lila asked.

"Not much. You?" Daniel replied.

"Same.

"Okay enough about me," James said. "How did you two get free?"

"Daniel got out first, and then he helped me," Lila said.

James' brows rose. "Really?"

"Yeah," Lila said.

James continued to stare at Daniel until it got awkward.

"What?" Daniel said.

"Nothing."

"Well, can you help us save the others?"

"Right "

He crawled over to Alexandra and cupped her cheek. Quickly, he retracted his hand.

"What is it?" Daniel asked.

"She's stuck in a loop watching her family get murdered over and over while she tries to save them," he said.

"Jesus..." Lila said.

"I'm going in," he said. "I'll be back in a jiffy."

He grabbed her shoulders with both hands, and his head lolled to the side, indicating he was no longer conscious.

Daniel glanced at his watch.

"How long do you think it'll take him to—"

"Ahhh!" Alexandra screamed and sat up; eyes wide open. "Make it stop!"

She shoved James, who let out a high-pitched shriek as he fell over and tumbled.

"Ow," he muttered. "Is this my thank you?"

Daniel was by Alexandra's side in an instant, hugging her tight to keep her from swinging her hands at anyone else.

"Alex!" he said. "Alex, it's Daniel!"

"You're all going to die!" she screamed. "All of you! Why aren't you listening to me? Why is no one listening to me? I'm trying to save you! I'm trying to save everyone! I'm... I'm trying..."

"Alex," Daniel called out again, softly this time "Alex, it's over. No more loops. No more dead bodies. It's over. Look around."

There was a desperation in her eyes as she took in her surroundings anew, holding on to Daniel's hands like it was all that was keeping her tethered.

She looked around, checking all the entrances as if expecting something or someone to emerge.

"I don't want to go back there, " she pleaded. "Please don't make me go back there."

James joined Daniel on Alexandra's other side and took her hand in his.

"You're awake now," he said. "Your family is safe. Your friends are all here."

Slowly but surely, Alexandra's panicked breathing began to slow until she found a steady rhythm.

"Are you with us?" James inquired.

Alexandra nodded.

"Thank you," she said.

James shifted his gaze to Daniel; his expression was asking, "You got this?"

Daniel nodded. He was now gently rocking Alexandra in his arms. "Go. Bring Sam back to us."

Reassured, James left them and made a beeline for Samantha.

Like he did with Alexandra, he first cupped her cheeks.

"Oh..." he said, his tone flat.

He lifted her to a sitting position, got behind her, and put his arms around her stomach, underneath her arms. Then like before, his body went limp.

No more than five seconds later, a piercing, gut-wrenching scream rents the air as Samantha awakens.

She screamed until she ran out of breath, and she screamed some more. And when her strength finally left her body, she collapsed in a loud and uncontrollable sobbing fit, held upright only by James' arms around her. It felt like her pain had been personal as well as physical.

Lila felt bolts of electricity racing through her body with each outburst. Both girls were broken and she could not help but wonder how much worse it would have been for her had Daniel not stepped in the way he did.

"I've got you," James was saying. "It's over now. I've got you."

His eyes were shut tight, and Lila could feel his powers taking effect even over her. It felt like her father's hug, her sister's laugh, and the taste of her grandma's cookies all smushed together—like everything that made the world feel good and right again.

The feeling abruptly faded away as the air started to grow tense.

"Well, aren't you lot just full of surprises," Warden Blackthorne said.

He was not physically present this time around.

Caught off guard, they put their emotions aside and jumped to their feet, unprepared but determined to face whatever he threw at them next.

"We played your game twice now and we won," Lila said. "So why don't you put on your big boy pants and come face us like a man?"

"You think the game is over?" His tone was mocking. "You think you've won?"

"We beat your stupid illusions!" Alexandra said.

Her defiance was astonishing considering the state she was in a mere few minutes ago. She really was tough as nails.

"Did you now?" he said. "Did *all* of you beat my 'stupid' illusions?"

"What is that supposed to mean?" Alexandra said.

"I think a few of you are starting to realize what I mean," he said. "But here's a hint: not all your friends are to be trusted."

Lila looked at James and as she expected, his eyes were fixed on Daniel with suspicion.

"Daniel," he said. "Tell me again, how exactly did you get out of the illusion."

"What the hell are you going on about?" Daniel snapped.

"Somehow, you were able to get out of the illusion before the rest of us. How did you manage that?"

"I already told you that!"

"No, you didn't," James said calmly.

"Yes, I did." He paused. "Well, maybe not you, but I told Lila."

"Well, I'm here now so tell me,"

"How about you back the hell up before I hurt you?"

There was a worried silence because James had not moved a step, least of all in Daniel's direction.

"I'm not trying to get confrontational. Just answer the question. How did you get free?"

"I already faced my fears; now, if you don't want me to face you next, I'd suggest you get the fuck out of my face!"

"I'm not in your face, Daniel," James said. "Is that what you're afraid of? Getting beat up by me?"

Daniel closed the distance between them so fast that no one saw him coming, least of all James. He floored him with one powerful swing.

"Daniel!" Samantha scolded.

"Oh my God!" Alexandra said.

"You wanna say that again?" Daniel said, ignoring everyone but James.

James was more stunned than hurt, but he quickly recovered and got up.

"James, back down," Samantha said. "That's enough."

"No. The warden said one of us was not to be trusted, and he's acting rather untrustworthy right now."

He rushed at Daniel, aiming for his midsection, but unlike him, Daniel had actual fighting experience and evaded his attack, then scored a clean hit to James' jaw, knocking him to the ground.

"You'd take the warden's words over your friendship?"

James lunged forward and tackled him to the ground.

"What would he gain from lying to us?" he said as he rained blows onto Daniel, whose arms were up to protect his face. He's already more powerful than anything we faced."

"He'd have us fighting each other instead of fighting him!" Alexandra said.

Daniel got his leg under James' stomach and kicked him back. In a flash, both men were up and ready to throw blows, but Alexandra got in the middle of the two men.

"Knock it off, James," she said. "And you too, Daniel!"

"You're not fooling me with your little act, Alex," Daniel said. I know you're on his side—not mine!

"What?" Alexandra said.

He tried to shove her aside, but she expertly grabbed his wrist and pinned it to his back, then forced him to his knees, where she held him in a submission hold. He struggled against her grip, but she did not let up.

"What are you talking about? I'm not on anyone's side. There are no sides!"

"Yes, there is!" James said. "And it's looking like he's not on ours."

"You're not helping!"

"Not helping?" James scoffed. "From the beginning, he's always known more than the rest of us..."

"Because he's seen more than the rest of us."

"...and now he conveniently breaks out of the illusion like it's nothing."

"What are you saying?"

"I'm saying he's always been suspicious, and now he's lying to us. He's not to be trusted!"

Daniel took advantage of the distraction and hit Alexandra in the gut with the back of his head, then went after James.

Samantha stepped in, but she was no fighter, and he shoved her aside with relative ease, barely breaking a stride.

Before he and James could exchange fists some more, however, both of them got lifted off the ground and pulled apart.

"Guys!" Lila said while casually suspending both men in mid-air. "The warden wasn't lying, but the hint was not for us. It was for him!"

"What?" James and Alexandra said in unison.

"Daniel broke out of the illusion," she said. "But he hadn't dealt with all his fears. One fear, probably the greatest one, ate its way out, and it's manifesting in reality."

"Yeah, I'm going to need more than that," James said.

"Remember when we first met in the cafe? He was in disguise because he didn't trust us. He has been hurt many times in the past, and his fear is this. His fear is us, his friends, turning against him! When the warden said some of our friends were not to be trusted, he was adding fuel to the fear in his heart. Daniel is no enemy, and he is no spy just because you dislike him, James! He's our friend, and right now, he needs our help just like we've needed his at one point or the other. Get it together!"

She gently lowered both men, and Daniel immediately scrambled away until his back hit the wall, and then he sank to the floor. He looked like a cornered animal with fear in his eyes.

"Oh my God," James said. "I was so... blinded. How did I not see?"

"Can you help him?" Samantha said.

"I can," James said. "But it's not as simple as it was with you and Alexandra. You two suffered through nightmares conjured up by your subconscious, but he's plagued by the darkness of his past. I think Lila is in the best position to understand."

Lila pursed her lips and blinked back tears as James approached Daniel.

"I'll hold him down for you," Lila offered.

"No," he said. "Don't cause him any more distress."

He hunched over and held up his hands to make himself less threatening.

"I come in peace," he said.

Daniel flinched as James extended his hand to touch his shoulder, but he did not attempt to run away.

"In his mind, he's reverted to his younger, more aggressive self," James explained. I sense such overwhelming pain spanning years of his life. The world hurt him so much that he learned to throw the first blow. But deep down, he's scared of everything and everyone. He recognizes that they can hurt him, and so he expects them to."

James retracted his hand and then moved to sit next to Daniel. He gestured for the others to join them, and they sat around in a circle.

"I'm James," he said. "That's Lila, and Alexandra, and Samantha. They're your best friends in the whole wide world. Me, I hate your guts too much to qualify, but we do get along when we're not butting heads. I know it's hard for you to believe it, but you're safe now, Daniel. You have friends who actually do love you this time. It's okay. I promise you that things will turn out alright for adult Daniel. You can let go now. We'll take care of him."

Daniel looked at each and every one of them and then back to James.

"Promise?"

"We promise."

His eyes softened; a mix of confusion and recognition shone through.

"Guys," he said, "what's going on?"

"You don't remember?" Alexandra asked.

"I... I think I was having a dream and..." He glanced over at James. "You hit me!"

"Okay, but you hit me first."

"I did what?"

Lila tackled him in a hug.

"Hey! What's this for?" Daniel asked.

"We're just glad to have you back, Danny," Samantha said.

"It's still Daniel."

Chapter 21:
ABSOLUTION

The warden's presence disappeared into the heart of the asylum after his hold on Daniel was broken, but the barrier remained intact.

Thanks to James' powers, the effects of the illusions quickly faded and their minds were sharp as ever, which was good because it was time to properly confront the warden once and for all.

They shared the remainder of their food, and then it was time to seek out Warden Blackthorne. The ground floor was clear, so they took to the stairs and searched out the floors above.

As they climbed, they sensed his presence growing stronger and stronger until they came to the cafeteria.

They pushed the door open, and there he was, seated at one of the tables in the center of the hall, eating something out of a plate as ghostly as he.

"When I first caught wind of the chief physician's demise at your hands, I assumed you five had gotten lucky." He rose from his seat, and the food vanished. "Doctor von Menschen was a brilliant man, but he could be careless. I assumed that was a flaw that you exploited in order to defeat him. In so doing, I underestimated you a lot in the same way the doctor underestimated you, I imagine. This slight on my part has cost me valuable energy I have harnessed over the year, and so I assure you, it will not happen again."

"That's a lot of big talk for a dead man," Daniel said.

"You will share the same ending as your friend," Samantha said. "And you should know, it was I, the worthless medium, who dealt the final blow."

The warden had a smile on his face, but it did not touch his eyes. His eyes burned with the promise of a slow, painful death.

He lifted the table with a flick of his hand and launched it at them.

No one flinched, and rightly so because it stopped in mid-air and gently came to rest somewhere to the side.

"Oh, look! I can do that, too," Lila said.

"You tried to break our spirits, and when you failed, you tried to break our minds," Alexandra said. "You failed at that too, and so you tried to tear us apart. You did all this because you were too much of a coward to face us head-on, weren't you? Because you're not so sure you'll win."

"Fascinating hypothesis," Warden Blackthorne said. "Do you care to test it out?"

"I mean, we're here, aren't we?" Daniel shrugged.

He picked up a rock and launched it right at Warden Blackthorne's head.

The warden caught it and crushed it.

"Good. We can hit you," he said. "Just checking."

"It's really not too late to surrender," James said. "The odds are not in your favor."

"Then allow me to even things out." Warden Blackthorne floated to the ceiling and stretched out his hands. "Come."

It was that scene from his office all over again.

Malevolent spirits began to climb out of the floor on either side of him; five menacing skeletal-looking specters.

"I mean, that is pretty even," James said. "I didn't expect you to play fair."

"James," Daniel said.

"Yeah?"

"Please shut up."

"Right."

"Attack," Warden Blackthorne ordered.

The specters took flight at once.

"Scatter!" Alexandra yelled.

One of them had already set its sights on James and made a beeline for him, but Samantha stepped in and punched a hole right through it, tearing open its midsection.

To her surprise, however, rather than dissipate into nothing, its body reformed, and instantaneously too.

"That's not good," Samantha said.

It came for Samantha this time and knocked her off her feet.

She did not get a chance to get off the floor as the malevolent spirit swooped in like a hawk going for the kill, but before it could claw out her eyes, it was pulled back and then brutally torn apart by telekinesis.

Even that did not stop it.

Again, the spirit recovered from an attack that should have ended it.

"What the hell are these guys made of?" James said. "It's like they've evolved or something."

"Look out!" Alexandra yelled out in warning.

Daniel ducked out of the way and ran for the counter.

The malevolent spirit swerved and followed him.

He grabbed a tray off the counter and held it up as the spirit struck. Its sharp, claw-like fingers tore through the metal tray like it was nothing, but he smacked it across the face.

"Guys, we might need a plan!" James yelled. "By that, I mean I need a plan! Fast!"

His voice came from the other end of the hall, and she found him running with a ghost hot on his heels.

With Lila holding off two of the malevolent ghosts, Samantha was the only one free to act. Working out her plan as she went, she ran after him.

"James, head towards Danny!" she yelled.

Surprisingly, neither of them questioned her instructions. James just did as she asked while Daniel continued to chuck dinner plates at his opponent.

Samantha doubled her speed heading just ahead of James as though to intercept him. She climbed onto a table and as James ran past, she leaped into the air.

Her calculation was on point and as the ghost rocketed after James like a horse with blinders on, she latched onto it, wrapping her arms around its neck.

"Gotcha!" she announced.

The ghost reared like a wild stallion and thrashed about, hoping to dismount her, but she held on tight. He flew up towards the high ceiling and then started to descend rapidly

"If a blow won't do the trick," she said. "Here's something more personal, you bastard!"

She reached up and grabbed both sides of his head. Her blue aura manifested like when she had been locked in battle with Doctor von Menschen.

"It is way past your forever bedtime," Samantha said. "Go. To. Sleep."

He screeched and then went poof.

Unfortunately for Samantha, that meant she was now free falling towards the ground at life-threatening speed.

"Coming in hot!" she screamed. "Help!"

Lila reached up and slowed her fall but before she could lower her to the ground, the ghosts she had been fending off broke free of her grip and attacked her.

Her focus shifted long enough to hold back one of them, but Samantha slipped through her grasp.

As the distance between her and the floor reduced, Samantha braced for impact, hoping to escape with one or two broken bones. Down below, Lila managed to briefly get the situation under control enough to slow her down further.

Unfortunately, that did not last long as the ghost literally tore away its upper half from the rest of its body, and like a rag doll, Lila was knocked over a table, leaving Samantha to fall for a third time.

Luckily, Lila had given James ample time to move in and soften her landing with his body. She had also slowed her landing enough to make sure neither of them died upon impact.

"And they say chivalry is dead," Samantha quipped.

"That definitely hurt," James wheezed. "You mind getting off now?"

She rolled off him and helped him up.

"This is not very effective," Samantha commented.

"You think?"

"I just saved your life. You have no right to be snippy."

"Cool. You think you can do that four more times?"

"Shut up."

In truth, Samantha couldn't. The malevolent spirit she exorcised was nearly as stubborn as Doctor von Menschen. Not to mention, the others did not share their energy with her. She barely had enough strength to exorcise one, much less four.

She quickly assessed the situation.

Daniel had run out of kitchen utensils to throw but had now found a stick. Alexandra was unarmed but she was doing a good job of evading. She was likely using her precognition to see the moves before the ghost made them.

Warden Blackthorne was still hovering above them. She had a feeling he was focused on regenerating his forces and that was why he was playing keep away.

"That won't do at all," she muttered. "Hey, Lila!"

"What?" Lila was back on her feet and had both her attackers pinned to the wall on either side of her.

"Any chance you could bring him down?" She gestures towards the warden.

"One sec," she said.

She slammed the ghost on her right into the wall and before he could recover, she sent a whole table flying at him. The table broke in two and buried itself in the wall.

With her hand free, she reached up to grab the warden and tried to pull. The effort was clear but the warden did not budge.

"I can't move him," Lila said. "He's too strong."

A stupid idea came to Samantha.

"Well, can you get me to him?"

Lila raised a brow.

"My powers have a greater effect with physical contact," she said. "If I can get a hold of him, I can weaken him and hopefully bring him down."

"I don't have enough strength left to lift you that high, and I'm definitely not throwing you up there," she said. "But how's your balance?"

"I was in gymnastics club back in high school."

"Good." She moved her fingers the same way she had done back in Warden Blackthorne's office, and chairs began to float. "You see where I'm going with this, yes?"

Samantha nodded.

"Good," she said. "Because if we're to catch him off guard, I need you to move fast. Keep your eyes on the prize and trust me to hold you up. Do you trust me?"

Samantha did not answer. She took off running.

At Lila's will, the chairs aligned themselves like steps in front of Samantha.

Pretending they were just steps, she kept running.

Ten. Twenty. Thirty. Forty steps. And then she jumped.

Summoning all her power and channeling it to her fists, she swung with all her might.

Samantha never got to land the blow because, mere inches away from his face, she came to a hard stop. And then an invisible force blasted her through the air.

"Sam!" someone screamed from below.

Wind rushed past her, and for a terrifying moment, she thought she would become a red stain on the wall, but her fall was cushioned, and she was lowered to the ground.

"You insolent children have no idea what real power is," Warden Blackthorne said.

A new ghost crawled out of the floor, replacing the one Samantha had destroyed, but it did not stop there. As they watched, another five appeared. And then another five. And another five.

"Okay, now that's just overkill," James said.

Lila pulled Daniel and Alexandra over and raised a telekinetic field about the five of them just as the ghosts launched their attack

"Well, it looks like we're massively screwed here," Daniel said breathlessly.

"Agreed," Alexandra said. "We could barely stay alive when they were five. Now there's twenty."

"I don't understand it," Samantha said. "I know he's on another level, but this is ridiculous. A ghost cannot use this much power without a host vessel. How can he still be this strong even after everything?"

"He's... He's not," James said.

"What?"

"There's negative energy all over the place so I couldn't sense it because I wasn't looking for it, but the negative energy is coming from somewhere," he said. "There are strings of energy coming from underground, and it's feeding the warden."

"That's why he's so strong!" Samantha said.

A particularly persistent ghost rammed into the shield, causing a visible shudder, but Lila did not flinch.

"So, if we sever the link or destroy the source, he'll be depowered?" she said.

"Pretty much," Samantha said. "I have to go."

"But we're already outnumbered here," Lila said. "And you're the only one who can actually hurt these things. Maybe James should—"

"No," James said. "Sam will find the source; she's the only one who has power over the ghosts, and Daniel will go with her."

"Why me?" Daniel said.

"Because someone needs to watch her back, and everyone else needs to be here if we are going to stay alive by the time Samantha returns."

"You think three of us can take on these monsters?" Alexandra said.

"It's not a matter of can. We will. Because we have to," he said. "And we will stop acting as individuals. We all don't have the kind of powers to face these things. It's time we stop pretending. So, Lila will fight them."

"Alone?" Lila said.

"You are not alone. None of us are," he said. "I trust you all with my life. Do you trust me?"

"I do," Daniel said.

"So do I," Lila said.

"Likewise," Samantha said.

Alexandra nodded.

"And do we trust one other?"

The answer was the same.

"Ever since we got here, we've been trying to find ways to contribute. I know I have. But now, I think it's clear what we all are and why we are here. Samantha is the medium between the living and the dead. Alexandra is the seer who guides us. Lila is the telekinetic; strong-willed and powerful, you get us through impossible obstacles. Daniel is the bridge between the past and the present."

"And you?" Alexandra said.

"Me?" James smiled. "I'm the cheerleader."

It was weird, but it made perfect sense. The situation was dire, and the odds were impossible, yet he had already managed to convince them they could do it. And then there was that glow again, emanating from him and bathing them all in warmth and confidence.

"We are a team and we are united not just in purpose but in heart and mind," he said. "For this fight, my strength will be your strength, and your strength will be mine. We will all act as one. I cannot swing the sword but I can lend my strength to your swing. I can steel your mind in the face of the impossible."

"And I can lend you my foresight and sharpen your instincts," Alexandra said.

"Now, you get it," James said. He turned to Lila. "You will fight with the strength of five. All you have to do is have faith. In us. In yourself."

Lila stepped forward and held up her hand; her fingers balled into a fist. She sharply uncurled them, and the force field exploded, sending every single ghost flying across the room. They hit the walls and burst into smoke, their particles scattering about.

"Whoa!" Samantha said in awe.

Even the warden was visibly perplexed.

Lila walked forward as the ghosts began to reform. It took much longer than before, as if their particles were reluctant to come together.

One of them formed halfway and flew at her from behind, but she glanced at it, and it became smoke once more.

Samantha was awestruck, and it was a feeling that everyone else shared. It was satisfying watching Lila put the ghosts down over and over, but there was work to do.

"You two have somewhere to be," James reminded them. "We've got this."

"Right."

Samantha and Daniel left the room and raced down the hall. It wasn't until they got to the top floor that Daniel asked,

"Where are we headed?"

"Down below," she said. "Doctor von Menschen's office."

"But we were there not too long ago. It was empty."

"We're not going into the office. Remember the third door to the left?"

"Yeah?"

"Bingo."

The elevator opened, and they set off running again.

"Is it just me, or are we faster than we used to be?" Daniel noted.

Samantha had not thought about it before, and now that she did, she saw it was true. They had been full-on sprinting since the cafeteria, and she wasn't even slightly breathless.

"Yeah, and I'm not even remotely winded," she said. "I feel like I could run a marathon."

They got to the pressure plates before the doctor's office and amazingly, they were able to get through the door before it closed by sheer speed.

They came to the doctor's office and faced the door on the left.

"Still sensing it?" Daniel asked.

"Stronger than ever."

She tried to open the door, but it was locked.

"Stand back," Daniel said.

He kicked the door in, and it fell off its hinges, to their surprise.

"Must've been rusty," he said.

They shone their flashlights into the room and found that they were at the top of a flight of stairs looking down at some kind of pit.

Even before she looked down, Samantha sensed what was waiting for them. Thousands of distraught spirits called out to her from below. She could sense their life force being siphoned to the floor above.

"Are those what I think they are?" Daniel asked.

Samantha nodded slowly.

"I guess we found the rest of the patients of Ravensbrook Asylum," she said.

They followed the stairs down into the pit, and the view became clearer and more horrifying.

The spirits were huddled around like prisoners with chains binding them to the floor.

"Is this hell?" Daniel muttered.

"It might as well be. He's got them doing for him the same thing we're doing for Lila; except they don't have a choice."

"Should we be worried that he's got the numbers on us even here?"

"No. They're not willingly lending their powers to him that's why he needs so many of them. Not to mention, they're ghosts, so not a lot of power to lend in the first place."

"And he's had them down here for fifty years?" Daniel asked.

Samantha did not bother to reply. She stepped into the midst of the ghost prisoners. As she moved, they gravitated towards her, curious enough to follow her but wary enough to keep their distance.

"Sam, wait, what are you doing?" he said. "It could be dangerous."

Again, Samantha responded to him with silence. She knew it wasn't dangerous. The faces around her were not dangerous. They were tired and they were miserable, and they were in a world of pain.

"Please," someone from among them said. "Please make it stop."

Other voices chipped in until she could hear nothing but then begging for an end to their suffering. They wanted to rest. They wanted peace.

"I'm sorry but I cannot end your suffering by my hands," she said. "Not without destroying you. The only way to help you find peace is to kill the warden, but as long as you all exist in this place, the warden is invincible."

Their pleadings were reduced to murmuring, and then someone else spoke,

"Then destroy us!"

"What?" Samantha said.

There were cries of agreement from the crowd, and soon the begging resumed.

"Wait! Stop! You don't understand. If I destroy you, you won't go on to find peace in the afterlife, you'll just be... nothing."

"It would be better to be nothing than to spend another second in this tortured existence as nothing but food for a monster!"

More murmurs of agreement.

Samantha looked to Daniel for help, but he was just as confused. This decision rested squarely on her shoulders

"No!" she said. "I won't do it! That would make me as much of a monster as Blackthorne. I refuse! I'll think of another way to save you. There is another way. There has to be!"

"Please! Take pity on us."

"If you won't do it for us, do it so the world can be free of Blackthorne."

"End our suffering please!"

They went on and on, each voice in agreement with the last. They wanted this. They *all* wanted this.

Samantha shut her eyes, but not before the tears escaped and streamed down her cheeks, and then slowly, she raised her hands.

*****

Never before in Lila's life had she ever felt more powerful, and yet never before had she felt more in control. Her powers came to her more naturally than ever. It was as subconscious as breathing and just as easy.

The tides of the battle remained at a stalemate, but she was not worried. Not even when Warden Blackthorne doubled his summons and she had to deal with forty specters zipping around the hall and looking for openings to hurt her. She had faith.

Behind her, James and Alexandra had assumed the lotus position on the floor and had not opened their eyes in some time. They, too, had faith in her to protect their bodies while they lent their powers and their energy to her.

Ultimately, however, the mission now rested on the shoulders of Samantha and Daniel. But there was not a thing to worry about because they had faith.

Up above, Blackthorne was growing more and more irate. The fact that Lila was putting away his forces and doing it without breaking a sweat was getting to him."

"How are you doing this?" he growled.

"I take it you haven't been eating your vegetables," Lila mocked.

Yelling in frustration, he doubled his army once more and then doubled them again. They attacked in unison, attempting to bury her under the sheer mass of them, but after a few seconds, during which the warden almost believed he had claimed victory, Lila blasted them all away.

"This is impossible!" Warden Blackthorne screamed.

His ghostly army sluggishly began to reform, but halfway through, they all crumbled to nothing.

"What... What is this?" the warden said. "What is happening?"

"It looks to me like you're running out of juice, which is a shame." She pushed off the floor and joined him in the air. "...because I'm still fully charged."

She shot forward and punched him right in the face, sending him careening through the air like an astronaut in space.

Bouncing off the wall, she landed a second blow.

This time, she landed on the floor. She pivoted, reached up, grabbed hold of him, and yanked him down.

Without his power source, the warden had no defense against her telekinesis and came crashing down. He cracked the tiled floor on impact, and his form shuddered.

He tried to stand up but fell on his hands and knees.

"H-how is this happening?" he said.

Lila stood over him.

"Have you ever heard of the power of friendship, Warden?"

"What?"

He lifted up his head, and she put her fist to his face with all the strength in her body; his head snapped to the side, and his body followed. If he had still been alive, he would have died right there.

The door to the cafeteria opened, and Daniel came in, carrying a sickly-looking Samantha in his arms.

For the first time since the power-up, Lila was scared.

"What happened?" she said.

"We found the source of his power. He had a pit full of ghosts bound and forced to feed him their energy. They begged Samantha to destroy them and free them from their suffering. I don't know what happened after—"

"It's okay, Daniel," Samantha said. "You can put me down."

He did as she asked, and she staggered forward. Lila tried to help her, but she waved her off.

She walked past her, right up to the warden, and waited for him to lift himself off the ground.

"Did I hear that right? You destroyed them?" He laughed. "Some medium you are. Even I could not be so heartless."

"My friend... is mistaken," Samantha said, her voice barely above a whisper. "I did not... destroy them."

"You're lying," he said. "They're gone. I can feel it. There was no other way to free them from those chains. No ghost could leave that chamber while I exist!"

"You should... really expand... your horizon, Warden," she said.

Lila did not know it was possible for a ghost to lose color in the face, but that was what happened to Warden Blackthorne.

"What did you do?"

Samantha dropped unsteadily to her knees and locked eyes with him.

"Why... don't you look... into my eyes and... see... for yourself?"

The warden's eyes widened in horror.

"No!" he said. "No, no, no! That's not possible! You couldn't have!"

He tried to get away, but with astonishing speed, she grabbed him by the neck.

When she opened her mouth to speak again, they heard not her voice but a multitude of voices speaking through her.

"Welcome to judgment day, Blackthorne," they said.

Smoky tendrils rose out of Samantha's body and transformed into ghost people. They numbered in tens, then hundreds. By the time they ceased manifesting, Lila was certain there were at least a thousand ghosts in the room.

They swarmed Warden Blackthorne, circling him until they had formed into a tornado with him in the center.

His hand emerged from the depths, clawing at the ground in an attempt to escape, but he was swept back in shortly after

Warden Blackthorne's screams were gut-wrenching as they ripped him to shreds. Had it been anyone else— barring the chief physician, of course— Lila would have been inclined to feel pity for him, but instead, she thought every bit of torture was well deserved. When the winds died down after a long minute, and the chaos eventually ceased, so did the screaming. And nothing was left of Blackthorne.

The ghosts lingered long enough to say their 'thank yous, 'and then they began to fade away.

"Is it over?" Daniel asked.

"The warden is gone," Samantha said. "For good."

Color had begun to return to her face, and she could stand on her own again.

"Banished to the afterlife?" James asked.

She nodded.

"Isn't that too good for him?"

"If there really is a God on the other side," Samantha said, "it's his problem now."

"So, you actually let yourself be possessed by a thousand ghosts?" Alexandra asked.

"I did," Samantha said.

"You were this close to actualizing your worst nightmare. What made you do something like that?"

"My choices were very limited. It was either that or destroy their very essence, and compared to that, this was easy."

"But how did you even know you could hold that many ghosts in one body without getting torn apart by the sheer number?"

Samantha's gaze was intense as she looked at Lila before she answered.

"I didn't."

*****

The sun was rising as the five of them descended to the lobby for what would be the final time.

As they came to the door, two ghosts appeared to them. It was Sylvia Grace and Mark Waters.

"Hello again," Sylvia said.

"Where's Billy?" Samantha asked.

Mark turned and pointed out into the yard. They saw Billy holding hands with an older woman there as he chattered away excitedly. As they watched, the pair slowly faded out of their sight, but not before Billy turned and waved to them.

Samantha buried her face in the crook of her elbow, and Lila put her arm around her.

"There aren't enough words we could use to thank you for your help," Mark said. "And honestly, not enough time."

"You helped us help you," Lila said. "Thank you for that."

"You can finally rest." Alexandra beamed.

"We can, and it's all because of you," Sylvia said.

Samantha lifted her head.

"Glad we could help," she said.

"Goodbye," Mark said.

"Goodbye," Sylvia said.

"Goodbye," the five of them chorused. And there was not a dry eye among them.

They stepped through the gates of Ravensbrook Asylum and looked down at the town. In the distance, they could see the early risers starting their day.

"You feel it too, don't you?" Samantha said.

"Yep," James said.

"Totally," Alexandra said

"Rainbows and sunshine," Lila said, nudging Daniel fondly in the rib.

Lila wondered if the people in town would look up and notice the calming peace that had washed over Ravensbrook Asylum, too.

The darkness that cast a shadow over Ravensbrook has been dispelled, and the lost souls, wandering and tormented, have finally been put to rest.

All wrongs have been righted, and the town is at peace.

Epilogue:
REFLECTIONS

The bell tinkled as Alexandra walked through the door of Raven's Cove. She immediately bumped into Wesley Hargreaves, who was clearing up a table.

"Hey, Alex!" she said. "Haven't seen you in a minute. What have you been up to?"

"Oh, nothing much," Alexandra said. Just been getting into ghost stories and such."

"Ah. I like a good horror novel every once in a while myself. Maybe you could recommend a couple for me?"

"Sure thing." Alexandra smiled, amused at herself.

"Anyway, your party's already seated over there." She cocked her head towards the corner booth where James was already waving at her.

Next to her, Daniel and Samantha seemed to be arguing about something while Lila was focused on making a spoon dance around on a table on the other side of the room.

The smile that stretched across Alexandra's face at that moment was automatic, and she could not have stopped it if she had tried. It just felt right.

She went over to join them at the table.

"Hey, guys!" she said.

Lila had not heard her coming and jumped in her seat. In the distance, the sound of a spoon falling on the floor could be heard.

They shared a look and burst out laughing while Wesley went over to investigate the table.

This was the first time they were meeting since they left the asylum on Sunday morning.

"That really was something, wasn't it?" Samantha said. "Just a few days ago, we say in this very booth listening to you talk about it."

"And now we've actually done it," Lila said.

"Am I the only one who laid awake thinking, 'Did that actually freaking happen?'" James said.

"Oh no," Alexandra said with a small laugh. "No, you weren't. I kept thinking about the many times we could have died and probably should have."

"We fought ghosts!" Lila said. "Like actual freaking ghosts! I can count the number of times the Ravensbrook Asylum came up in my history classes, and now we can say we defeated the warden. Except, we can't!"

"Imagine if we tried to tell people. They'd probably think we were playing a prank."

"How's everything back at home, Lila?" Alexandra asked.

The table grew quiet as the atmosphere turned serious.

"My mom hasn't changed, I'll tell you that much," she said. "I told her what really happened the night of the accident, and as I expected, she didn't believe me. But I did say a thing or two to her that left her very stunned."

"And your sister?" Daniel asked.

"We're cool. The problem was me all along because I could not forgive myself so I thought there was no way she could forgive me. We talked. There was a bit of crying, but not me, and we had plans for this weekend and the next. Got a lot of lost time to make up for."

"I'm happy to hear that, Lila.," Samantha said. "We all are."

"And um... I called my dad as well. He was very surprised to hear from me, and I'll go see him next week. I have a feeling we have a lot to talk about."

Alexandra nodded.

"Sounds like you benefited the most from asylum therapy," she teased.

Silence fell over the table, but it wasn't because there was nothing to say. It was more like there was something to say, but no one wanted to go first.

It was Daniel who broke the ice.

"I feel like we're all thinking it, but I'm going to bite the bullet and ask, what's next for us?" he said. "I can't go back to being strangers, that's for sure. I've never been so close to any group of people in my life."

"Same," Lila said.

"Ditto." James nodded

"Me neither," Samantha said.

"Actually, this is going to be kind of awkward, but I have something to say," Alexandra said. "I'm actually an undercover cop."

She ducked out of the way of a flying napkin from Daniel, but there was no way to escape Lila's punch to the arm.

"Okay, okay, fine, you got me. I'm not a cop." She laughed.

Despite the positive response to her humor, however, she could sense the need for a serious answer, and as usual, they were subconsciously looking to her for it.

She took a deep breath.

"I know I tend to see the future, but in this case, I don't know where the path ahead will take us," Alexandra said. "Maybe we'll drive around town in a brightly colored van solving supernatural cases, or maybe we'll move to LA and consult for the police; who knows? Truth be told, I never thought this far ahead in the first place. I mean, who would be crazy enough to follow a girl they met on the internet into an abandoned asylum to fight ghosts?"

Four hands went up around the table, and she cracked a smile.

"But you four *are* my best friends. It was true when we were in the asylum, and it's true now. Whatever comes next, whatever the future holds, I want to be side by side with you guys when I face it."

James turned away and rubbed his eyes.

"Damn allergies," he said.

"Need a tissue?" Daniel teased.

"Shut up."

"Now, that's no way to talk to the bridge between the past and the future, is it, Mr. Cheerleader?"

"Daniel, I swear to God—"

Wesley interrupted just then, bringing a tray over to their table.

"You guys ordered without me?" Alexandra said, feigning offense.

It did not last as Wesley sat down a glass of iced tea in front of her.

She jerked her head towards Daniel. "He ordered for you. You two must be close. He got your usual order right, down to a T."

"Of course he did." Alexandra rolled her eyes.

Daniel reached across the table and took her hand in his. "Yeah, we're *really* close."

She smacked him with her free hand, and he leaned back, laughing heartily.

They waited until Wesley was gone before they resumed conversations.

"Well, now that we've established that we're best friends in real life too, my sister's birthday is coming up if anyone wants to come. She's big on birthdays, and she doesn't mind the extra guests."

"Meeting the family already?" Samantha said. "You sure move fast, Miss Horren."

"Zip it, Miss Cunnington."

"Will there be cake? I love cake!" Lila asked.

"Fuck cake, will there be booze?" Daniel asked.

"Yes and yes."

"I'll be there," Lila and Daniel said in unison.

CONCLUSION

As the final echoes of Ravensbrook Asylum fade into silence and we step out from its shadowed halls into the light, I find myself pausing to reflect on the journey we've undertaken together. It has been a path through darkness and light, horror and hope, bound by the unwavering spirit of those who dare to confront the past to shape a brighter future.

I want to extend my deepest gratitude to you, dear reader, for joining me on this intricate journey. Your willingness to explore the depths of Ravensbrook Hollow and to stand alongside Alexandra, James, Lila, Samantha, and Daniel as they faced the specters of their own fears and those of the asylum has been the greatest honor. Through your eyes, the haunted halls of Ravensbrook came alive, and the spirits trapped within found a voice.

This story, though woven from the threads of imagination, speaks to the enduring human struggle against the darkness within and without. It is a testament to the power of unity, the strength found in vulnerability, and the courage to confront the unseen. The characters you've journeyed with are a reflection of the many facets of bravery and resilience that reside within us all, reminding us that even in the face of overwhelming darkness, there is light to be found.

"Lost Echoes: The Dark Asylum" was not just a tale of supernatural encounters but a narrative of redemption, of souls lost and found, of battles fought within the heart and mind. As you followed the story of these brave souls banding together, overcoming their fears, and facing the darkness head-on, it was a journey not just within the confines of a haunted asylum but within the intricate landscapes of their own hearts and minds.

It is my hope that this story lingers with you, not just as a memory of fear and suspense but as a beacon of the belief that no darkness is too dense to be pierced by the light of determination and compassion. The journey of Alexandra and her companions is a mirror to our own lives, where every day, we face our own Ravensbrook Asylums, our own shadows, with the hope and the belief that light exists, waiting to be found.

Thank you for allowing me to share this story with you. Thank you for walking through the darkness to find the light on the other side and for believing in the power of stories to transform and transcend. As we part ways, remember the journey through Ravensbrook is not just a tale of the past but a mirror reflecting our own inner battles, reminding us of the light we carry within, capable of illuminating the darkest of places.

May the courage of Alexandra, James, Lila, Samantha, and Daniel inspire you to face your own shadows with a renewed sense of hope and strength. Until our paths cross again in the pages of another adventure, I wish you light, courage, and the strength to face your own shadows with the certainty that you are not alone.

With heartfelt thanks and the hope for future journeys shared,

EJ Castille

EJ CASTILLE

Made in the USA
Las Vegas, NV
11 March 2025